SETTING FREE THE KITES

ALEX GEORGE

G. P. PUTNAM'S SONS | *New York*

PUTNAM

G. P. PUTNAM'S SONS
Publishers Since 1838
An imprint of Penguin Random House LLC
375 Hudson Street
New York, New York 10014

Copyright © 2017 by Alex George

The Library of Congress has catalogued the G. P. Putnam's Sons hardcover edition as follows:

Library of Congress Cataloging-in-Publication Data
Names: George, Alex, 1970– author.
Title: Setting free the kites / Alex George.
Description: New York : G.P. Putnam's Sons, 2017.
Identifiers: LCCN 2016036566 | ISBN 9780399162107 (hardback)
Subjects: LCSH: Teenage boys—Fiction. | Male friendship—Fiction. | Life
change events—Fiction. | Loss (Psychology)—Fiction. | Maturation
(Psychology)—Fiction. | Maine—Fiction. | Psychological fiction. |
BISAC: FICTION / Literary. | FICTION / Coming of Age. | FICTION / Historical. |
GSAFD: Bildungsromans
Classification: LCC PR6107.E53 S48 2017 | DDC 823/.92—dc23
LC record available at https://lccn.loc.gov/2016036566
p.   cm.

First G. P. Putnam's Sons hardcover edition / February 2017
First G. P. Putnam's Sons trade paperback edition / January 2018
G. P. Putnam's Sons trade paperback ISBN: 9780399576485

Printed in the United States of America
1   3   5   7   9   10   8   6   4   2

Book design by Gretchen Achilles

Praise for
SETTING FREE THE KITES

"A warm, relatable—at times heartbreakingly so—story of two boys becoming men in 1970s Maine . . . George authentically relays the dynamic, difficult nature of families."

—*Columbia Daily Tribune*

"George's effortless and beautiful prose flows off of the page to construct a timeless narrative of love, loss, kinship and how the connections we make will almost always find a way to affect us for the rest of our lives."

—*Oxford Citizen*

"George combines wit, sorrow and nostalgia into a story readers young and old will not forget. . . . Heartbreaking and real."

—*Vox Magazine*

"*Setting Free the Kites* is a serious but breezy work, a sad but delightful story, and just right for thumbing through at the beach this summer."

—*Down East* Magazine

"A mesmerizing and eloquent read . . . This is a book that takes hold of your life, so much that you forget the individuals are fictional and assume them as characters in your everyday life. . . . Highly, highly recommended."

—*Jenn's Bookshelves*

"Heart-rending . . . A beautifully told, nostalgic tale about friendship, George brings to life true, strongly independent characters . . . An effecting, emotional read. So many excellently crafted details are packed into its pages, poignantly capturing the rapid change of emotions during adolescence."

—*Portland Press Herald*

"A dandy book."

—*St. Louis Post-Dispatch*

"A moving novel of friendship, family, loss and reconciliation . . . An emotionally resonant novel."

elf Awareness

"This generous, poignant novel addresses family, friendship, and dealing with catastrophic loss. . . . A beautifully wrought work for fans of literary fiction and coming-of-age novels."

—*Library Journal*

"[A] touching story . . . George is masterly in his rendition of Maine landscapes and the emotional swings of adolescence."

—*Publishers Weekly*

"A lovely meditation on young friendship and the harsh realities of growing up."

—*Book Riot*

"It's sort of early to be carving titles into the marble 'Best of 2017' lists already, but it would be a surprise if I didn't end the year as impressed and moved by this novel as I am right now. . . . With echoes of Stephen King's *Joyland* and *The Body* as well as John Knowles' *A Separate Peace*, *Setting Free the Kites* features unforgettable characters and a nice little twist."

—*The Day* (New London)

"George's writing has tremendous voice, one that brings these adolescent boys to life as few others do."

—*Seattle Book Mama*

"Replete with soaring emotion. *Setting Free the Kites* is a coming-of-age novel driven by the forces of hope. Alex George skillfully proves that the tethers of a painful past can be cut, freeing us to rise above our circumstances if only we have fearless hearts."

—SARAH McCOY, *New York Times* and international–bestselling author of *The Mapmaker's Children*

"I think I fell a little in love with Alex George's *Setting Free the Kites* when I heard the beautiful title. Luckily, the book itself—colorful, poignant, winning and touching—does not disappoint and seduces like a spring breeze. Mr. George, please consider me one of your new and ardent admirers."

—GEORGE HODGMAN, author of *Bettyville*

ALSO BY ALEX GEORGE

A Good American

To AAS, with love

SETTING FREE THE KITES

PROLOGUE

HAVERFORD, MAINE
2016

Nathan Tilly gave me the story I'm going to tell, but it is the old paper mill that sets my memories free.

I READ THE REPORT in the *Haverford Gazette* the previous week. The mill has not been operational for more than fifty years, but now the land has been sold to a supermarket chain, and the old building is to be razed to make way for a customer parking lot. The news has prompted vigorous local debate. Some are angry that the city council has allowed part of our municipal heritage to be sold off. Others are excited at the prospect of fresh bagels. Such is progress.

For myself, I'm sorry to see the old place go. I want to pay my last respects, watch the thing go down.

THE LOWER END OF Bridge Lane is lined with mud-encrusted pick-ups and vans. I have to double back and park on the other side of the river. It is a beautiful, fresh spring morning. The faintest of breezes is coming in off the ocean. As I walk across the bridge I can hear someone shouting instructions through a bullhorn.

Warning signs have been posted along the road, keeping the curious at bay. **AUTHORIZED PERSONNEL ONLY. HARD HAT REQUIRED.** I keep my distance. A huge crane is parked in front of the old building, its arm stretched high into the sky. A wrecking ball hangs at the end of the crane's thick steel rope, fat and heavy with the threat of violence. The mill's giant wooden doors have been padlocked shut my entire life, but now they are open wide, and early-morning sunlight falls into the cathedral-like space where vast pulping machines once rumbled from dawn to dusk, the town's beating heart. Workmen in reflector vests walk in and out, murmuring into walkie-talkies. I guess they are checking all three floors for uninvited visitors before the walls start crashing down.

The mill's redbrick chimney rises tall and straight into the sky. By lunchtime it will be gone.

At precisely nine o'clock there is a long, shrill blast from a whistle. A man climbs into the cabin of the crane and turns on the ignition. As the engine rumbles to life, the arm of the crane begins to move from side to side, and the wrecking ball starts to swing.

The old mill has been on the brink of demolition for years. Up and down this part of the southern Maine coast, from Biddeford to Brunswick, abandoned industrial buildings have been rescued and revivified, artfully repurposed for twenty-first-century living. Those ancient spaces have been reborn as art galleries, office suites with double-height ceilings, and organic delicatessens selling squid-ink pasta from Umbria and artisanal cheeses from Vermont. Everyone has been waiting for a similar metamorphosis to happen in Haverford. It hasn't been for want of trying: in 2004 a consortium of property speculators from away went crazy for the mill's exposed brickwork.

An architect was commissioned to design a warren of luxury condominiums with reclaimed-timber floors and glinting chrome appliances. But the town lacked the necessary real estate mojo to pull it off. No matter how pretty the artist's impressions in the brochure looked, nobody was buying. Not a single unit was sold, and the promised renovation never happened. The place has remained abandoned and deserted ever since.

The wrecking ball is swinging fiercely now, slicing through the air in ever more violent arcs. The crane operator begins to rotate the cabin, gradually turning it toward the old walls. I feel my body stiffen in anticipation of the first impact. When it comes, there is an infernal roar of collapsing brick, crushed wood, and splintering glass. That's when I feel a release within me, a quiet letting go. The crane operator edges the caterpillar tracks forward a few feet, and moments later another slab of wall disappears. A fog of atomized red brick hangs over the rubble. I watch for a few minutes and then turn away. There is nothing more to see.

As I walk back over the bridge, I think about those two gravity-defying summers, almost forty years ago, when the old mill gave us shelter, and Nathan Tilly's gift for boundless hope gave us wings. Nathan loved the mill so much. Inside those old brick walls, the light of uncomplicated happiness shone down on us, as warm and as comforting as the sun.

But such a bright light casts long, dark shadows.

I open the door of my car and climb in. I rest my hands on the steering wheel and gaze back across the bridge. The wrecking ball is still swinging hard, making its way toward the mill's chimney.

I do not want to see the chimney fall. I drive away.

1976

ONE

Sometimes life-changing moments slip by unnoticed, their significance becoming apparent only in the light of subsequent events. But Nathan Tilly was never one for the subtle approach.

The summer of 1976 had been long and humid. The horseflies had been larger and more vicious than in past years, which was saying something. They had swarmed around me, taking painful chunks out of my sweet, thirteen-year-old flesh. My legs and upper body bore the scars of months of relentless attacks. For me the smell of summer was not the salty tang of the ocean, nor the ambrosial scent of young blueberries, but the sour chemical whiff of antiseptic cream that my mother would slather on my bumpy mosaic of bites, a constellation of unending irritation. On the first day of my eighth-grade year at Longfellow Middle School, my shoulders were still itching from the horseflies' diabolical attention.

My discomfort was also, I am sure, a physical manifestation of the anxiety that I was feeling that day. I had been dreading the start of the new school year all summer. Every blissfully unscheduled day of vacation was, to me, just one step closer to seeing Hollis Calhoun again.

For most of the previous year, Hollis Calhoun had bullied me without mercy. He undertook a campaign of terrors small and large. Some of it was innocuous enough—an unanticipated cuff around the back of the head in the corridor, a sharp elbow jab to the ribs in the cafeteria line—but he also liked to corner me out of sight of others and inflict more elaborate, sustained cruelties. He crowded in on me, heavy and huge, obliterating the world beyond his fists. His violence was claustrophobic as well as cruel. There was a warped intimacy in all those carefully administered punches and kicks. He would scrutinize my face intently as he hurt me, delighted by the fear in my eyes.

For all his thuggery, Hollis possessed a nuanced understanding of the psychological mechanics of terror. He took care to ensure that his attacks were never predictable. Not knowing when they might come, I was in a constant state of high alert. Sometimes he would leave me alone for days, which had the paradoxical effect of ratcheting up my sense of impending dread. When I finally saw him lumbering toward me, I felt something oddly close to relief that the wait was over. The threat of Hollis Calhoun's fists that marauded across my fevered imagination was worse than any blow they could land in actuality.

There had been nothing I could do to make Hollis stop, since he didn't appear to want anything from me. My terror seemed to be an end unto itself. He never told me what I had done to deserve his attention, and always the same unanswered question would fog my panicked brain as he approached me with that malevolent look in his eyes: *Why me?*

Hollis was a year older than me, and I had consoled myself with the thought that at least he would be graduating to high school in the fall. Then, a week before the school year ended, Hollis had cornered me in the boys' locker room. He pressed one side of my face into the cold floor, his knee in the small of my back, and told me that he was being held back a grade. He would be at Longfellow again next year. He banged my head against the tiles a couple of times, as if this was somehow my fault.

As I pushed open the door to my classroom, the prospect of seeing Hollis Calhoun again, combined with the ferocious itching beneath my shirt, had plunged me into my own universe of self-pity. I sat down at the nearest desk and opened my bag. As usual, my mother had left me a folded note. Her choice of quotation that day seemed especially apt.

The Lord is my helper; I will not fear. What can man do to me?

HEBREWS 13:6

That was indeed the question. I had spent much of the past three months anxiously imagining what abominations Hollis had in mind for me. I looked up gloomily and noticed an unfamiliar presence in the row ahead. Most of my classmates were already slumped in bored disaffection over their desks, but a new boy I did not recognize sat bolt upright in his chair. His hair was as black as the leather on my mother's Bible. He wore a green cable-knit turtleneck sweater, which looked insufferably hot on that warm morning. While I was surreptitiously examining him, he turned and looked right at me. Our eyes met for the briefest of moments, and then I looked away. New arrivals were to be treated with extreme caution until their position in the classroom pecking order could be calibrated. I bent down and pretended to look for something in my bag. The new boy didn't turn back around, though. He kept looking at me.

THE DAY DRAGGED ON impossibly slowly, but not slowly enough for me. As the hands on the clock above the blackboard crept toward the final bell, I could feel the fear rising in my throat.

As soon as classes were over I ran to fetch my things, hoping for a quick escape, but Hollis Calhoun was already waiting for me, leaning against the door of my locker. To my dismay, he seemed to have grown even bigger over the summer. We looked at each other without speaking. There was nothing to be said. Hollis twisted my arm roughly behind my back and began to march me against the tide of students who were streaming toward the exit. The corridors became more deserted as we walked toward the back of the school. Like a nostalgic lover, Hollis was taking me back to one of our old haunts. He stopped in front of the boys' locker room and pushed me inside.

He grabbed my shirt and shoved me up against the wall, snapping my head backward. The summer evaporated in an instant. Pinned there by his fists, I felt as if we had never been apart. Hollis was peering beadily at me. I averted my gaze and said nothing. After a moment he relaxed his grip, took a half step away from me, and put a ferocious knee into my thigh. I yelped and dropped to the ground. He pushed me over onto my back with his foot. Pain began to radiate across my lower body. Killer dead legs were a specialty of his. He held me down and went to work on my upper arms, pressing and pulling my skin into fat knots of pain. He found the worst of my horsefly bites and pinched them with brutal relish.

"Oh, this is just like old times, isn't it?" he whispered. "Are you ready for another year of fun?"

Before I could answer Hollis hauled me to my feet and dragged me to the nearest stall. He flung open the door and pushed me inside. Still holding the collar of my shirt, he flipped up the lid of the toilet. He kicked the backs of my legs and I collapsed to my knees.

"I thought we might try something new," said Hollis. He grabbed my hair and pushed my head into the toilet bowl. I just had time to take a deep breath before he pulled the chain. He held my head firmly in place as water sluiced through my mouth and up my nose. When he finally yanked me out of the bowl I sucked air into my lungs and then began to cough. Hollis did not relinquish his grip on my collar. "We're just getting started," he told me. To my disappointment, I felt the prickle of tears at the corners of my eyes.

Just then there was a loud bang, and Hollis lurched into me. The door of the stall had been flung open. Standing there was the new boy from class that morning.

"Let him go!" he yelled.

Hollis and I were both too surprised to speak. Neither of us really wanted to be interrupted. Hollis was too busy enjoying himself, and I didn't want my humiliation made worse by a witness. As we stared at our intruder, he began kicking Hollis on the shins. In that tiny stall there was nowhere for Hollis to go. Laughing, he let go of me for a moment and tried to push the boy away. His attacker responded by stepping in closer and hammering his fists against Hollis's chest. He was no match for Hollis physically, but what he lacked in strength he made up for with sheer ferocity. The stall was crowded with the three of us squeezed in there. The new boy was by the door and I was still kneeling in front of the toilet bowl. Sandwiched between us, Hollis had no room to defend himself properly or mete out retribution. The boy stepped in to deliver another flurry of punches, which Hollis swatted away. He had stopped laughing by then. Now the fight was conducted almost entirely in silence. All I could hear was the boy's heavy breathing and a few grunts from Hollis whenever a punch landed on target. I cowered on the floor, hoping not to be kicked. My head and shirt were soaking wet. The world beyond the stall vanished. The three of us were so focused on the strange, unequal struggle within its walls that we failed to hear the door of the locker room open.

The shout of anger that followed we heard well enough.

TWO

Ten minutes later, the three of us were sitting on a bench in a deserted school corridor. The janitor who had interrupted the fight had hauled us out of the stall, one by one, grabbing us by the scruffs of our necks like newborn kittens. Identifying Hollis Calhoun and the new boy as the main antagonists, he had propelled them angrily in front of him toward the principal's office. I—obviously the victim of whatever malfeasance was being perpetrated—had been left to trail behind them.

Now I was wedged uncomfortably in between the other two boys. My shirt was soaking wet, and the brisk efficiency of the school's air-conditioning was starting to make me shiver. Hollis Calhoun glowered over my head at my new classmate.

"You got a name, hero?" he muttered.

The boy turned to look at him. "Nathan Tilly," he said.

"You've got nerve, interrupting us like that," said Hollis.

"More nerve than you, that's for sure," said the boy.

For a gratifying moment it looked as if Hollis had swallowed his tongue.

I turned toward Nathan Tilly. "I really wouldn't—"

"Do you always pick on people half your size?" asked Nathan. "Scared of a fair fight, are you?"

Hollis's neck had turned red. "The only person who should be scared right now," he said, "is you."

Nathan Tilly picked an invisible piece of lint off his sweater. "Oh, I'm scared all right." He held up a hand and began to count on his fingers. "I'm scared that my mongoose is going to run away. I'm scared that my father is going to fall off his boat and drown himself, because he's a lousy swimmer. I'm scared that Frank Lucchesi is going to stay on as manager of the Texas Rangers and run the team into the ground."

"You have a mongoose?" I said.

"I'm scared that the Russians are going to blow us all to smithereens," continued Nathan Tilly. "I'm scared that I'll never fall in love. And, just between you and me"—he leaned in conspiratorially— "I'm a tiny bit scared of spiders. You know, the fat, hairy ones." He paused and looked directly at Hollis. "But one thing I am not scared of," he said, "is you."

I gazed at Nathan Tilly in wonder. Hollis Calhoun was staring at him, too.

When we had read "Rikki-Tikki-Tavi" in seventh grade, we'd done a whole unit on the mongoose. "Mongooses are illegal in this country," I said.

"Maybe they are, maybe not," said Nathan Tilly carelessly.

"Why do you have a *mongoose?*" I asked.

"To catch snakes."

"Snakes?"

"This was when we lived in Texas," explained Nathan Tilly. "Our backyard was full of copperheads and cottonmouths. My mongoose loves to kill snakes, but he hasn't found a single one since we moved to Maine. I think he's bored." He turned to Hollis. "That's why I'm scared he'll run away," he explained.

Hollis was still unable to speak.

"Is he a *pet?*" I asked.

"Well, we keep him outside. He's tethered to a rope, near the house. Otherwise he'd disappear into the forest and we'd never see him again."

I imagined the mongoose hitching a lift south, back to Texas and the snakes. "Where in Texas are you from?" I asked him.

"A small town in the west. Nowhere you've heard of."

All I knew about Texas was that the Johnson Space Center was in Houston, and President Kennedy had been assassinated in Dallas. In my imagination it was a vast desert, populated by rugged, dusty cowboys with big hats. It couldn't have been much more different from coastal Maine.

"When did you move here?" I asked him.

"At the start of the summer."

"Do you like it?"

Nathan Tilly looked at me. "You sure do ask a lot of questions," he said.

"Sorry," I said, blushing.

"What's *your* name?" asked Nathan.

"Oh, don't you know? This is the great Robert Carter." Hollis had finally recovered the use of his voice. "But he's far too important to bother with people like you and me."

"He doesn't *look* very important," said Nathan.

Hollis gave me a quick cuff on the back of my head. "His family owns the amusement park outside of town. I just spent the summer working there, earning crap wages." He looked at me with contempt. "I didn't see *him* working, though. He was probably sitting by his swimming pool being fed ice cream by his butler."

I closed my eyes. So that was why Hollis had been picking on me—he thought I was a member of the town's privileged elite. When he hit me, he was (literally) striking a blow for the downtrodden proletariat. I shouldn't have been surprised. Hollis wasn't the first person to imagine that my family was wealthy. I'd been encountering the same assumptions and petty jealousies since kindergarten.

"We don't have a butler," I said wearily. "Or a swimming pool."

"I didn't even know there *was* an amusement park," said Nathan. I looked at him gratefully.

"Listen," said Hollis. "When they ask us what was going on back there, we'll tell them that we were fooling around, okay? Just a little bit of fun. Nothing serious. Got it?"

The last thing I wanted was to give Hollis Calhoun's bullying the additional fuel of self-righteous vengeance. I nodded. "Nothing serious," I repeated.

"What about you?" said Hollis to Nathan. "Do we have a deal?"

Before Nathan could answer, a familiar voice called my name, followed by the anxious clip of sensible shoes hurrying down the corridor. My mother came to a stop in front of the bench. She clutched her handbag in front of her like a shield, as if it might ward off whatever unpleasantness was about to happen. She looked me up and down. "Robert," she said. "You're soaking wet. What's been going on?"

Hollis Calhoun shifted a little closer to me, radiating menace. "We were just having a bit of fun," I mumbled. "Nothing serious."

My mother glanced between Hollis and Nathan Tilly. "I got called into school because of a bit of *fun?*" she said. Hollis stared down at the space between his feet, smirking. Nathan Tilly looked my mother in the eye and winked at her. To my astonishment, she blushed. Without another word, she turned away and pushed open the door to the principal's office.

The three of us sat in uneasy silence for a few minutes. I wondered what story my mother was being told. Over the years she had spent many hours in tense conference with school principals, but never because of me. My flawless behavioral record was about to be compromised, and she looked as if her heart was going to break. I gazed resentfully at Nathan Tilly. This was all his fault. Whatever private misery Hollis Calhoun might have inflicted on me would have been preferable to the public circus of recrimination that I would now have to endure. I had never told anyone about Hollis's bullying, because my silence allowed me to contain the damage he could cause. The last thing I needed was well-meaning adults clucking in disapproval and trying to make things better. I knew they would only make things worse.

More footsteps echoed down the corridor. When I looked up I was surprised to see a man approaching us. (I had seen countless mothers arrive to collect their children from the principal's office, but I couldn't remember ever seeing a father show up before.) The man had an untamed beard, peppered with gray. A dark blue sailor's cap was pulled down over his forehead at an incongruously jaunty angle.

"Ahoy!" called the man, his deep voice booming down the deserted corridor.

"That's my dad," said Nathan, unnecessarily.

Mr. Tilly stopped in front of us and looked at his son. "Didn't take you long to be sent to the principal's office, did it?" he said. To my surprise, his face broke into a wide grin. "Excellent work, Nathan. First-class." He turned to me. "Who are you?" he asked.

"This is Robert Carter," said Nathan.

Nathan's father looked at me. "Why are you so wet, Robert Carter?"

I felt Hollis's flat eyes on me. "We were just having a bit of fun," I said.

"Really. Fun for whom, I wonder," said Mr. Tilly. This was met with three blank looks. "Oh, I see," he said cheerfully. "Honor among thieves, is it?" He removed his cap and tucked it under his arm.

"Well, we'll get to the bottom of it soon enough." With that he turned and pushed through the door of the principal's office.

After a moment Hollis spoke. "If we all keep quiet, they won't be able to prove anything."

"Which would be great for you," said Nathan.

Hollis looked at him. "And for *you*."

"What about Robert, though?" said Nathan.

"I'm fine," I said anxiously.

Just then the door to the office opened and the principal's secretary stuck her head out. "You can come in now," she said.

The principal of Longfellow Middle School, Mr. Pritchard, was in the twilight of a long and dispiriting career. He had taught eighth-grade English for twenty years, and his heart still beat blackly with the accumulated disappointments born of unsuccessfully cajoling generations of sullen thirteen-year-olds into reading *Huckleberry Finn*. But if his time as an educator had been unfulfilling for everyone involved, now Mr. Pritchard had found his true métier. He was a born administrator. He loved to impose order upon chaos. Insubordination and rule-breaking were not tolerated. Sanctions were imposed swiftly and without mercy.

As we filed in silently, Mr. Pritchard glared at us from behind his desk. My mother and Mr. Tilly were sitting to one side. We shuffled to an awkward halt in the middle of the room. Principal Pritchard looked us over, not bothering to hide his irritation.

"We might as well begin," he said. "We called your mother, Hollis, but apparently she was too busy to come in." He did not sound surprised. I guessed that Hollis's mother and the principal were already well acquainted. "So, gentlemen. Restroom stalls are designed to accommodate one person, not three. And they really just have one function. So will someone explain what the three of you were doing?"

There was a long silence. Finally Hollis spoke up. "We were just having a little bit of fun," he said.

"A bit of *fun*," said Mr. Pritchard.

"You know, fooling around," elaborated Hollis.

Mr. Pritchard's eyes settled on me. "Would you agree, Robert? You were just fooling around? Because it looks as if you were fooling around more than anyone else."

I didn't dare look up. I didn't want to see the disappointment on my mother's face. "Just a bit of fun," I agreed.

"That's a big fat lie." Nathan Tilly pointed at Hollis and then at me. "He was flushing his head down the toilet. And before that he was hitting him and kicking him. I heard it all."

My mother stiffened in her seat.

Mr. Pritchard looked at me. "Is that true?"

"Of course it's true," said Nathan's father. "He's soaking wet, for God's sake. How else do you explain that?"

"We were just fooling around," said Hollis again.

Mr. Pritchard cleared his throat. "And what were *you* doing in the boys' locker room so long after the last bell, Nathan? You should have been out of the school gates and on your way home by then."

"I got lost," said Nathan.

"Lost?" echoed Mr. Pritchard. As the word hung in the air, the question seemed to morph into an accusation.

"It's his first day," said Nathan's father. "Haven't you ever taken a wrong turn before?"

"I'm just trying to establish what happened here," answered Mr. Pritchard stiffly.

"He's already told you," said Mr. Tilly. "Robert was being bullied, and Nathan tried to stop it. My son's done nothing wrong." He pointed at the principal. "You have a bullying problem. And I want to know what the hell you're going to do about it."

Mr. Pritchard looked rattled. He didn't like having his prosecutorial process disrupted by rowdy parents. "First of all," he said, bristling, "we don't use that kind of language here."

Nathan's father frowned. "*What* kind of language?"

"What you said. That word." Mr. Pritchard paused. "H–E–double hockey sticks."

There was a moment's silence, and then Mr. Tilly began to roar with laughter. A rich, deep, thunderous gale of unbounded hilarity ricocheted off the office walls. He was laughing so hard that he bent forward and grabbed his stomach as it shook—it was, quite literally, a belly laugh. Mr. Tilly's amusement was infectious. As I watched him, it was impossible not to smile, too. I glanced across at Nathan, who had begun to laugh as well. My mother was looking at her shoes, but the corner of her mouth was twitching upward into a grin. Hollis smirked. The only person who was not laughing was Mr. Pritchard, who sat behind his desk, his cheeks pink with anger.

Nathan's father did his best to compose himself, but it was clear that he was having difficulty keeping a straight face. "I'm sorry," he said, obviously not sorry in the slightest, "but do people really talk that way around here?"

"Some of us do," said Mr. Pritchard, tight-lipped. "You're not in Texas anymore, Mr. Tilly."

"Oh, don't I know it. In Texas people would be more worried about the fact that students are being bullied instead of objecting to my language." Mr. Tilly had stopped laughing now. "I should give you a *real* four-letter word to complain about."

I decided that I liked Nathan's father.

Mr. Pritchard had picked up a pen and was stabbing its nib into the topmost piece of paper on his desk. He finally looked up at me. "Has this ever happened before, Robert?" he asked.

"No," I said.

"That's a big fat lie, too," said Nathan. "I heard them talking in the locker room. This was going on last year, too."

"Is that true?" asked my mother sharply.

"You need to get your house in order," Nathan's father told Mr. Pritchard. "Who knows how much longer this would have gone on if Nathan hadn't intervened? I want to know what you're going to do to stop this from happening again."

Mr. Pritchard went very still for a moment, and then he stood up. "I don't think we'll need to worry about that," he said.

We all looked at him, surprised.

"This matter is closed," said Mr. Pritchard. "I can assure you, Mr. Tilly, and you, Mrs. Carter, that everything will be taken care of. You may all go. Except you, Hollis. You stay."

Hollis shot me a poisonous look as my mother ushered me out of the room. We stood in the empty corridor with Nathan and his father. My mother's face was pale. I wasn't looking forward to the trip home.

"I'm Leonard Tilly," said Nathan's father, extending his hand toward my mother.

They shook. "Mary Carter."

"It's a pleasure to meet you."

"I wish the circumstances had been different," said my mother. She turned to Nathan. "Thank you, Nathan," she said. "That was a brave thing you did." She nudged me.

"Yeah, thanks," I mumbled.

Nathan beamed at us, oblivious to the bucketfuls of discomfort he had heaped upon me. My mother was right. It *was* a brave thing that he'd done. And he wasn't scared of Hollis Calhoun, not one bit. Nathan Tilly, I decided, was either a hero or an idiot. Whichever it was, I couldn't help but like him.

"Well look," said Mr. Tilly, "I think this calls for some sort of celebration." He rubbed his hands together. "Good conquering evil, a triumph for the underdog, all that stuff. We should all go and have some ice cream, or gin, or something. What do you say?"

"We really need to be getting home," said my mother. "Robert's brother is in the house on his own, and he doesn't like to be left alone for too long."

This wasn't true, and she knew it. Whenever he had the house to himself Liam played his records as loud as he could, gleefully rocking back and forth in his wheelchair, rattling the window frames with all the noise.

"Perhaps another time, then," said Mr. Tilly.

"That would be *great*," I said.

He looked at me kindly. "We'll plan on it," he said. "And don't worry," he added, turning to my mother, "we'll mainly eat ice cream. No more than a glass or two of gin, I promise."

My mother smiled wanly.

"Quite an eventful first day of school, all in all," said Mr. Tilly, ruffling his son's hair. "Are you ready to go home?" Nathan nodded. They turned and began to walk down the corridor. As I watched them go, something occurred to me.

"Mr. Tilly?" I called.

He turned back to look at me.

I cleared my throat. "Do you really have a mongoose?"

"Of course we do."

I couldn't help myself. "But aren't mongooses *illegal*?"

Nathan's father grinned at me.

"Maybe they are, maybe not," he said.

THREE

The following morning I walked into school in a state of high agitation. I didn't know what kind of punishment Mr. Pritchard had given Hollis the afternoon before, but I was sure that he would exact retribution from me in proportionate terms.

My mood wasn't helped by the awkward display of parental hand-wringing that I'd endured the previous evening. When my father had arrived home, my mother had pulled him into their bedroom for a whispered conference. When they emerged, both of them wore the same expression of saddened concern. What worries us, said my father more than once over the course of the painful conversation that followed, is that you never asked us for help. I had denied them the opportunity to swoop down and fix everything; my silence about Hollis had prevented them from playing the role of involved and caring parents. *That* was what was so disappointing. As I listened to them talk, the thought occurred to me that if either my mother or my father had been paying the slightest attention, they would have noticed that something was wrong. But my happiness, or lack of it, didn't make even the tiniest ping on their emotional radar. My brother was like a World War II bomber dropping strips of foil into the air, scrambling their screens. Nothing else registered.

I was late and hurried down the corridor. Mr. Pritchard was waiting for me outside my classroom. "Ah, Robert," he said. "I thought you would want to know that I've rescinded my earlier decision about Hollis Calhoun's academic development."

"Hollis?" I frowned. "I don't—"

"Boys like Hollis don't care about rules. No matter what punishment I gave him, he would have kept on bullying you, maybe worse than before. Am I right?"

I nodded.

"Then I realized that there was one thing I *could* do." Mr. Pritchard gave me a small smile. "Last night, with my blessing, Hollis graduated. We did a little grade management, shall we say, and as of this morning he is no longer a student at Longfellow. He's where he belongs, which is in high school, where he can push around people his own size."

I looked around me. "So he's not—?"

"No," said Mr. Pritchard. "He's not."

The heavy weight of dread that had been pressing between my shoulder blades disappeared. I felt light, free, able to fly.

"I won't pretend that it doesn't stick in my craw that Hollis is getting rewarded for his bad behavior," continued Mr. Pritchard. "The boy is an idiot, and lazy, too. But this looked like the best result for you, and the best result for the school."

"Thank you," I breathed.

"Don't thank me," said Mr. Pritchard. "Go and thank Nathan Tilly. If he hadn't made such a ruckus, then Hollis never would have been caught, and you'd still be in the same predicament."

I nodded and pushed open the classroom door, still blinking in wordless astonishment. Hollis was gone! I couldn't believe it.

Nathan was already at his desk, his hands resting calmly on the table in front of him. I slid into the seat next to him and told him the news. The words were no less amazing when I heard myself say them out loud. "Hollis is gone." *Hollis is gone.* Nathan greeted the news with almost as much jubilation as I did.

"That's amazing," he said.

"It's because of you," I said.

Nathan waved this away but couldn't help grinning. "My dad wants to take us out for ice cream this afternoon, like he promised. If you walk home with me after school, he'll drive us back into town. He can drop you at your house afterward."

"Where do you live?" I asked.

"Out on Sebbanquik Point."

Sebbanquik Point was a small promontory just north of town that edged into the dark waves of the Atlantic. It was a bleak, isolated spot, covered with tall pine trees. Sometimes I bicycled out that way.

My mother would be busy with Liam. She wouldn't notice if I was late getting home.

"That sounds great," I said.

IT WAS A WARM AFTERNOON. When school ended Nathan Tilly and I slung our backpacks over our shoulders and trudged out of the school gates together. We walked in silence for a little while. The road out to Sebbanquik Point was a narrow lane that had only recently been blacktopped, lined on both sides by tall banks of hedgerow. At the crest of a hill, the ocean came into view for the first time. We stood there for a moment and watched the whitecaps of the waves as they rolled toward the shore. Overhead a couple of gulls hovered, motionless in the air.

"I like it here," said Nathan.

"Why did you move to Maine?" I asked.

"My dad has always dreamed of being a lobster fisherman. Like, ever since he was a kid. He finally convinced my mom to move, so we came here and he bought a boat."

"What did he do in Texas?"

"He worked in an office."

"That's quite a change," I said.

Nathan nodded. "He's grown that beard since we got here, too. He wanted to look more like a sailor."

"How's the fishing going?"

"Well, that depends how you look at it," said Nathan. "He never catches much. In fact he hardly catches anything. But he loves to check his traps every day. That makes him happy."

My parents knew several lobstermen who went out onto the ocean each morning before the sun came up, rain or shine. They were sad, hard men. I wondered what they thought of the cheerful amateur from Texas with his sailor's cap joining their ranks.

"What about your mom?" I asked. "Does she like it here?"

Nathan kicked at a stone and sent it skittering into the shoulder. "She misses home," he said.

"You have any brothers or sisters?"

"No, it's just me and my parents. What about you?"

"One brother."

"I wish I had a brother," said Nathan. "It would be fun to have someone to mess around with on the beach."

"Liam doesn't go outside much," I said.

"Why not?"

When my brother had first been diagnosed, I had been too young to be able to pronounce the name of his disease. Those long, alien words were foreign and frightening on my tongue, each complicated syllable freighted with menace. Now I would not say the name out loud, even though I could. To name it was to acknowledge what we all knew to be true, that eventually it would win.

"He's pretty sick," I said.

"That's too bad," said Nathan.

I remained silent. As usual, talking about Liam had drawn all words out of me.

We turned a corner, and Nathan pointed. "That's our house," he said. Up ahead stood a solitary two-story building, its silhouette framed starkly against the vast expanse of pale northern sky behind it.

Two-thirds of the way along the roof, Nathan's father was perched on the shingles, one foot on either side of the apex. He stood perfectly still and appeared to be looking out toward the ocean. On his head was the sailor's cap that he'd been wearing the previous afternoon.

"What's your dad doing on the roof?" I asked.

"Can't you see?" said Nathan. "He's flying a kite."

I scanned the sky over the house. Finally I saw it—way up high, a flash of scarlet. The line between the tiny lozenge of color and Nathan's father was invisible, but their perfect and total stillness mirrored each other so precisely that it was impossible that they were not connected. But Mr. Tilly had not glanced at the kite once. His gaze remained turned toward the ocean.

"Come on," said Nathan. We began walking.

As we got closer, Nathan shouted, "Dad!"

Mr. Tilly turned in our direction. He looked down at us and raised his arm in greeting. As he did so, he slipped. His body lurched sideways as he tried to regain his balance, and I saw his mouth open into an O of surprise. His foot couldn't find any purchase on the sloping roof, and he spun in an unsteady pirouette, his arms windmilling, before toppling sideways. As he fell, the side of his head smashed against the shingles. The sailor's cap went flying, and he tumbled downward in ghastly slow motion. The gutter that ran around the bottom of the roof halted his progress, but only for a moment. There was a terrible crack as the molded aluminum gave way, and then Nathan's father rolled off into nothingness.

We ran.

Mr. Tilly was lying on a narrow strip of grass that edged up to the side of the house. He looked as if he could have been enjoying a brief nap in the afternoon sun had it not been for his right arm, which was bent at a grotesque angle halfway between his elbow and his wrist. The sight of the misshapen limb caused a tide of bile to rise in my throat. Finally I remembered to breathe and gulped down some air.

We stared down at Mr. Tilly's body. A matrix of angry cuts and bruises spanned his forehead and cheeks. His mouth was hanging open. There was a smearing of dark red where his teeth should have been. A small groan emerged from his throat. He coughed painfully and half opened his eyes. He squinted foggily at us.

"Hello, boys," he croaked. The words emerged barely intact from his punctured mouth. "We might have to wait for that ice cream." A glistening pearl of dark blood filled his right nostril. A thin white nylon line emerged from between the fingers of his left hand and stretched into the sky. I looked up. The scarlet kite hovered above us, only now its presence felt more sinister, like a bird of prey readying to strike.

"Don't die, Mr. Tilly," I said, my mouth dry with terror.

"Go fetch your mother, Nathan," he said. "She's on the beach."

Nathan stared down at his father. "I'm not leaving you," he said. "I'm never going to leave you."

"You're a good boy," said Mr. Tilly, "but I really need you to go." He closed his eyes. "The kite was just an excuse to be on the roof, you know," he murmured.

Nathan knelt down beside him. "What do you mean?"

"When I'm up there I can see your mother as she walks up and down by the ocean. That's why I do it." He smiled. "I love to watch her."

There was something so absolute about the stillness that overcame him then that I knew at once that he was dead. As life drained out of Mr. Tilly's pulverized body, his grip on the kite line loosened. Before I could stop it, the nylon line slipped free of his fingers and was tugged away by the wind.

That was when Nathan turned away and sprinted down the side of the house. He disappeared around the corner, toward the ocean.

"Nathan!" I yelled. "Come back!"

But he did not come back. I looked down at the dead man. Not sure what else to do, I dutifully began to pray for Mr. Tilly's soul.

Moments later I heard footsteps approaching. I turned around to see Nathan running toward me, followed by a woman. "Leonard!" she screamed. She threw herself on top of the dead man and began to beat her fists against his chest. The pummeling made Mr. Tilly's head twist to the side, which caused the blood in his nose to trickle across his cheek in a single dark rivulet. Finally the punches slowed, and then stopped. Mrs. Tilly laid her head against her husband's chest. Her face was turned away from me.

In the stillness that followed I glanced at Nathan. He was staring up into the sky, watching the scarlet kite. By then it was no more than a speck of color in the distance, dancing away from the earth. Nobody said anything for a long time.

Finally, Mrs. Tilly wrapped her arms around her dead husband and wrestled him into a sitting position. She clung to him, letting out a low moan of despair.

In the spot where Mr. Tilly had been lying was a misshapen cake of brown fur. It was, I realized dully, about the size of a mongoose.

Nathan fell to his knees and inspected the flattened body for signs of life, and then his face dissolved into a waterfall of silent tears. While he wept, Mrs. Tilly held her husband in her arms, swaying gently. She did not look at Nathan once.

They looked like the two loneliest people in the world.

FOUR

They chose the smallest chapel in Haverford, but it was still too big.

Holy Trinity Church of Christ was squeezed between the town library and the automated car wash. The only indication that the building was a place of worship was a modest wooden cross above the front door. The church couldn't have held more than a few dozen congregants when it was full, but there were only five of us at Leonard Tilly's funeral. Nathan and his mother were in the front pew. My parents and I sat behind them.

Nathan was wearing a dark suit several sizes too large for him. He stared straight ahead all the way through the service, not once glancing back at us. Mrs. Tilly dabbed at her eyes with a small handkerchief. During the hymns they stood with their hymnals open but neither made any sound at all. My father mumbled the words in his usual tuneless way, and I sang cautiously along in my unsteady treble. It was left to my mother to carry the melody, which she did with her customary verve. I glanced at her halfway through the third verse of "Nearer, My God, to Thee" and saw that she was crying.

There was nothing my mother loved more than a good funeral.

She wept as she listened to the choked-up eulogies, she wallowed in the somber beauty of the mournful hymns. It didn't matter whether she knew the deceased. It was the shared grief of the living that she sought, the congregation's dazed sadness at the finality of their last good-bye.

Every service my mother attended was just another rehearsal for the main event, for the funeral that was yet to come.

MY BROTHER, LIAM, had been a beautiful baby. Our house was filled with photographs of his little face grinning impishly into the camera. He was a happy child, delighted with everything he saw, quick to learn new things. My mother loved to put him in the stroller and parade him around the town. She sat with the other mothers at the town playground and watched as Liam happily dug holes in the sandbox with his plastic spade. But he had been slow to walk and never quite outgrew his initial unsteadiness on his feet. His infant totter morphed into an inelegant waddle. He began to fall down more and would lie on the ground sobbing, waiting to be picked up. Soon my mother began to follow him around, an anxious shadow, ready to haul him back to his feet whenever he fell. By the age of two and a half, he didn't want to leave his stroller. He screamed when my mother undid the straps and lifted him out. Rather than running off to play, he would try to clamber back into his seat. My mother did her best not to worry, but somewhere deep within her a seed of unspoken terror had been planted, and it grew until she could no longer turn away from the truth.

So began a nightmare of appointments and examinations. Liam was prodded and poked and observed as he struggled to walk across a room. Cautious, inconclusive reports led to more referrals and further scrutiny. My parents' world was finally blown apart in the office of a consultant neurologist in Portland. Liam, he told them, suffered from Duchenne muscular dystrophy.

My parents sat there, as still as death, saying nothing, waiting for more.

It was a slow, wasting disease, explained the doctor. Over time Liam's muscles would atrophy until he was no longer able to walk at all. Once he was in a wheelchair, other problems would present themselves. Long periods of immobility would result in scoliosis, a vicious curving of the spine, which would cause a compression of the lungs. It was usually respiratory problems that killed Duchenne sufferers first.

And no, said the doctor, in answer to the question that had not been asked. There is no cure.

My parents clutched each other's hands, unable to escape those four words.

How long? whispered my father.

It varies, answered the consultant. The majority of patients die before the age of twenty, but there are exceptions. Some can go on longer, with luck and careful treatment.

Then my mother whispered an even bigger question: *Why?*

We don't know exactly what causes the disease, admitted the neurologist. We think it results from a genetic mutation that inhibits the production of muscle protein. But there are thousands of such proteins, and we haven't identified which one is responsible. What we do know from the data is that it appears to be hereditary, and it seems almost exclusively to affect boys.

His words echoed around the room, but my mother could not let them in. Four days earlier she had sat in another doctor's office and been given the date, about twenty-eight weeks away, when I would be born. Scarcely able to form the words, she asked whether her new baby would have the disease, too.

The doctor leaned back in his chair. Statistics, he said. You know what people say about them, so take this how you will. The studies suggest that if your new baby is a boy, the chances are about fifty-fifty that he'll develop Duchenne as well.

My mother gazed down at her still-flat belly, numb with fear.

The great-granddaughter of Irish immigrants from Cork, my mother had been raised a devout Catholic. All her life she had found comfort in the unworldly rituals of her faith, and never more so than back then. Every night she knelt down beside her bed, her Bible clasped between her hands, and prayed for a baby girl, as fiercely as she had ever prayed for anything.

Seven months later, as she lay in the delivery room with her arms around my purple, minutes-old body, the nurse bent over and told her that she had a son. The odds of future heartache doubled in an instant and eclipsed all joy.

LIAM'S CONDITION CONTINUED to deteriorate. Physical therapists came and went. My parents massaged my brother's feet and stretched the tendons in his young legs to ease his discomfort. He continued to walk, but with increasing difficulty. School was hard from the start. In first grade the other children made fun of his slow, unusual gait, and when they pushed him to the ground, he was unable to get back up. He would lie sprawled across the playground and yell at his tormentors while they stood over him and laughed. Sending Liam off to school each day was torture for my mother. He could not take the bus that passed by the end of our road—the steep steps at the driver's door were too much for him—and so every morning my mother drove him. She helped him out of the car and watched as he limped off without a backward glance. For the rest of the day she would dangle me off her knee and tickle me under the chin, but her mind was inside those school gates.

By the time I was three years old, Liam needed full-length orthoses, grotesque plastic contraptions that sheathed his legs from his buttocks down to his ankles, in order to keep him standing upright. Stairs became a torment. That winter my father converted his ground-floor study into a bedroom for Liam. He painted a dazzling mural across one wall, a dramatic jungle panorama with beautiful creatures peeking out from behind verdant fronds of exotic foliage. I didn't like to go in there, fearful that all those monkeys, zebras, and parakeets would make me weep with envy. I knew I should not complain, should not begrudge my brother this one small thing. But I ardently, secretly wished that my father would paint *my* bedroom wall, too.

On a therapist's recommendation, my parents purchased a trampoline. Each afternoon my mother lifted Liam into the center of the rubber circle, where he would perform a series of exercises. Lift one leg, lift the other leg. He fell down frequently, but as his balance improved, my brother learned how to generate enough momentum to launch himself skyward. In those moments when he was airborne, his mutinous legs were no longer trapped beneath the weight of his body, and he yelled with glee, every bounce a tiny glimpse of freedom.

All this time, my parents were watching me. Every time I stumbled or tripped, they were skewered by an ice-cold needle of fear. They would wait for me to do it again, looking for a pattern that would spell the death of hope. But there was no pattern, not for me. I was just a clumsy child, manifestly healthy, charging about without a care in the world. I spent my days climbing trees and flying up and down the neighborhood sidewalks on my bike. By my fifth birthday

I was almost as tall as my brother, and finally my parents allowed themselves to believe that they would be spared a second dose of heartbreak. As she lifted her wreck of a son in and out of the bathtub each night, my mother knew that there was a world of grief to come, but at least the scope of the tragedy was finite now.

SOON AFTER MY BROTHER turned twelve, he was confined to his wheelchair, and his body began its next phase of deterioration, a curvature of the spine that began to warp his young body into a gruesome knot. Navigating school corridors and classrooms was becoming increasingly difficult, and while nobody could push Liam over on the playground anymore, he still had to endure the cruelties of his classmates. My mother begged him to let her homeschool him, but he refused. My brother possessed a stupendously obstinate streak. Everybody would have understood if he had opted to stay home, which was precisely why he refused to do it. People were always making allowances for him, and it drove him crazy. All Liam ever wanted was to be treated the same as everyone else. It was unfortunate that my parents were the people least equipped to indulge him. Instead they fretted and hovered over him, ceaselessly vigilant and impossibly suffocating. It took Liam months to convince my father that he should be allowed to have a job at the amusement park, just like every other kid in his class. Over my mother's hysterical objections, he worked for two summers in the admissions kiosk, tallying receipts and keeping track of daily attendance. I don't remember a time when he had been happier.

At school, my brother threw himself into everything. He directed a production of *Oklahoma!*, edited the school magazine, and played clarinet in the wind band. He had started learning the instrument because the controlled breathing would strengthen his weakening lungs, but he quickly discovered a profound joy in the music he created. Tunes poured out of him, released from beneath his fingers as they fluttered across the instrument's silver keys. Every day our house was filled with rich, woody melody. The clarinet's high, hopeful tone cleaved through the walls, bearing us all along on its joyful river of notes.

It wasn't all Poulenc sonatas and Finzi bagatelles, though. Liam loved his clarinet, but his deepest passion was rock and roll. His favorite bands were the Ramones and the New York Dolls, and there was nothing he liked more than listening to their records in his bedroom with the volume turned up too loud. The heavy *whomp whomp* of the bass would reverberate through the house like an earthquake. My parents would exchange baleful looks as the walls shook, but they never asked him to turn the volume down. I, on the other hand, was constantly being reprimanded for clomping up the stairs or blowing my nose too noisily. My parents couldn't forget, not even for a moment, that Liam would die too soon, and so they indulged him at every turn, terrified that one day they would look back and wonder if they could have been kinder. I was expected to abide by the household's many rules, but my brother always got a free pass.

Sometimes Liam would call me into his bedroom and insist on playing a particular song for me. I watched him bounce up and down in his wheelchair, invigorated by the brutal onslaught of noise that came out of the speakers. I desperately wanted to like my brother's music. I craved a bridge that would allow us to traverse the chasm of his disease and let us escape the fact that I was going to live and he was going to die. But as much as I tried, I couldn't enjoy the anarchic, coiled anger of Liam's musical heroes.

"Hey, Robbie," he would tell me, "when you're older, we'll take a trip to New York together, just you and me. We'll hang out on the

Lower East Side and watch the bands." He would wave at whatever record was on the turntable. "Imagine hearing these guys play live!" By then his limbs were as thin as the bones beneath his skin, the flesh and muscle atrophied into extinction. His left lung was dangerously compressed. I would nod, baffled by his ability to make plans for a future that we knew would never come. I would eventually creep away and put on one of my mother's Elton John records to becalm my jangled nerves. All I could hear in Liam's music was fury, but he saw beauty in those bruising three-chord explosions. But that was my brother all over. He was always able to ferret out joy where others could not.

WHEN THE SERVICE FOR Mr. Tilly ended, our little group walked quietly out of the church. In a corner of the adjacent graveyard was a rectangular pit next to a hill of freshly excavated dirt. The coffin was carried to the graveside on the shoulders of six men I hadn't seen before. I supposed there were volunteer pallbearers the church could call on if the deceased didn't have the requisite number of friends to do the job. We stood and watched as the men lowered the coffin into the ground.

The minister opened his prayer book and began to speak. Nathan stood on the other side of the open grave, standing stiffly next to his mother. I watched Mrs. Tilly curiously. She wore a dark gray coat that went all the way down to her ankles, and her blond hair was tucked up beneath a large black hat. Much of her face was hidden behind a pair of oversize sunglasses, even though there were dark clouds scudding low across the sky. She looked like a movie star trying to pass incognito.

Nathan and Mrs. Tilly did not look at each other while the minister spoke. They shared the studied indifference of strangers standing side by side on a platform, waiting for the next train to pull in. When the prayers were finished, Mrs. Tilly bent down and threw a handful of earth onto the lid of the coffin. She turned to Nathan, but he shook his head angrily and put his hands into his pockets. After a pause, my father stepped forward and a second volley of soil landed on the coffin. My mother went next, and then she nudged me. As I threw my handful of dirt into the hole I could feel Nathan's eyes on me.

As I stepped back, Nathan turned from the grave and began to walk away. His mother set off after him, murmuring something I could not hear. The minister watched them go and then nodded to the gravedigger, who was standing to one side, leaning on his shovel, waiting to get to work.

My parents and I walked back through the cemetery. The only sounds were the scrape of the gravedigger's blade as it bit into the mound of earth and the rhythmic thud of soil landing on mahogany.

Nathan was standing just outside the cemetery gates. A few yards away, his mother sat behind the steering wheel of an old Impala. She was smoking a cigarette with the window rolled down. She said something to Nathan, who did not reply. Finally Mrs. Tilly threw the butt of her cigarette out of the window and backed the car out of the parking lot. Nathan did not look up as she drove away.

My mother nudged me. "You should go and see if he's all right."

"He looks fine to me," I said.

"Robert," she said gently. "How is he going to get back home?"

I scuffed my shoe against the gravel pathway and shrugged.

"Nathan was kind to you in the locker room last week." My mother put a hand on my shoulder. "So now he needs you to be kind back. Remember Proverbs: '*Do not let kindness and truth leave you. Bind them around your neck. Write them on the tablet of your heart.*'" She smiled at me, and I knew the game was up.

My father's cheery agnosticism had never been a match for my mother's faith. I had been raised on a strict regime of regular attendance at Mass and the dutiful saying of prayers at bedtime. When my mother quoted the scriptures, it was as if she were casting a spell over me that I was powerless to defy.

I looked across the parking lot at Nathan Tilly. I would not let kindness leave me. I walked toward him.

FIVE

Nathan looked up as I approached. "She shouldn't have done it," he said.

"Shouldn't have done what?" I asked.

"She shouldn't have *buried* him." His eyes were dark. "She should have scattered his ashes into the air and set him free."

I didn't know how to respond. "Do you want to come back to my house?" I asked him. I pointed toward the station wagon, where my parents were pretending not to watch us through the windshield.

Nathan turned to look at them for a moment. "No thanks," he said.

"How are you going to get home?"

He shrugged. "I suppose I'll walk."

"At least let us give you a ride," I said. "It might rain."

"Okay," said Nathan. "Thanks."

The four of us drove in silence out to Sebbanquik Point. My heart performed an anxious somersault as the Tillys' house came into view. There was no evidence of the accident. I don't know what I was expecting—a flag fluttering at half-mast, perhaps, or yellow police tape cordoning off the area—but the place looked the same.

ALEX GEORGE

Nathan's father was dead, and life was going on without him, exactly as before.

Mrs. Tilly's car was not in the driveway.

"Are you sure you'll be all right on your own, Nathan?" asked my mother as we pulled up. "Wouldn't you prefer some company right now?"

Nathan glanced at me. "Some company would be okay," he said.

My mother twisted around in her seat and fixed me with an unambiguous look. "Dad can come and pick you up in a while," she said.

I had been ambushed. "I'll see you later, then," I said reluctantly, and opened the car door. Nathan clambered out the other side. As my parents backed out of the driveway, Nathan pulled a key out of his pocket and unlocked the front door. I kept my eyes firmly on the ground, unwilling to look up at the roof. I wanted to ask Nathan whether he stayed awake at night, like I did, replaying his father's fall over and over again in his mind. Since the accident I had been unable to escape the nagging thought that if we hadn't appeared when we did, Mr. Tilly never would have waved at us, never would have lost his balance, and never would have fallen.

We stepped into a hallway floored with flagstones. "I'm going to change out of this stupid suit," said Nathan. "I'll be right back." He set off down the hallway and then I heard footsteps as he climbed the stairs.

Off one side of the hallway was a study. I wandered in. The room was empty apart from a table and chair in the middle of the room. On the table there was a typewriter and a glass ashtray half-full of crushed cigarette butts. A curtain was drawn across the room's only window. I pulled back the fabric and watched the dark waves of the Atlantic smash into the rocks farther down the coastline.

My family lived in a neighborhood in the middle of Haverford, a

42

couple of miles inland. The view from my bedroom window was of our fenced-in backyard. There was a crabapple tree and a pond, whose waters were never troubled by more than an occasional breeze. It was a safe place, and that was what I liked. The ocean outside Nathan Tilly's house was ferocious, untamable. I let the curtain fall back in place.

I sat at the desk and pressed down on one of the typewriter keys. A thin metal arm rose up in a tight parabola, and the blackened ribbon rose to meet it. I allowed the hammer to hover for a moment and then took my finger away.

"There you are." Nathan was standing in the doorway.

I turned to face him. "What is this place?"

"My mom's study. It's where she spends most of her time."

"Doing what?"

Nathan pointed to the table. "She types. At least, that's what it sounds like. I've never actually seen a single piece of paper with words on it." He paused. "I don't think she puts paper into the typewriter—she just sits there and hits the keys all day." He looked at me. "Hey, I want to show you something. Come on."

We went through the house to a utility room next to the kitchen. A mountain of unfolded clothes was perched on top of a washing machine. Cleaning supplies had been stuffed into a dirty yellow bucket. In the corner of the room was a freezer, humming quietly to itself. Nathan opened it, reached inside, and removed a black trash bag. He carried the bag into the kitchen and put it in the middle of the table.

"Open it," he said.

The top of the bag had been secured with a green plastic twist. I unwound it.

"Go ahead," said Nathan. "Take a look inside."

I opened the bag, and then I yelled in terror.

Gazing out at me were two yellow eyes, fogged by death.

It was Nathan's mongoose.

The creature's jaw was frozen open in a rictus of horrified surprise. It was baring its small, pointed teeth at me, as if I were one last rattlesnake to confront. "What's this doing in your *freezer*?" I gasped.

"I wanted to keep him," explained Nathan. He reached into the bag and pulled out the mongoose. The fur on its back was frozen into tufted peaks, each one crested with a dusting of ice. Whatever kind of postmortem care Nathan had administered, there was no mistaking the fact that the mongoose had been badly squashed by Mr. Tilly's fall.

"It's frozen," I pointed out.

"If you put him in the oven he warms up pretty fast," said Nathan.

And so we put the dead mongoose on a baking tray and warmed it up. Soon it had defrosted sufficiently for us to be able to wiggle its paws and turn its head from side to side. Once it had lost its ghostly patina of ice, the mongoose looked almost lifelike again.

"What's its name?" I asked.

"Philippe. After Philippe Petit."

I looked at Nathan blankly.

"You know, the guy who walked between the Twin Towers on a tightrope a few years ago. Can you imagine?" Nathan's eyes shone. "What do you think it must have felt like, being that high off the ground? With nothing to support you, nothing to catch you if you fell?"

I frowned. "It sounds awful."

"You don't think it would be amazing? Suspended in midair over New York, balancing on a rope!"

"The guy must be crazy," I said.

"Of course he is," agreed Nathan cheerfully. "He thinks that the usual rules don't apply to him."

"The usual rules?"

"You know. Gravity. Physics. Laws of all kinds, actually. He was arrested when he climbed off the rope."

After we put the dead mongoose back into the freezer we sat in the kitchen and each drank a glass of milk. I thought about Mr. Tilly's funeral.

"I liked your dad a lot," I said.

"I can't believe he's gone," said Nathan. "It's like there's this big black hole inside me now, and it's going to keep on growing until there's nothing of me left."

I said nothing, thinking about my brother. I knew about big black holes.

"Dad and I used to do everything together," said Nathan. "He took me places, taught me stuff. We had adventures." He was silent for a moment. "Now that he's gone, I don't know what I'm supposed to do anymore."

"Your mom will take you places," I said.

Nathan shook his head. "The only places *she* goes are inside her head."

"What sort of things did you do with your dad?"

"I'll show you. Come on."

Nathan led me to a wooden shed that stood behind the house. He pulled back the latch and ushered me inside. There were two large windows, one looking toward the house, the other toward the ocean. The walls, floor, and ceiling had all been painted dazzling white. There was a long table in the middle of the room. Forests of color-flecked paintbrushes stood in grimy glass jars. There were hacksaws of various sizes, hammers, pliers, spools of thread, and a regiment of glue pots. A heavy iron vise was fixed to the edge of the table. From its grip emerged a complicated, three-dimensional matrix of pale balsawood rods. But it was the display on the walls that really caught my attention. Kites were mounted in neatly ordered rows. There were squares, rectangles, and fat diamonds of tautly drawn fabric, a glorious riot of color.

"This is my father's workshop," said Nathan.

I looked around the room at the kites. "He *made* these?"

Nathan nodded. "Pick one," he said. "We'll take it out to the beach and fly it."

"Really?"

"He didn't make them to hang on a wall, Robert."

I didn't need a second invitation. I pointed to an orange lozenge with flashes of bright yellow jagging diagonally between its corners. "That one."

Nathan unhooked the kite. "We'll need that," he said, pointing to a spool of nylon line that lay on the workbench. I picked it up.

The moment we stepped outside, the fabric began to billow and snap in the breeze. Nathan steadied himself as the kite came to life in his hands. Just beyond the workshop was a weathered wooden staircase leading to the beach. I followed Nathan down the steps. The beach was in fact a cove, cut off at both ends by jagged promontories of rock.

"Dad and I came down here to fly kites," shouted Nathan above the wind. He pointed to the southern end of the cove, where a squat, windowless hut sat by the water's edge. Next to it an old wooden pier stretched into the ocean. "His lobster boat and traps are in there," said Nathan. But something else had caught my attention. All along the beach there were columns of sun-bleached stones stacked one on top of another. No two piles were quite the same shape or size.

"What are those?" I asked.

"My mother builds them," said Nathan. "If she's not in her study, she's down here."

I remembered Mr. Tilly standing on the roof, watching his wife.

I wondered which column she had been working on when he fell. "What are they for?"

Nathan shrugged. "They remind me of some kind of army," he said. The columns stretched up and down the shoreline, windswept sentinels, vigilant against the onslaught of the ocean and whatever dangers lurked over the horizon. "Sometimes she builds them too close to the water, and the tide knocks them down." He paused. "Those are never good days."

We wandered among the ghostly piles of stones. It felt as if they were watching us. At the ocean's edge, Nathan threaded the white line through a tiny metal eye in the center of the kite's frame. Then he handed the spool back to me.

"You first," he said.

Still holding the kite, he began to walk down the beach. The line unraveled with each step he took. When he was about thirty yards away from me, Nathan turned and held the kite out in front of him. "Start running on three," he shouted.

I nodded.

"One, two—three!"

I began to run along the sand, lifting the line high above my head, tugging it upward as I went. The kite caught a gust of wind and streaked into the sky. I allowed the nylon to unspool quickly, giving the greedy winds what they wanted. Nathan joined me by the water's edge. We watched the kite bob and weave above us. I could feel the tug of every gust of wind in my fingers. I lost track of time then. There was nothing except the kite and me, and the thin cord that connected us. At some point Nathan stepped forward and took the line from me. I surrendered without protest but did not take my eyes off the kite. We stood side by side, hypnotized by its gentle dance. Neither of us said a word.

Then without warning Nathan reached into his pocket and

pulled out a penknife. Before I knew what was happening, with one quick motion he cut through the line. The kite spiraled upward until it vanished into the clouds.

"What did you do that for?" I demanded.

"My dad wouldn't have wanted his kites trapped in that workshop." Nathan smiled at me sadly. "He may be buried in the ground, but I can still set his kites free."

IN THE WEEKS THAT FOLLOWED, Nathan and I walked back to Sebbanquik Point most days after school. I never saw Mrs. Tilly on those visits, but I certainly heard her. The door to her study remained shut, but the rhythmic clatter of typewriter keys could be heard throughout the house. I marveled at her industry; she never stopped, not even when she lit another cigarette—which, judging by the wisps of smoke that were always curling beneath the study door, she did every few minutes. I thought about Nathan's theory that there was never any paper in the typewriter. I imagined Mrs. Tilly hunched over the keys, telling stories to nobody but herself.

Nathan and I didn't spend much time in the house. Each afternoon we hurried out to his father's workshop and took another brightly colored kite off the wall. We trooped down to the beach and, standing amid his mother's silent crowd of stone onlookers, launched each one heavenward, feeling the caress of the late-summer breezes shiver down the line.

While we watched the kites dance over our heads, Nathan told me stories from before they'd come to Maine. He told me about epic fishing expeditions with his father, crazy road trips, and domestic adventures involving exotic species of wildlife I'd never heard of. He told me about driving into the Texas desert in search of the dry winds that whipped across the hot, empty scrubland. They would pull off the road and throw his father's kites into the huge white sky. My own stories about growing up in Maine seemed pedestrian in comparison, but Nathan was interested in hearing about the amusement park. He wanted to know everything about the place. He made me promise that I would take him there soon.

It was only when Nathan pulled out his penknife that we stopped talking. He would cut the string, and then we would silently watch as the kite climbed higher and higher into the sky, until we could no longer see even the faintest speck of color.

We walked back to the house without saying a word.

SIX

My father, Samuel Carter, was a serious man who had the misfortune to be destined to be involved in an unserious business. It was a burden that he did not wear lightly.

This burden manifested itself in physical form: specifically, thirteen acres of less-than-prime real estate, located just south of the Haverford city limits. On those thirteen acres there existed a magical world, full of enchantment, excitement, and fun. That, at least, was what the brochure said.

The name of this magical world was Fun-A-Lot.

From Memorial Day to Labor Day, the elaborately filigreed gates of Fun-A-Lot opened to welcome visitors who had had their fill of the natural glories that Maine had to offer and were looking for some man-made entertainment.

And what entertainment it was. At Fun-A-Lot a person could step back in time to the days of Arthurian legend. The court of Camelot had been re-created on the coast of southern Maine—**OLDE ENGLAND IN NEW ENGLAND,** as the legend above the gates put it. Teenage knights clanked about in ill-fitting plastic armor and damsels swept up and down the pathways in bodices garlanded with ribbons. There were jousting contests every afternoon: park employees mounted two tiny Shetland ponies and charged gently at each other, wielding plastic lancets for the edification of the watching crowds.

All the traditional amusement park entertainments were on offer, as well. There were devices designed to make visitors lose their lunch by sending them rocketing skyward or plunging toward the earth at unnatural velocities and angles. There was a Tilt-a-Whirl, bumper cars, and a large Ferris wheel. A roller coaster built on an elaborate scaffold of crosshatched wood soared over the other attractions. The excited screams of the riders could be heard throughout the park.

There were also more sedate pleasures to be enjoyed: booths where visitors could throw darts at playing cards, or pitch a baseball, or try to hook plastic ducks with a wooden pole. And because this was fantasy, not real life, every stall had a large sign that read: **PRIZE GUARANTEED EVERY TIME**. Children all longed for the five-foot-tall furry lobster on display in each booth; instead they won rivers of Taiwanese flotsam: giant sunglasses, glow-in-the-dark whistles, and erasers shaped like footballs.

All park employees wore medieval costumes and were required to talk in English accents and address guests using antiquated turns of phrase—the air was ripe with *verilys*, *sires*, and *prithee*, *fair maidens*. My father insisted on teaching all new recruits this mangled argot himself. His own English accent was a hybrid of down-east Maine and faux Cockney. It made Dick Van Dyke in *Mary Poppins* sound like Laurence Olivier. In a way it was perfect, this mauling of the English language. From the logo of the local dentist that was emblazoned in the center of every knight's shield to the faded pennants that flew from the molded plastic turrets, the whole place was a riot of artificiality, a festival of cheese.

But authenticity was never really the point. When I was younger my father had bought a miniature golf course from an amusement park that was going out of business in Oklahoma. He had shipped the whole thing halfway across the country on two giant trucks and rebuilt it, hole for hole. Unfortunately the park in Oklahoma had had a Wild West theme, and consequently the golf course was decorated with cacti and teepees and gin joints in dusty border towns, rather than castles in the English countryside. Every winter my father promised himself that he would turn all the gunslinging cowboys into wizards and court jesters, and the squaws into medieval maidens, but he never had the time. And so the cowboys and Injuns remained amid the tranquillity of Arthurian England, rifles drawn and tomahawks raised, like a weird glitch in the space-time continuum.

Refreshments, too, were anachronistic and of an unmistakably American variety. The concession stand did a brisk trade in plastic baskets of fried chicken, hot dogs and hamburgers, and alarmingly yellow popcorn.

My father had a joke he liked to tell. How do you make a small fortune in the amusement park business? he would ask. Well, you start with a *large* fortune . . . I had heard him deliver this line more times than I could count, and he always told it with the same wry smile that meant it wasn't really a joke at all. The profit margins were impossibly narrow. It cost an awful lot to deliver a summer's worth of fun on that scale, and my father had only a handful of weeks each year to recoup the money to pay for it all. He fretted his way through every day of the summer season. He was spoiled for choice when it came to things to worry about, but there were two fears that particularly weighed down his already embattled psyche. It was entirely typical of my father that they were the two things he was incapable of doing anything about.

Fear of fire was the thing most likely to keep my father awake at night. Ever since amusement parks had been built, so had they been incinerated. Entire parks had been swallowed by infernos, razed to the ground by a single wayward spark. My father would gloomily stare up at the roller coaster's immense wooden scaffolding and call it fun-size kindling. He compulsively checked fire extinguishers and ran weekly fire drills, yelling at staff with the apoplectic zeal of an army sergeant.

But no amount of precautionary drills could do anything about the weather.

When it rained, nobody came. People didn't want to watch jousting contests or go on the Ferris wheel if it meant getting soaked by drizzle whipping in off the Atlantic. It took only a few wet days more than the seasonal average to wipe out the park's profits for the year. The little transistor radio in my father's office was tuned to an oldies station that gave the local forecast every fifteen minutes, and his eyes were always flickering skyward, on the hunt for the first treacherous whiff of dark cloud. The gloomier the meteorological outlook, the more morose my father became. Whose bright idea was it to start a business in Maine that depends on *sunshine* to make money? he would complain every time it rained. Who would be crazy enough to contemplate such a thing?

MY GRANDFATHER, Ronald Carter, had been crazy enough, although it's doubtful he ever thought about the weather. He was never in it for the money.

Grandpa Ronald had been toiling quietly away behind a desk in an insurance adjustment agency in Augusta, processing claims and checking boxes, when he discovered that a wealthy second cousin in Peoria, Illinois, had died without leaving a will, and that he was her closest living relative. It did not take him long to decide what to do with the money that had unexpectedly landed in his lap. As a youth, my grandfather had loved tales of Arthurian legend. He used to lie in his bedroom reading those stories of heroic derring-do, ardently wishing that he lived centuries ago and half a world away. Now—this was in 1946—he bought a parcel of land by the coast and spent a sizable portion of his inheritance turning his childhood obsession into his own peculiar reality. Visitors were always welcome to pay the entrance fee and enjoy the attractions, but my grandfather built Fun-A-Lot for himself. He spent every waking hour in the park, cocooned within those plastic ramparts. He was always too busy enjoying himself to spend much time with his only son.

When my father realized that he would never be able to compete with the park for Grandpa Ronald's affections, he began to hate the place. While he was growing up, he was the only kid in his class who *didn't* have a summer job there. Instead he took backbreaking work on blueberry farms, harvesting the crops. After high school he escaped to the University of Maine, where he studied fine arts. I've always suspected that his choice of degree was really an act of self-defense, as far removed from my grandfather's world as he could get. During the summer months he bused tables at restaurants in Orono, refusing to return to Haverford while the park was open. He began to envisage a future for himself, one free of cotton candy and penny arcades.

Over the years Grandpa Ronald developed an inviolable routine of unabashed hedonism during the summer season. Each morning he sat in the front car of the roller coaster for the first ride of the day. He gripped the metal bar and screamed and yelled along with everyone else as the cars hurtled through corkscrew turns at stomach-churning speeds. The morning of June 23, 1959, was no different. He strapped himself into the safety harness and waved to the ride operator as the roller coaster trundled away from the platform and began its first climb into the sky.

Perhaps it is possible to have too much fun. Perhaps there is a limit on the amount of delight that one person is permitted in their lifetime, and Grandpa Ronald had just used up his quota. Perhaps his daily diet of greasy, high-cholesterol fare from the concession stand came home to roost. Whatever the reason, when the cars came to a shuddering halt two minutes and forty-seven seconds later, my grandfather was no longer shrieking along with his fellow fun seekers. As the rest of the crowd clambered out of their seats, none of them noticed that the passenger in the front car was no longer moving. Somewhere along those swooping parabolas, a massive heart attack had ripped the life out of him. Thanks to the tight-fitting safety harness, he remained bolt upright in his seat, and nobody realized what had happened. He was sent on two more rides before the operator noticed that the boss's head was slumped forward as the cars pulled in.

I've often thought Grandpa Ronald probably wouldn't have objected to those last valedictory spins around the roller-coaster track. He went out doing what he loved best. But his unexpected death condemned my father to precisely the fate he had been working so hard to avoid. My grandmother had tolerated her husband's obsession with the park with resigned patience, but she had no interest in overseeing operations herself. The morning after the funeral she begged Sam to abandon his studies and return to Haverford. Revenues were steady, expenses under control—it was a viable, modestly profitable business, she told him, but any sale now would be disastrous. The vultures would be circling, sensing blood. The rides could be dismantled and sold, but she wouldn't get more than a few cents on the dollar for them. And nobody would ever want to buy the land.

As Sam listened to his mother, a small geyser of disappointment welled up inside him, and it had been bubbling away quietly ever since. To his chagrin, he found himself skewered by both guilt and filial duty. Even in death his father was as selfish as ever, derailing his plans. He couldn't allow Grandpa Ronald's dream to be sold off at a knockdown price. Besides, the town needed the park. Without it, the tourist trade would pass Haverford by. Kids needed summer vacation jobs. Nobody came knocking, begging him to save the town, but my father knew what he had to do. He quietly packed up his dreams, quit his studies, and drove back to Haverford, to his destiny.

IN THE YEARS THAT FOLLOWED, Sam remained a reluctant steward of his father's legacy, but he discovered consolation in unexpected places.

During his second season in charge, he noticed the green-eyed beauty in admissions who tallied up each day's take. When he finally summoned up the courage to talk to her, she told him that her name was Mary and that she was home for the summer, staying with her parents and saving as much as she could before her final year at Smith. He had laughed anxiously at that. They had dinner two nights later. When she left for Massachusetts that fall, Sam was not sure how he was ever going to live without her. At Christmas, he gave her a ring. My parents were married a week before Fun-A-Lot opened its gates for the next season. They never had a honeymoon.

The frenetic chaos of the summer months was nothing but a torment for my father. He spent every minute of those long days wheeling from one potential disaster to the next. By Labor Day he was like an exhausted boxer, pummeled and on the ropes. The park was not much better. Sun-faded paint peeled off every surface; tired motors coughed and spluttered. Every fall my father gently tended the place back to health. He repaired whatever had broken over the course of the season, a process that took a little longer each year. He stripped down and rebuilt each tired piece of equipment, trying to stave off decrepitude. Fixing things with his hands was its own reward, and he relished the solitude of the deserted park after the crowded hysteria of the summer. But his greatest pleasure he saved for when winter descended, and the cold and snow drove him inside to the workshop.

Unlike his father, Sam never rode the rides himself. He regarded them primarily as contraptions that were liable to go wrong. There was one exception: my father adored the park's antique carousel. As a child he'd been bewitched by the spectacle of the wooden horses prancing by, three abreast. He had loved to cling on to those elegant equine necks and ride in ceaseless, ecstatic orbits. He loved the bright pipe organ melodies and the delighted squeals of his fellow riders—these gentle pleasures were far more intoxicating than the daredevil thrills on offer elsewhere. He could stay there all day, riding his chosen mount as it moved up and down its silver pole.

The carousel's charms had never faded for my father. It stood in pride of place at the center of the park and still drew the longest lines every summer. Like everything else, it was in need of constant care and attention. The horses were old, their saddles worn thin by the backsides of thousands of holidaymakers. And so each winter, when the snow came, my father retired one horse from duty and carved a new one from scratch. Every Memorial Day there would be a gleaming new steed waiting to be ridden, still smelling of fresh paint and varnish.

But Sam loved the old carousel horses too much to let them go. He kept them all in a corner of his workshop, a cavalry of retired stallions. Their painted coats were faded, but still they stamped and snorted, teeth bared and forelegs raised for the next step that would never be taken.

SEVEN

If my father's sentiments about the amusement park were mixed, my own were less complicated. I loved the place, simply and without equivocation.

When I was younger I spent all my summers at Fun-A-Lot. During the season my father would bring me to work with him every day while my mother stayed home with Liam. I would roam up and down the gravel pathways from morning to dusk, free to go wherever I liked. By the time I was six I knew every inch of the place as intimately as I knew the corners of my own bedroom. The smell of pastry baking in the kitchen every morning for that day's cream horns was more familiar to me than my mother's own cooking. The fact that there were a couple of thousand strangers swarming everywhere didn't make it feel any less like home.

But for all that I was surrounded by people all day, my existence was a solitary one back then. I was allowed to clamber on and off the rides as I wished, as long as there was no line. I learned the ebb and flow of the crowds and knew which rides were most popular at which time of day. There were children everywhere, of course, but I was too shy to talk to them. Instead I constructed epic adventures in my head, creating new worlds out of the one I knew so well. There was a secret trapdoor in the haunted house that led to a magical place where the ghosts were real. If you gripped the handles of the Tilt-a-Whirl in a particular way, it would spin you into another dimension so that when you climbed off the ride, you had stepped back in time. I discovered that if I ate cherry-flavored cotton candy while walking counterclockwise around the carousel, I became totally invisible for ten minutes.

When I got bored of playing on my own, I enlisted the unwitting help of others. Sometimes I was a detective, hot on the trail of a suspected criminal. I would track my quarry for hours. I was an expert in not being spotted. I knew all the good hiding places and could instantly vanish into the crowd. I watched my targets as they stood in line for rides and waited patiently for them while they went up in the Ferris wheel. I was as relentless as a bloodhound. All interesting developments were reported back to HQ via the invisible two-way radio on my wrist.

When I saw a family that I particularly liked, I would pretend that they had adopted me and would follow them around. My talent for invisibility was especially helpful here, but every so often a grown-up would notice that they had an extra kid trailing along with them. They would crouch down next to me, always with the same expression of annoyance and concern on their face, and ask me where my own parents were.

IT WAS THE END of October when I first took Nathan to the park. I'm not sure which of us was more excited. I wanted to show the place off to him, eager for his approval, and Nathan had been pestering me for a visit. By then my father was well into his fall maintenance schedule, and the pathways were strewn with parts of disassembled machinery. As we walked through the deserted park, I pointed out the various rides and attractions, relishing my role of tour guide. It was easy for me to conjure up the sights and sounds and smells of a busy day in the middle of the season. I could see the vast swarm of humanity roaming hungrily up and down the paths; I could hear the happy screams of children; I could smell the pungent aroma of fried onions at the back of my nose. Nathan knew none of that—he saw lifeless banks of bulbs, not the kaleidoscope of a thousand brilliant lights—but his eyes were shining with excitement all the same.

We meandered along the paths, chattering constantly, making our way toward the mammoth frame of the roller coaster. The cars had been taken off the track and were lying upside down on the wooden deck where customers waited to climb on board. Nathan walked up to the edge of the platform and peered down at the rails.

"Are those safe to walk on?" he asked.

I shrugged. "I think so."

"Good," he said, and hopped down onto the track.

"What are you doing?" I said.

Nathan turned to me. "I'll be careful, I promise."

"Careful? What do you mean?"

"I'm going for a walk," he said. He turned and began to make his way along the roller-coaster track.

"Nathan," I said. "Don't be dumb. Come back."

The initial gradient was gentle enough that Nathan could walk along the rails without any trouble. After a few steps he turned to face me. He was only a few yards away, but the distance between us had never been greater.

I enjoyed riding the roller coaster, but as the cars hurtled along the hairpin bends, shaking my bones and pulling me this way and that, it was the protective harness across my chest that gave me comfort. That reassuring pressure against my thumping heart told me that I was safe.

"Come back," I said again. "Let me show you the rest of the park."

"I'll have a better view of everything from up here."

"But it's not safe!"

After a short, straight run, the track made a vicious jackknife to the left and went into its first dip. When Nathan reached the corner, he called out, "I can see the ocean from here!" He stood quite still, looking out toward the coast. Behind him there was nothing but sky. After a moment, he began moving again, out of my line of vision. I sprinted down the steps of the roller coaster and along the asphalt pathway that ran parallel to it. All I could see was the underbelly of the track, so I ran up a hill, away from the ride. When I turned to look back, I could see Nathan again. He had reached the bottom of the first dip and had begun to clamber up to the next peak. This was the highest point of the ride, more than a hundred and fifty feet off the ground. A narrow iron ladder ran alongside the rails to allow access for maintenance, and Nathan was climbing it, pulling himself upward rung by rung. Dwarfed by the massive heft of the roller coaster, his progress toward the summit was barely perceptible, but he never stopped. Not for one second were his limbs frozen by fear or doubt. He kept moving, away from me, away from the ground, away from everything.

Finally, Nathan reached the crest of the ride. The track immediately plunged downward at an even steeper gradient than the one he had just climbed. He looked down and waved at me. He yelled something, but the words were caught by the wind and swept away.

"Nathan!" I yelled. "Come down!"

If he heard me, he pretended not to. He sat down in the middle of the track, his knees tucked up under his chin, and gazed upward at the sky, aloft and alone.

EIGHT

The snow came early that year.

It arrived in one giant, overnight fall, a week before Thanks-giving, a silent ambush from the sky that left us beneath a dazzling blanket of white. I gazed through my bedroom window at the new world outside. Within hours the snow would be plowed up, shoveled aside, trampled down, and driven over. Life went on. You can't afford to be sentimental about the weather in Maine. This far north, the unrelenting tyranny of cold fronts—icy winds off the Atlantic, snow from the north, and the vast lakes to the west—feels as if it will never, ever end. Days are short, too short for living, it sometimes feels. The sun metes out its miserly hours, a spectral presence in the washed-out sky.

With the snow came the next phase of my father's seasonal repair schedule. His workshop was full of motors of varying shapes and sizes, and now he spent his days taking each one apart, replacing worn parts, cleaning and oiling them, and then putting them back together again. He was cocooned in his workshop; it was the one time of year when he wasn't anxious about the weather. Winter had thrown all it had at him and could not touch him now.

Nathan and I often biked to the park after school, our knuckles blue from the cold. (After we had set free all of Mr. Tilly's kites, there was no reason to spend much time at Sebbanquik Point, except to defrost the mongoose from time to time and play with him. The door to Nathan's mother's study remained firmly shut while we were there.) My father was always pleased to see us. He took our arrival to mark the end of his formal workday. He stopped whatever job he had been doing and fetched the block of unvarnished cedar from the back of the workshop—the block that would eventually become the newest horse on the carousel. He chiseled and scraped away at the wood as we talked. As the weeks went by the head and neck appeared, then two prancing forelegs. My father worked by eye alone. He did not consult pictures or even look at the old wooden warriors that still lurked in the corner of the workshop. There was no need. Every contour of that horse was already buried somewhere deep within him. I liked to watch him carve. A contented stillness settled within him—a million miles away from his usual anxious mode of existence.

THE ROAD OUT TO Sebbanquik Point was a minor one, and so was sometimes left unplowed for days after a fresh fall of snow, rendering it impassable for most cars. By December the school bus couldn't make it through the snowdrifts, and Mrs. Tilly's Impala was no better. After he had missed a few days of school, Nathan and I agreed that he should come and stay with us. There had been a guarded telephone exchange between our mothers. At the end of it, my mother put the receiver back into its cradle.

"Did she say yes?" I asked eagerly.

My mother had an unreadable look on her face. "Until the weather improves or that road is properly cleared, yes."

I punched the air in delight. My mother wiped her hands on her apron, as if trying to clean something off them. She turned to my father, who was sitting at the kitchen table. "I worry about her, Sam, all alone out there," she said. "This is her first winter in Maine. She has no idea what she's in for. Lord knows this isn't Texas. I wonder if she has enough food or gas."

"I could go and check on her from time to time," said my father. "See if she has what she needs."

My mother looked out the window at the snow. "I don't think that woman has the first idea what it is that she needs."

"How does she get by, now that her husband's gone?" asked my father.

"Heaven only knows," said my mother. "Poor woman. Bringing that boy up all on her own."

"Nathan said his father never made any money with the lobster boat," I said.

My mother frowned. "So how did they ever pay their bills?"

I shrugged. I didn't care. I was just excited that Nathan was coming to stay. We put up a cot in my bedroom and cleared a space in my chest of drawers for his clothes. Later that day my father and I drove out to Sebbanquik Point in the station wagon to pick him up. There had been more snow that morning, and the Tillys' driveway had not been cleared. My father looked at the untouched banks of white that lay between the road and the house. From the trunk of the station wagon he took three shovels and handed one to me. We trudged toward the house. My ears were already aching with the cold. The front door opened on my first knock. Nathan stood there, two shopping bags of clothes at his feet. He looked at us expectantly.

"Go put your snow clothes on, Nathan," said my father. "We're not leaving just yet."

We spent the next hour shoveling a trench so that the Impala could reach the road. I could feel the sting of frostbite through the tips of my gloves, but the steady rhythm of the work soon had me perspiring freely. Every so often I would rest, but never for long—as soon as I stopped moving I could feel the trickles of sweat soak through my T-shirt and chill my skin. During one break I looked up toward the house and saw Mrs. Tilly watching us from an upstairs window. She remained motionless until she raised her hand to her mouth and took a long drag on her cigarette.

When we had dug a path wide enough for Mrs. Tilly's car to pass through, we went inside. Nathan put the kettle on the stove. A small cloud of steam rose from each of us into the warm air. As we waited for the water to boil, the door opened and Nathan's mother stepped into the kitchen.

Despite all the time I'd spent at Sebbanquik Point, I'd only ever seen Mrs. Tilly twice before—once when her husband fell off the roof, and once at his funeral—so this was the first time I'd had a chance to get a good look at her. Her blond hair was pulled back from her face in a thick ponytail. From across her husband's open grave I had thought she exuded a certain foxy mystique, but now, to my disappointment, she looked just like every other mother I knew. The most noticeable thing about her was the overpowering reek of stale cigarette smoke. (My mother always smelled of clean linen and freshly baked bread.)

"You must be Robert," she said to me.

My father took a step forward. "And I'm Sam Carter," he said. "Robert's father. We were at your husband's funeral service."

"Yes, of course." Mrs. Tilly smiled at him, and then her eyes began to skitter about the room. "Thank you for clearing the driveway," she said.

"You need to get some chains for your car," said my father. "Otherwise I don't think you'll be going very far."

"We never had to worry about snow in Texas," said Mrs. Tilly, looking out of the window.

"There are a few tricks you should probably know," said my father. "Would it help if I explained a few things?"

"Only if it's not too much trouble," said Mrs. Tilly.

Nathan turned to me. "Want to go down to the beach?" he said.

I could almost feel the tips of my fingers again. "Not really," I said. "I'm still freezing."

"As you can see," observed my father, "some of the natives cope with the cold better than others."

Two minutes later I was grumpily trudging through the snow. There was no way I was going to allow my father to mock me like that in front of Mrs. Tilly, and so I'd reluctantly followed Nathan back out the door. When we reached the top of the wooden staircase that led down to the beach, I stopped and stared. The snow below me was impossibly white; the ocean next to it was almost black, and ethereally still. It looked as if the cold had bled all color out of the world. I had never seen the shoreline look more stark, or more beautiful.

Nathan bent down and scooped up a handful of snow. With three deft smacks he formed a tightly packed ball, then threw it at me. I pulled my head back, laughing, as the snowball sailed past me. We scrambled down the stairs onto the pristine expanse of white beach. There I quickly made a snowball of my own and hurled it at Nathan's head, missing by a mile. After that we ran, shouted, and threw snow at each other. Usually we missed; once or twice one of us scored a direct hit, provoking howls of triumph and despair. Pretty soon I forgot about the cold.

As the battle continued, we made our way down the beach until we were in the midst of Mrs. Tilly's columns of stone. Sheathed in white, they looked like a village of malnourished snowmen. We weaved in between them, making tactical use of the protection they afforded. Nathan was crouching down behind one of the taller statues when I let fly with a particularly vicious shot. Rather than hitting Nathan, my snowball smacked into the pillar in front of him. The column collapsed beneath the impact, leaving a glistening corona of scattered stones.

Slowly Nathan got to his feet. I was panting heavily. "I'll get you next time," I warned him.

Nathan waved at the stones lying on the ground. "We have to rebuild this," he said.

"What? Why?"

"My mom checks on them every day. She gets mad if they're not all perfect. Like it's a sign that something bad is going to happen."

I wondered if all the columns were intact on the day Mr. Tilly fell off the roof.

The largest stone was still where the base of the column had been. Nathan squatted down and picked up another one. Together we reconstructed the statue as best we could, guessing the order and orientation of the stones. By the time we had finished I was shivering again.

"We should go back in," I said. Nathan nodded. When I reached the top of the wooden staircase I turned and looked back toward the beach. In the middle of those anonymous pillars of white stood the column we had rebuilt, its stones dark against the surrounding snow.

Back in the kitchen, Mrs. Tilly and my father were sipping their coffee by the stove. I felt a twinge of guilt about my errant snowball. "Are you boys ready to get on the road?" asked my father.

Nathan picked up the shopping bags that he had left at the door. "Ready and waiting," he announced.

My father turned to Mrs. Tilly. "Thanks for the coffee, Judith," he said.

Mrs. Tilly walked us to the kitchen door. "Be good," she told Nathan.

"Of course," said Nathan.

They didn't hug.

We made our way down the track we had cleared. As Nathan and I clambered into the station wagon, I looked back toward the house. Mrs. Tilly was watching us from the kitchen window. She had lit another cigarette. As my father put the car in gear and pulled away, she exhaled against the glass and disappeared behind a wall of white smoke.

NINE

Nathan fit right into our family routine. We walked to school when the weather permitted; otherwise my father drove us there on his way to the park. By the time the school bell sounded at the end of each day, it was already dark outside. We did our homework at the kitchen table while my mother cooked. That was the one time of day when we stopped talking. From the moment that we woke up to the last exhausted exchanges across the darkness of my bedroom, the words never stopped. We teased each other, we told each other stories—some true, some not—we joked and bickered and argued. We developed our own code, an opaque shorthand of in-jokes and obscure references that often had us snorting with laughter at the dinner table while my parents and Liam looked on, bemused—which of course simply added to the pleasure of our private lexicon.

Not once in the river of words that flowed between us did Nathan ever talk about his mother. If he ever wondered how she was doing, all alone out at Sebbanquik Point, he never mentioned it to me. She never featured in any of his stories. At first the echo of typewriter keys and the chime of Mrs. Tilly's carriage return had seemed like an exotic soundtrack to my visits to Nathan's house, but now I began to understand how lonely he must have been there. I wondered what was so important that his mother couldn't step away from her desk for two minutes to check on us. One afternoon I cycled to the Haverford public library and asked if they had any books by Judith Tilly. The librarian checked her card catalog and told me that no books had ever been published by anyone of that name.

Every night after dinner Nathan and I sat on Liam's bed while he played us records. My brother's bedroom had become a shrine to his musical heroes. Tattered posters of David Johansen and Iggy Pop covered the walls, obscuring the jungle mural that my father had painted for him years before. My brain always felt as if it were being scrambled by Liam's music, but Nathan seemed to enjoy it. He gazed admiringly at the strange-looking men who glared and pouted from the album sleeves. He would lean over and show me when he found a musician's name that he particularly liked. In this way we discovered Johnny Thunders, Richard Hell, Sylvain Sylvain, and Rat Scabies. Then of course there were the Ramones—Johnny, Dee Dee, Joey, and the rest, a nightmarish clan if ever there was one. I remember wondering what their parents must have thought of their notorious offspring. For some reason—weirdly, since everyone had such obviously fake names back then—it never occurred to me that the Ramones weren't actually brothers. When I finally realized the truth, I was too mortified to admit my mistake.

The expansion of Nathan's musical horizons became Liam's pet project. I sat on the bed and watched as the two of them bonded over squalling, three-minute blitzkriegs of noise. Nathan was a quick learner. It did not take him long to acquire a basic working knowledge of the New York Lower East Side music scene. His enthusiasm quickly eclipsed my own tepid responses. Sometimes, when they put on a song they especially loved, Nathan jumped up and down on the spot, waving his arms around as if he were in a mosh pit, and Liam rocked back and forth in his wheelchair, playing an imaginary drum kit and doing wheelies. Once he lost his balance and performed a spectacular backward somersault onto the carpet. The ensuing crash brought my mother scuttling in, but Liam was laughing too hard to pay much attention to her scolding.

By then my brother's scoliosis was so advanced that his upper body was permanently contorted in a vicious twist to the left. Nathan showed none of the awkwardness around Liam that we had become accustomed to. Most people were so overcome with well-meaning sympathy that they couldn't look at him without dissolving into inarticulate fits of compassion. But Nathan understood that my brother didn't need anybody's pity, even if the rest of us sometimes did. Liam liked him enormously as a result.

Every Tuesday evening my parents went out for their weekly bridge game. Liam took their absence as license to play his music even louder than usual. On one such night, Nathan and I were sitting on my brother's bed while he lectured us about music he hated—which was pretty much everything. Liam was rigorous and unstinting in his derision of all music that didn't fall within his narrowly defined tastes. Even Pink Floyd and Led Zeppelin were dismissed as bombastic dinosaurs, self-indulgent fops. (*Concept album?* he raged. Pile of *shit*. How's that for a concept?) But he reserved his greatest scorn for the hippies with their acoustic guitars.

"Joni Mitchell? Cat Stevens?" Liam wagged his finger at us in warning, as if listening to that stuff might lead us to Lawrence Welk. "Have you listened to the lyrics? Every song is a fucking question. But this!" My brother brandished the New York Dolls album that was lying in his lap. "This has *answers*." He lowered the needle onto the vinyl.

As the skull-shaking noise of "Personality Crisis" blasted into the room, Nathan and I looked at the photograph on the record sleeve. The five band members were lounging on a sofa, looking moodily at the camera. They were a long-haired, androgynous bunch in platform boots and flamboyant outfits. Between them they wore more eyeliner than a chorus line of dancing girls.

"Those guys are the ultimate badasses," said Liam. "They want to fuck the system. Break the rules."

"They're rock stars," said Nathan. "They *should* be badasses. That's kind of their job, isn't it?"

"So?" I said.

"Well, what about us?" said Nathan.

"What *about* us?" asked Liam.

"I don't see any rule-breaking going on around here," said Nathan. "Not much system-fucking. Very little badassery."

"What do you have in mind?" asked Liam.

Nathan shrugged. "Don't you ever get the urge to do something crazy? I mean, if the New York Dolls can break the rules, why can't we?"

"Because they're rock stars," I said.

"But who says we can't break the rules, too?" said Nathan.

My mom, I wanted to say.

"So go on, then, big shot," said my brother, grinning. "Do something crazy."

I gave Liam a warning look, but Nathan had already stood up. He gazed out of the window into the darkness of the backyard. By then several weeks of accumulated snowfall covered the ground. Nathan pointed to the perfectly symmetrical hillock of snow that stood immediately outside the window. "Is that a trampoline?" he said.

Liam nodded. It had been years since my brother had been able to do his balancing exercises in the backyard. The springs were rusty with disuse, but getting rid of the thing would have been an admission of defeat, an acknowledgment that things were never going to get better, and so my parents had left the trampoline where it was.

Nathan looked at me. "Your bedroom's right above us, isn't it?"

"No way." I shook my head. "You can't jump out of my window, Nathan."

"Sure I can," he said.

"Don't be stupid."

"It's not stupid. The trampoline will catch me."

"You really *are* crazy," said Liam.

"Put another record on until I get back," said Nathan to Liam. He turned to me. "Come on."

"I'm not going anywhere," I said. "If you want to kill yourself you can do it on your own."

"Okay." Nathan shrugged and walked out of the room.

I shot Liam a dirty look and then ran up the stairs after Nathan. I found him kneeling on my bed, fiddling with the window latch.

"I just need to— Ah." The latch clicked and he pushed the window open. Freezing air rushed into the room. Nathan put his head out and looked down. "Well, look at that," he said.

I crossed the room and peered out of the window. Immediately beneath us was the trampoline, a raised circle of white.

"Come on," I said. "You're not really going to do this. Let's go back downstairs."

"Of course I'm going to do this," said Nathan.

"But nobody's jumped on that thing in years," I said.

"It's a trampoline," said Nathan. "What could go wrong?"

There were so many answers to that question, but all the words caught in my throat, trapped by the memory of Nathan's father falling to his death down the side of a house much like this one. "Just come downstairs, okay?" I said.

Nathan hauled himself up onto the window frame. Slowly he squeezed himself through the open space until there was more of him outside than in. He looked down at the ground with a thoughtful expression on his face.

"It would be a good idea," he said, "not to miss."

"Come back inside," I pleaded.

Nathan glanced past me, into the warmth and safety of the bedroom, and I could tell that he was considering abandoning the whole idea. But the moment passed, and he turned back to contemplate the target below him. He shifted his weight a little further forward.

"What's going on up there?" shouted Liam.

Nathan didn't move. He kept staring out into the backyard.

I cleared my throat and called down to my brother. "Everything's fine," I yelled. "We're just— I don't think Nathan's going to—"

Nathan jumped.

I rushed to the window. The two seconds that it took for his body to plummet to the ground were long enough for me to imagine all the terrible things that would happen next: the thud of Nathan's body hitting the ground; the wait for the ambulance; the subsequent police interrogation—would they think I pushed him? was I going to be a *murder suspect?*—my parents' fury; Mrs. Tilly's sorrow; and my guilt, my guilt, my guilt. My best friend had jumped out of a window and I had done nothing to stop him.

Nathan's body landed exactly in the middle of the trampoline. The force of the impact sent the snow that had been lying undisturbed for weeks flying into the air, momentarily obscuring him from view. An instant later, the trampoline catapulted him back through the snow, and I watched in horror as he flew through the night air. He landed on the ground, several feet away from the trampoline. His body lay facedown in the snow, horribly inert. I stared at him from the bedroom window.

"Oh my God!" yelled Liam. "He did it! He actually did it! He fucking jumped!" His voice jolted me out of my shock, and I turned and raced for the stairs. I flung open the back door and tore across the yard to where Nathan was lying. When I arrived by his side he still hadn't moved.

"Nathan!" I said. Tentatively I reached out and touched his shoulder. He was wearing one of his cable-knit sweaters, warm enough for inside but not much use in the snow. I had already begun to shiver myself. "Nathan," I said again. "Can you hear me?" Still he didn't move.

"What's going on?" shouted Liam. He had opened his bedroom window but the trampoline was blocking his view.

I looked down at Nathan's crumpled body. "He's just—" I whispered. "He's not moving."

One of my mother's favorite albums was *Ladies of the Canyon* by Joni Mitchell, and a line from one of those songs came back to me now. *You don't know what you've got till it's gone.* The understanding of everything that I was about to lose smashed into me, and with it came a terrible fury. I grabbed Nathan's shoulder and shook it. "You idiot," I yelled. "Why did you have to go and ruin everything?"

I sniffed, loudly and messily, a trumpet of angry tears and snot.

Nathan rolled over. "Are you *crying*?" he said.

I was so surprised that I just stared at him.

"You are," said Nathan, propping himself up on one elbow and looking at me closely. "You're actually—"

He couldn't speak anymore after that, on account of the fistful of snow that I smashed into his face.

I STORMED BACK INTO the house, leaving Nathan lying in the snow. The sound of his laughter rang in my ears as I slammed the door shut behind me. By the time he came inside a few minutes later, I had retreated to the kitchen and was making myself a cup of hot chocolate. Nathan went into Liam's bedroom and told him what had happened, which made me feel even more stupid. Of course Nathan was fine: the trampoline had taken all the force out of his fall from the window, and the foot of snow on the ground had softened the impact of his landing. After some further discussion, Nathan climbed back up the stairs to my bedroom and jumped out the window again. And again. Now each leap was accompanied by kamikaze shrieks of glee from Nathan and whoops of encouragement from Liam. I sat at the kitchen table and glumly sipped my drink, mortified by my tears.

I tried my best to shake off my lingering embarrassment, but a week later I could still hear Nathan's laughter chasing me inside as he lay in the snow.

TEN

There was a fresh snowfall on Christmas Eve. My father and I spent the afternoon clearing the driveway and the sidewalk in front of the house while my mother and Liam worked in the kitchen. Christmas lunch was always a monumental production, the table groaning beneath mountains of food that we would eat for weeks afterward. But all that culinary industry was no act of celebration. Christmas had become a ritual of preemptive mourning for my family. My mother offered up turkey and all the trimmings in the unspoken fear that each holiday might be Liam's last. Every gift she wrapped, every ornament she hung on the tree, every wreath she positioned just so—this was all done in the shadow of what she knew was to come.

Late that night, my father lifted my brother into the backseat of the station wagon and drove us to midnight Mass at St. Mary's. The familiar melodies of the carols were a warm reminder of the pleasures of the day to come, as sure a sign of the holiday as the fresh scent of pine needles from the Christmas tree. Liam sang along with the rest of us. He had a beautiful voice, although his compressed lung meant that he could only sing softly. During the final verse of "Hark! The Herald Angels Sing" I glanced at my mother. Her lips were not moving, and she was not looking at the hymnal clasped in her hands. Her eyes rested on my brother. She was listening to his quiet song.

CHRISTMAS DAY DAWNED BITTERLY cold, but with a brilliant blue sky. The sun was dazzlingly bright on the snow.

Just before lunchtime my mother gazed out of the kitchen window. She wore the same sweatshirt that she wore every Christmas morning. The word HALLELUJAH! was emblazoned in sequins across her chest. "Do you think they'll make it?" she asked my father.

"Who?" I asked.

My father cleared his throat. "Nathan and his mother are coming for lunch."

"What?" I said. "When did you—"

"I invited her that afternoon when we cleared the driveway to their house," said my father. "While you and Nathan were at the beach." He paused. "She's not a big talker, is she? I was really just trying to fill the silence in between sips of coffee."

"You did the right thing," said my mother. "It's the first Christmas since Nathan's father died. They'd have been all alone, and we couldn't have that."

"Why didn't you tell me?" I said.

"We thought it would be a nice surprise," said my father.

Just then Mrs. Tilly's car appeared around the corner. It was moving quickly, far too quickly for the road conditions. As it approached the house, the Impala's brake lights went on, but instead of slowing down, its wheels locked up. The car skidded to a stop, its progress halted by a small bank of snow in front of our house. We waited for Nathan and his mother to climb out, but nothing happened. The windows were fogged up. Then the driver's window opened and a cloud of smoke billowed into the cold air.

"She's poisoning that poor boy," said my mother crossly.

"Maybe she's nervous," said my father.

A minute or so later the window rolled back up again, and the driver's door opened, but not very far. The car had stopped right in front of our mailbox and the door could only open a few inches before it knocked against it. We watched as the car door nudged the mailbox gently a couple of times, and then, to my astonishment, Nathan's mother began bashing it repeatedly, with increasing violence. The mailbox shuddered but did not move.

I looked at my father. "Should we go and help?" I asked.

Before he could answer, there was a ferocious squealing of tires. The Impala's wheels were spinning uselessly. The engine whined alarmingly, but the car was firmly stuck in the bank of snow. Through the fogged-up window I thought I could see Mrs. Tilly hit the steering wheel with her fists. Finally she gave up and switched off the engine. The passenger door opened, and Nathan appeared. A few moments later Mrs. Tilly climbed out of the same door, looking somewhat disheveled. She wore a dark green puffer coat that went all the way down to her ankles. The coat had a hood, which she pulled over her head, making her look like an ambulatory Christmas tree. Nathan and his mother made their way up to the front door, where we stood waiting for them.

My mother stepped forward. "Merry Christmas!" she said as she grabbed Mrs. Tilly's hand. "Judith, it's so nice to finally meet you!"

"I'm sorry about your mailbox," said Mrs. Tilly.

"Let me pour you a sherry," said my father kindly.

As we went inside Nathan beamed at me. "I got you a present," he said. "I made it myself." From behind his back he produced a plastic bag. I peered into it and saw a handful of thin wooden poles wrapped in bright green fabric. It took me a moment to realize what I was looking at.

"A kite," I breathed.

MY MOTHER'S ROAST TURKEY was delicious, and the gravy and roasted vegetables were all up to her usual high standards. Mrs. Tilly had accepted only tiny portions, and she spent the meal staring down at her food, pushing it around the plate instead of actually eating anything. She looked as if there was nothing she would have liked to do more than crawl under the table and disappear. I wondered why she had agreed to come. My parents, though, weren't going to have their Christmas dinner spoiled by an untalkative guest. They gamely tried to coax the conversation along.

"So, Judith," said my father. "Did you ever get those snow chains for your car?"

Mrs. Tilly shook her head. "I never got around to it."

"Are you managing all right without them?" said my mother. The question seemed redundant, given that Mrs. Tilly's Impala was stuck in a bank of snow in front of our house.

"Well, most days I just stay home," she said.

My parents exchanged looks.

"You're awfully isolated out there," said my mother.

"That was part of the appeal of the place." Mrs. Tilly prodded at a piece of turkey. "Leonard worked in an office for seventeen years, when we lived in Texas. When we arrived in Maine he built a bonfire and burned all his suits." She paused. "Leonard was a terrible lobster fisherman, but he loved being out in the boat on his own, alone on the ocean. And I liked living out of town. We both enjoyed the solitude."

"Do you miss Texas?" asked my mother.

"Every day," said Mrs. Tilly. "I swear I don't know how you people get out of bed. These winters are so long."

"Mary and I don't know anything else," said my father cheerfully. "Maybe that's a good thing. Ignorance is bliss, and all that."

"Maybe," said Nathan's mother doubtfully.

"Have you considered moving back to Texas?" asked my mother.

I stared down at my plate. It was the one question I had never dared to ask.

Mrs. Tilly shook her head. "We're going to stay in Maine."

I'd been holding my knife and fork so tightly that the metal had left anxious indentations in my flesh.

"I'm pleased to hear it," said my father. "We would hate to see you and Nathan go."

"Yes, well." Mrs. Tilly picked up her wineglass and drained it in one needful swallow. "If it were just up to me, we'd have gone back already. But Nathan doesn't want to leave."

"Mom," said Nathan.

"I was an only child, and so was Leonard. And so is Nathan. He's always been a bit of a loner, just like his parents." Mrs. Tilly looked across the table at me. "Then he met you, Robert."

I felt my cheeks start to burn.

My mother smiled. "As thick as thieves, aren't they, living in each other's pockets!"

Nathan was staring at his plate.

"Anyway, that's why we're staying," said Mrs. Tilly. "Nathan doesn't want to go back to Texas. Not unless Robert comes, too."

"My goodness," said my father.

Ever since Nathan had jumped out of my bedroom window I had been quietly dying of embarrassment about my tears that night, fearful that I had revealed too much. Now all that worry vanished in an instant, like a wonderful conjuring trick. I could barely see the food in front of me. All I could feel was the blood roaring through my veins, the thrilling pulse of secret elation.

WHEN THE MEAL WAS OVER we went outside and pushed Mrs. Tilly's Impala out of the snowdrift. By the time we had heaved the car clear, everyone's faces were as flushed as mine and Nathan's.

As we walked back inside, Nathan nudged me. "Let's go and fly that kite," he said. He assembled the balsawood frame and showed me how to pull the fabric taut across it. The finished kite was an elongated lozenge, elegantly proportioned, perfectly sized. Nathan attached the white nylon line with a complicated-looking knot. He handed it to me. The kite weighed almost nothing, but I could feel its resilience beneath my fingers. We went out into the backyard, our footprints leaving trails in the snow. The winter light had begun to fade. I gave the kite to Nathan. The thread unspooled through my fingers as he walked toward the pond at the far end of the yard. He turned to face me.

"Ready?" he called.

My fingers tightened around the plastic reel. "Ready!"

And then the kite was aloft. There was a brisk breeze from the east that made it dip and flutter in the sky. I felt the tug of the line and let out more, and then some more. I watched as the vivid green flash grew smaller and smaller. The kite hung in the air, high above us. It was the most beautiful thing I had ever seen in my life.

We stood there for fifteen minutes or so, taking turns to hold the line, not speaking, our eyes lifted up to the heavens.

Nathan was staying in Maine because of me. We stood in the snow with the sun going down and the winter wind rushing in off the ocean, but I didn't feel the cold.

Then, the next time Nathan gave the line back to me, I saw what was in his hand.

"Oh no," I said.

Nathan said nothing.

"Please don't. Not this time."

The blade of the penknife shone dully in the afternoon twilight. "You know how this goes," he said.

"But this kite is *mine*," I said. "You gave it to me."

"I gave it to you so you could set it free."

"I don't *want* to set it free. I want to keep it."

Nathan handed me the penknife. "It's your kite, Robert," he said. "You choose." He turned and walked back to the house.

I stood alone in the middle of the yard for what felt like an eternity. Now every gust of wind chilled me to the bone. My toes became numb. I could barely feel the plastic reel through my gloves.

I looked up sadly into the sky.

When I finally trudged back to the house the sun had disappeared. I was so cold I could barely talk.

"There you are!" said my mother. "We thought you were never coming back in."

"Where's Nathan?" I asked.

"He and his mom already left," said Liam.

I looked down at my shoes. The snow that had compacted around the bottoms of my pants had begun to melt.

"Come into the kitchen and get warm," said my mother. "I'll make you some hot chocolate."

"Where's the kite?" asked Liam.

THAT NIGHT I COULDN'T SLEEP. I lay awake and stared at the ceiling. The happiness I'd felt over Christmas lunch had vanished along with my kite. I'd felt a keening, jagged sense of loss as I'd watched it disappear into the sky.

At eleven thirty I climbed out of bed to go downstairs for a drink of water. At the end of the corridor, my parents' bedroom door was framed by a pale silhouette of light. I could hear them talking, but their voices were too soft for me to make out the words. Suddenly my mother raised her voice sharply. I crept closer until I could hear more clearly.

"It's not right," my mother said. "How can you say this is right? Liam is going to die, Sam. He's going to die, and you and I are going to watch him die, and then we will bury him. How can that be anything other than terribly *wrong*?"

"It's not a question of wrong or right," replied my father. "It is what it is. Call it the natural order of the world."

"This isn't *natural*," said my mother.

"Illnesses, diseases, they happen."

"Not to us. They shouldn't happen to *us*."

"Oh, Mary. We don't get to choose. You know that."

"What if this was his last Christmas?"

My father was silent for a moment. "Liam's life will be as long as it's supposed to be," he said.

"But it's scarcely *begun*," moaned my mother.

"All the more reason to be grateful for every day we have."

I leaned against the wall, desperate to escape but unable to move.

My mother had started to cry. "He's so young," she sobbed.

"I know." My father sighed. "But we don't get to choose when people die, Mary. We just have to love Liam as much as we can while we have the chance. If we do that, his death won't be sadder, just because he's young."

"How can you say that?"

"Because our son is happy, fulfilled, and loved. *That's* what matters. Age is just a number."

"Just a number," echoed my mother tonelessly.

"So let's not ever say that Liam died too soon. Let's just say that he lived a good life."

"He's seventeen years old," whispered my mother.

"Yes, and he's had seventeen years full of joy and wonder."

"But it's not *enough!*"

A terrible bark escaped my father's throat. "Well if that's how you feel, take it up with that God of yours."

There was a stunned, awful silence.

"Can't you be at least a little bit kind?" said my mother.

"All those candles you lit. All those prayers you said. What good did any of it do?"

"Don't blame me for wishing that things were different!"

"I don't blame you for anything. But wishing for something doesn't make it so. You know that better than anyone, Mary. The answer to most prayers is no."

"Sam, please—"

"But still you go to church! Still you get down on your knees and beg for a miracle!"

"At least it's *something*," said my mother. "Praying seems like a better bet than not praying, however long the odds may be."

"Maybe we should play the hand we've been dealt, rather than always wishing for different cards."

"Go to hell, Sam." I heard my mother stand up and walk across the room. "I'll pray if I want to pray."

"Mary, come back to bed."

"Don't—just don't."

"Please." My father's voice cracked. "We can't do this alone."

There was a long silence before my mother spoke again.

"I'm not alone," she said. "I have God." Then she burst into tears.

I listened to my parents cry, two separate cycles of tears and snatched breath, a jarring counterpoint of misery. I left them then. I didn't go downstairs for water but tiptoed back to my room.

I'd always assumed that my mother and father had propped each other up as they'd struggled through Liam's illness, but now I realized that they were as alone as I was. Grief did not bring people closer. Loss turned you inward and shut you down.

Back in bed I watched the clock on my bedside table as Christmas Day expired, one neon minute at a time.

1977

ELEVEN

That spring my brother's breathing became more labored. His respiratory system was slowly collapsing in on itself, and he found it increasingly difficult to swallow. Eating and drinking became a struggle, and Liam shrank before our eyes. His face became a ghoulish mask of the boy we used to know. My mother bought a set of new pillows to prop up his frail, brittle body, cocooning it from the unforgiving world of sharp objects around him.

A nurse began to come to the house every day. Her name was Moira. We knew her from St. Mary's—she regularly attended Mass and often delivered scripture readings in a soft Irish brogue that always sounded wonderfully warm to me amid the hard, flat vowels of the locals. She must have been in her sixties, I suppose. Each morning when she arrived she disappeared into Liam's bedroom. She kept up a cheerful dialogue while she tended to him, and we heard them both laugh frequently.

My mother suffered through these visits. She had always been the one to care for her son, and it was difficult for her to step back and watch a stranger administer to his needs. She stood wretchedly in the hallway, wishing she could be on the other side of the bedroom door.

There was no more argument about Liam's going to school, but he still insisted on completing his assigned coursework at the kitchen table each day. The house began to echo with his prolonged fits of coughing. At night I lay in bed and listened to my parents clomp wearily up and down the stairs to help Liam drink a few sips of water and turn him from one side to the other—he was too weak now to roll over on his own. The threat of infection became almost as dangerous as the disease itself: Liam's body was too decimated to resist the assault of other people's germs. Visitors were no longer welcome; my mother stood sentry at the front door and politely refused to allow guests across the threshold. Liam slept for much of the day, and during those moments of respite my mother cleaned the house obsessively. Every surface sparkled with freshly applied disinfectant.

It didn't work, of course. Not even my mother could quarantine the house forever. In the last week of March, Liam caught a cold. Within two days it had mutated into pneumonia.

Only certain bleak memories of that first hospital visit remain with me now. My brother's pummeled body, what was left of it, lying in the hospital bed. Liam cracking jokes from behind the plastic mask of his respirator while the rest of us looked on, hollow-eyed with fear. The digital display above his head that tracked the oxygen saturation level in his blood. I remember those green glowing digits best of all; I stared at them for hours, silently willing them upward.

We returned home after three days.

Things changed after that. I saw a fresh terror behind my mother's eyes. For years, Liam's death had been the first thing she thought of when she woke up every morning and the last thing she thought of before she fell asleep at night. Now she knew that she would never be ready.

After that first hospital stay Liam was issued with a portable respirator, which my father tethered to the wheelchair, its mask always within reach. The unending effort of pulling air in and out of my brother's ruined body exhausted him. One evening I sat on his bed and watched as he held his clarinet to his lips. His fingers rose and fell over the keys, trying to conjure up a melody, but no notes emerged. He didn't have the strength in his lungs to blow air through the instrument. Finally, he laid the clarinet down across his lap.

"That's that, then," he said.

"Try again tomorrow," I suggested.

"Do you know what music practice does, Robbie? It changes you physically." Liam held up a hand and scrutinized it. "These fingers aren't like yours," he said. "They've been trained. They've developed muscle memory. They can do all sorts of clever things. These are talented fingers. The only problem is that they belong to me." He paused. "There's no point having clarinet-playing fingers if you don't have clarinet-playing lungs."

Just like that, there were no more melodies floating through the air, filling the house with light. For years the clarinet had lain on top of Liam's chest of drawers, ready to be picked up and played whenever the impulse took him. But he didn't want to look at it anymore. He packed the instrument away.

For some days after that, Liam stayed in his bedroom. Moira still came every day, but there was no more laughter from behind the door. My parents and I crept around the house, listening for clues. Finally the silence was shattered one afternoon by the riotous, squalling guitar riff of "I Wanna Be Your Dog." The music was so loud that the sugar bowl on the kitchen table rattled. My mother had never been a big fan of the Stooges, but I couldn't remember the last time I'd seen her smile so widely.

For the rest of that day we were treated to a selection of Liam's angriest records, all played at the same ear-bleeding volume. The noise was pounding, relentless. I couldn't imagine what it must have sounded like in his bedroom. It was never possible to gauge Liam's mood by the music he played, since every track seethed with the same fractious aggression, but I guessed that he was trying to obliterate the memory of his clarinet-playing by the sheer amount of noise coming out of the speakers.

Just before supper, the music stopped. I heard the bedroom door open, followed by the low whirr of the wheelchair motor as it trundled toward the kitchen. When Liam appeared, we all turned toward him. "There you are," said my father.

"I need to think about the future," announced Liam.

"What do you mean?" asked my mother.

"It's time to think about college."

"College," said my father.

My mother sat down in the chair next to Liam. She reached out and took his hand in hers. "We can certainly look at all the options," she said. Then she stood up and left the room.

THE REST OF THE SPRING was marked by the frequent arrival of thick, heavily embossed envelopes in the mail, postmarked from across the country. Liam sat at the kitchen table and read through each university prospectus, making notes on a yellow legal pad. There were piles of glossy brochures, stacked and arranged according to a complex system of preference and priority. Then, with my mother's help, Liam began the process of filling out application forms. The two of them spent days carefully completing questionnaires, collating documents and transcripts. I couldn't remember the last time Liam had been so excited. He loved to discuss the relative merits of different colleges and what courses he might take. These disquisitions usually took place over supper, once the papers had been cleared away for the day.

Liam would explore his academic options, contemplating future career paths. My parents listened in numb silence. Liam seemed oblivious to their distress. I watched them wilt under the weight of his words but was unable to stop him. My brother's illness trapped any rebuke in my throat. I could no more tell him to shut up than he could stand up and dance to one of his lousy records. And so we sat and listened to Liam talk about a future that we all knew would never come.

TWELVE

Each year in the weeks leading up to Memorial Day, Haverford performed its metamorphosis from a sleepy backwater of winter hibernation to a crucible of moneyed hysteria. The streets were swept daily and the municipal flower beds bloomed. Everything was designed to charm each fresh flock of tourists into parting with their hard-earned cash. Locals opened their arms in welcome, just wide enough to coax the money out of people's pockets. Shop shelves groaned beneath mountains of newly arrived nautical schlock. Everywhere you turned there was another lobster, one more anchor, a new confection of sea glass. Racks of postcards stood sentry outside every establishment, four for a dollar. The images were brilliant, Technicolor sharp, and of a place I hardly recognized. Ice cream parlors reopened and the restaurants in town took on extra staff. People rented out their spare rooms at whatever rates they could get away with. Along the roads in and out of town a caravan of white-washed trailers appeared, each one promising the freshest seafood in Maine. Every year enterprising locals cooked up new moneymaking schemes. There were historical walking tours or boat trips to be taken, a thousand boxes of saltwater taffy and hand-carved lighthouses to be purchased. Memories were for sale on every corner. Everyone was hustling to make a buck.

This seasonal squall of industry was no more than opportunistic scavenging, of course. The townsfolk picked off the tourist dollars that Fun-A-Lot left behind, as nakedly hungry as the squadrons of gulls that followed the trawlers that edged along the ocean's horizon toward Nova Scotia. It hadn't always been this way, though. Haverford's shameless courting of the tourist trade was a relatively new phenomenon.

THE HAVERFORD PAPER COMPANY was founded in 1872—so proclaimed the inscription in the limestone lintel above the doors of the paper mill that sat on the banks of the river that ran through the town. For the first fifty years of its existence the company had employed more Haverford residents than all the other businesses in the area combined. People came to the town from across the state and beyond, looking for jobs. The mill was the sun around which everything else orbited. Tons of pulp and newsprint were produced every day and shipped off to all points south. Orders rolled in, new jobs were created, profits rose. Houses were built to accommodate the growing population of workers. Whole new neighborhoods sprouted up, sprawling inland on a crest of optimism and prosperity.

Then came the Depression. The Haverford Paper Company survived, but it never recovered. The mill limped on for several more decades after that, suffering one setback after another—increased competition from Wisconsin and New York, a reluctance to embrace new technologies, complacent management, an icy economy. The place finally closed its doors for good in 1964.

The building had been an unshifting landmark of my childhood. I often cycled past its fortresslike walls but never really gave the place much thought. For all its familiarity, it felt entirely alien to me, forbidding in its silent, industrial vastness.

Since the closure of the mill, Haverford had been forced to reinvent itself, and my family's quixotic enterprise on the outskirts of town was the best it had to offer. This was Maine, after all: every summer there were carloads of cash passing the town by as tourists stormed up Interstate 95 to the natural glories further north. And so, in the absence of any viable alternative, Haverford stuck out a leg and pulled up its skirt. Little by little travelers were lured off the road, hoping to buy themselves a few hours of peace on their journeys to elsewhere. Without the amusement park, tourists would have had little reason to stop, but thanks to Fun-A-Lot the town soon had itself a small tourism industry.

Not that anyone was remotely grateful. In Haverford the park was spoken of with barely veiled resentment. My father's battered station wagon—the same car he had been driving since I was born— could not convince people that he wasn't printing money all summer long. Jealousy will always eclipse reason. My father didn't seem to mind, though. He worked like a dog to keep the park going every year and didn't expect a word of thanks from anyone. The satisfaction of quietly beating the odds had become its own reward.

THE DAY BEFORE the season began, after the final coats of paint had been applied and before the first guests walked through the front gates, Fun-A-Lot looked as fine as it ever did. Every tattered pennant had been mended, every lightbulb shone brightly. The paths were litter-free, the lawns pristine. In pride of place on the carousel, my father's newest horse—the beast that Nathan and I had watched come to life over the course of the long winter—stood ready for action, its hooves joyfully aloft.

Now that we were finished with middle school, Nathan and I were old enough to apply for summer jobs. My father warned us that we would receive no preferential treatment, no cushy gigs. This didn't bother me. I had seen the dead-eyed stares of the park employees as they struggled through the tedium of each day and knew that we would be numb with boredom by the second week, no matter what we did. But even with my low expectations, I was dismayed when my father told me that I was going to spend the summer working with Lewis Jenks, the maintenance man.

Lewis Jenks had worked at Fun-A-Lot longer than anyone, my father included. Grandpa Ronald had hired him when he first opened the place, and he'd been there ever since. Lewis Jenks scared me. He was a cantankerous old man who scowled at visitors and coworkers alike as he marched along the gravel paths with his toolbox tucked under his arm. He always wore the same tattered blue overalls and work boots that were on the brink of falling apart. He had a snowy beard and a dramatic mane of white hair, which always reminded me of God. (That was one reason he terrified me.) He had lost his front two teeth, which lent him a sinister air on the rare occasions that he opened his mouth to speak. In all the years I had known Lewis Jenks, I had never seen him smile.

"Follow him around," said my father. "Find out how everything works. You'll learn a lot. Then you'll be able to help me in the fall. We'll get things fixed much quicker if there's two of us."

"Isn't he a bit—I mean, he always looks scary," I said.

"Oh, no. Lewis is a pussycat."

"Are you sure?" I was thinking about that scowling, toothless maw.

"Oh, and by the way," said my father. "Within a day he'll start telling you about all the stuff I've messed up over the years. He'll have you believe that this park wouldn't even be standing if it wasn't for him fixing my mistakes."

"Is it true?"

"Of course it's not true." My father looked at me. "Just don't believe anything he tells you."

"What about Nathan?" I asked.

"He's going to be working in the kitchen."

"I think he was hoping for something else," I said.

Nathan had set his heart on being the park mascot, a furry green dragon that wandered through the park waving at visitors, hugging small children, and generally adding to the sum of human happiness in any way that a furry green dragon could. My father was very proud of his mascot. No matter that he had stolen the idea after seeing a picture of a full-size cartoon mouse strolling through the crowds at Disneyland. No matter that the inside of the costume was so encrusted with the sweat of a generation of teenagers that it could stand upright without anyone inside it. No matter that the dragon's tail was lumpy and half detached from its rear end, or that its wings drooped in the August heat. Everyone loved the dragon. The dragon was the big leagues. The dragon was prime time.

"I don't doubt it," said my father. "Nobody *wants* to work in the kitchen. But it's an important job. In some years, food sales keep us afloat. There's profit in hot dogs and cotton candy."

Sure enough, Nathan was unable to hide his dismay when I told him the news.

"It's an important job," I told him.

"Oh *please*," said Nathan.

"In some years, food sales keep us afloat."

Nathan wasn't listening. "I could have done great things with that dragon." He sighed.

"Maybe next year," I said.

"In the meantime, there's a mountain of potato salad in my future."

"At least you don't have to wear a stupid costume," I told him. My own misgivings about my forthcoming apprenticeship with Lewis Jenks had taken an additional knock when I discovered that I would be required to wear an outfit. You could calibrate a person's seniority at the park by the flamboyance of their clothes. The older boys—the noblemen of Fun-A-Lot—wore brightly colored crushed-velvet pantaloons. I, though, was issued a brown tunic, woolen tights, and a small green hat. I was a lowly serf.

On the morning of the first day of the season—the Saturday of Memorial Day weekend—I donned my uniform and gazed at myself in the mirror. At least Nathan would be hidden away in the kitchen, protected from ridicule. I would be spending my days in full view of the paying public. The potential for humiliation seemed limitless.

There was also the worrying prospect of reentering Hollis Calhoun's sinister orbit once again. I hadn't seen Hollis since we had left him in Mr. Pritchard's office nine months earlier, but I knew he'd be working at the park again that summer, and I wasn't looking forward to running into him. I sighed and put on my little hat.

On the drive to the park that first morning my father talked all the way, tapping the steering wheel, a bundle of nervous energy. The opening day of the season always pulled him in several different emotional directions. He was excited, hopeful, and worried, all at once. At the start of every summer he told himself that the sun would shine every day and nothing would go wrong. The cash registers would keep chiming all the way to Labor Day. It was a monumental triumph of optimism over experience. I sulked in the passenger seat. My tights had already begun to itch.

At the park I made my way to the maintenance hut, where Lewis

Jenks worked. The gates didn't open for another hour, but there were people everywhere. Many were dressed in outfits sillier than mine, but this failed to cheer me up. I plucked miserably at my tunic and wondered how Nathan was doing. We had agreed to meet up at the end of the day to compare notes.

I knocked on the door of the hut and waited. After a moment there was a gruff response, and I went in. Lewis Jenks was sitting at a desk that was covered in tools, spools of colored wire, and oily rags. He was carefully holding two slices of thick white bread. By his feet there was a small transistor radio, from which emerged the atonal squawk of a saxophone. Lewis looked at me and raised his snowy eyebrows in greeting.

"Robert Carter," he murmured.

I stepped inside. "Hello, Lewis," I said.

"D'you like sardines?" he asked.

I shrugged.

"You should try 'em," said Lewis. "Breakfast of champions." He took a huge bite of his sandwich. He sat back in his chair and chewed with evident satisfaction. "What are you supposed to be in that outfit?" he said, his mouth half full. "One of Santa's pixies?"

"I'm supposed to be a peasant."

"A peasant?" Lewis grinned, and I saw the gap where his front teeth should have been. "Your grandpa would be proud. He was a good man. Gave me my first job after the war. I didn't know much about fixing things back then, but neither did he. So I worked it out as I went along, and he was none the wiser." He gave me a look. "You know much about fixing things, Robert?"

"Not much," I admitted.

"Your daddy doesn't, either. He works hard, but I spend a lot of time putting right all the mistakes he's made." I said nothing. Lewis chewed thoughtfully. "He told you I was going to say that, didn't he?"

"No," I said.

Lewis grinned again and took another bite of his sandwich.

I felt my cheeks redden. "They're elves," I said.

"What are?"

"Santa's helpers. They're elves, not pixies. Pixies live at the bottom of your yard. Elves live at the North Pole."

"Is that so," said Lewis.

"The point is, I'm not an elf *or* a pixie."

"That's right," said Lewis. "You're a peasant."

"A peasant with a stupid green hat."

Lewis finished his sandwich. "Well, whatever you are, I hope you're ready to work." He held out his hand toward me. His massive palm was webbed by dark veins, soiled by years of grease and dirt. His fingers were callused and crooked. As we shook I noticed that the thumb on his right hand looked all wrong. It was twice as thick as any of his fingers but half the length it should have been. There was no joint where it could bend. It simply lay there, fat and grotesque, a useless stump. At first I thought that the tip must have been cut off, but there was a thick, gnarled nail at its end.

"You're wondering about my thumb," said Lewis.

I looked up at him, abashed. "What happened to it?"

"I lost it."

"How?"

"That's a question for another time." Lewis held up his other hand and spread it wide. His left thumb looked as it should—long and strong and perfectly in proportion to the rest of his hand. He crooked it ruefully. "I'll tell you this, though. I could have done with another one like this."

"But you've still got—something."

"This?" Lewis held up his stub of a digit. "This isn't my thumb, Robert. It's my toe." I looked again. Thick and ugly and hairy, the toe had no business being there, but it looked just familiar enough to create a sense of violence performed on the usual order of the world. I couldn't pull my eyes away from it. "The miracles of modern medicine," said Lewis. He pointed down at his large, dust-covered boot. "They cut it off my foot and grafted it onto my hand. Figured I could use it more up here than down there."

"Do you miss it? Your toe?"

"Not as much as I miss my damn thumb." Lewis sat back and put his hands behind his head, his toe disappearing into his thick white hair. "Let's talk about this job," he said. He nodded toward a gray walkie-talkie the size of a brick that sat on the desk. "Whenever that thing goes off, we grab the tool kit and fix what needs to be fixed."

"Okay," I said.

"Now, hear this?" Lewis pointed at the radio. A saxophone was playing a squalling, jagged solo. Behind it I could hear the clatter of drums and dark, spiky piano chords. It sounded terrible. "Do you know what that is?"

"It's jazz, right?"

"Well, yes, it's jazz. But it's a special *kind* of jazz. It's called bebop."

"Bebop?" I'd never heard of it.

Lewis nodded. "Right now you're listening to the most important American musician of this century," he told me. "His name is Charles Parker, although everyone called him Yardbird. Bird for short."

As I listened to the tuneless honk of the saxophone, I thought that even Liam's records were preferable to this.

Lewis was watching me. "You don't like it?"

"I *hate* it," I told him. To my annoyance, Lewis burst out laughing. The saxophone had been replaced by a vinegary trumpet. "Can we turn it off?" I asked.

"Hell no," said Lewis cheerfully. "You wait and see. In a couple of weeks you'll love it." Then he began to whistle along to the trumpet solo that was playing on the radio. Lewis kept perfect time with the instrument, tracking every flurry of rapid-fire notes and each syncopated twist and turn. It was a pitch-perfect performance, his whistle as sweet to my ears as the trumpet was sour.

"That was *amazing*," I said when he'd finished.

He pointed to his mouth. "My cousin Billy knocked my front teeth out when I was eight. Been able to whistle like the devil ever since."

Just then the walkie-talkie crackled with static and a disembodied voice filled the room. "Lewis. Lewis. Please come to the batting cage."

Lewis looked at me. "You ready?" he said.

I put on my green hat, suddenly not quite so bothered by it. "Ready," I said. Lewis handed me the walkie-talkie and picked up his tool kit, and we walked out into the sunshine. As he closed the door behind us, I could hear Charlie Parker playing on into the empty room.

OVER THE COURSE OF that first day, we rewired the control console for the Tilt-A-Whirl, replaced the rear axle on the caboose of the kiddie train that drove around the perimeter of the park, fixed two ancient cash registers, reattached the striped awning in front of the popcorn stand, and (twice) unjammed the pitching machine at the batting cage. I say "we," but it was Lewis alone who did all this. I just trotted along behind him, peering over his shoulder and holding tools for him, furtively glancing at his misplaced toe whenever I had the chance. He kept up a gruff commentary as he worked, explaining what he was doing and why, but none of it made much sense to me.

I thought I knew the park as well as anyone, but Lewis Jenks showed me a whole new world that day. Behind the brightly painted rides and banks of shining lights lay a parallel universe of grease-encrusted motors and ugly breaker circuits. As I gazed at each new mess of machinery and electronics, I began to understand my father's unending anxiety. Multicolored wires sprung like spaghetti from behind every panel that Lewis pried open. It was extraordinary just how much there was to go wrong.

THAT FIRST NIGHT, after closing time, I waited for Nathan by the front gate. I was eager to tell him about Lewis and his transplanted toe. All around me older kids were breezing out of the park in chattering groups, pleased to have finished their first day of work. Nathan finally appeared, looking tired. A pungent aroma wafted off him as he approached. I wrinkled my nose.

"Is that fried onions I smell?" I asked.

Nathan nodded.

"Did you cook them or roll around in them?"

"This year," announced Nathan, "I am to be the onion king. The *onionmeister*. Every fried onion eaten in the park this summer will be my work." He paused. "I am working toward a more perfect onion."

"You can give the state-of-the-onion address," I said.

Nathan became very serious. "I learned so much today," he said. "There's a lot that goes into frying an onion properly. You have to peel it right, then cut it right, then cook it right. The rings must be the correct width—too narrow and they crisp up too quickly, too wide and they can be too chewy. And then you have to caramelize them. That's an art all to itself." He rubbed his fingers together over an imaginary stove. "All it takes is a bit of sugar. But you have to know when to sprinkle and how much to use."

"I'm impressed," I said.

"This is an important job. Actually, this is *the* most important job. The burgers and hot dogs? They're just one item on the menu. But onions—onions are served with *everything*. So the kitchen really relies on me. And remember what you said—food sales keep the park afloat! If I mess up the onions, people will stop buying food. Then the park will close, and we'll all lose our jobs. The tourists won't stop in Haverford anymore. The money will dry up, businesses will shut down, and people will move away. It will become a ghost town."

"You seem to be bearing up under all the pressure," I said.

"Also there's a girl," said Nathan. "She works the cash register at the concession stand. With fair hair and blue eyes?"

"Ah," I said. "That would be Faye."

"Do you know her?"

Like all the boys in Haverford, I knew Faye. Even though we had never spoken, I had been watching her avidly since I was in fourth grade. Faye was a year older than me, and that alone would have been enough to ensure that we would never come into each other's orbit. I was a rule follower, an obedient observer of school etiquette, and so I never would have dared to talk to someone in the grade above me unless spoken to first—and that was never going to happen. But there was a more compelling reason I couldn't approach Faye: she was, without question, the most beautiful girl I had ever seen. She was so heart-stoppingly perfect that all I could do was look at her in furtive awe. I had watched her glide past me down the school corridors, usually pursued by a posse of older boys, and felt both anguish and relief that I would never stand a chance with her. Faye's divine untouchability inoculated me against being crucified by doomed desire. I was able to appreciate her charms privately, without complications or humiliations.

"Sure," I said. "I know Faye."

"What do you know about her?"

"I know that she's already in high school, and she probably has a hundred boyfriends."

But Nathan wasn't listening to me.

"*Faye*," he murmured to himself.

Nathan, it occurred to me then, was not a rule follower.

THIRTEEN

I started to enjoy my days in the park with Lewis. We were kept busy moving from one worn-out piece of equipment to the next, patching things up as best we could.

We were often confronted by frustrated customers who wanted to moan about whatever had gone wrong, even if all that achieved was to delay getting the problem solved. People appeared to believe that they were entitled to be as rude as they liked to staff, as if it were one more perk included in the admission price. Lewis always adopted the same posture while guests hurled abuse at him. He tilted his head to one side and gazed intently at the speaker as if he were giving the matter his full attention, but he never reacted to any of it, not once.

"How come you don't get mad at all the things people say?" I asked him after a man had complained for several minutes while his wife and children had scowled in aggrieved silence next to him.

"Can't get mad if you don't hear it," said Lewis.

"What do you mean?"

"I tune 'em out," he explained. "These people have a lot of things they need to say, but I don't have to listen."

"How can you not? They're standing right in front of you."

Lewis's eyes twinkled. "I listen to Charlie Parker solos in my head.

He can blow awful loud sometimes." He looked at me. "Don't get angry at those folks, Robert."

"But they're so rude!"

"Can't blame 'em for that. They're all miserable."

"But they're on vacation!" I said.

He looked at me. "You've never had a summer vacation, have you?"

It was true. My father had never taken a day off while the park was open. I'd spent every summer of my life in Maine.

"Here's how it works," said Lewis. "You spend all year working your ass off, doing overtime and staying late in the office, dreaming about spending time away, just you and your wife and your kids. So you save up. You plan. You count the days. It's only when you're actually on vacation that you remember that you don't actually *like* spending time with your family. There's a reason you work late. Your kids drive you crazy with their whining. Your wife nags you all day long. And of course this vacation is costing an arm and a leg. By the third day you're checking the calendar, figuring how long until you can crawl back to that job you hate so much." He beamed at me. "That's the most valuable thing about full-time employment, Robert. It keeps you away from the people you love."

Full-time employment! The words made me giddy. Each morning I proudly climbed into the station wagon with my father, ready for another day of adult responsibility. People depended on me to do my job and to do it well. Every Friday afternoon my father handed me a small brown envelope filled with folded banknotes. The money felt good in my back pocket. An honest wage for honest work.

Lewis was a good teacher. Each week I learned a little more. He began to let me have a first try at fixing things. Sometimes I could do it, sometimes I couldn't. Lewis never got impatient, even when there was a long list of problems that needed our attention. He would show me what to do and then would wait until I had fixed it myself. There was pride, I discovered, in mending things. Occasionally Lewis sent me out into the park to perform minor repairs on my own, while he sat back in his chair and listened to his beloved bebop.

As the season progressed I also stopped worrying about my costume. I had come to realize that my ridiculous hat and tunic made me invisible. I began to watch the guests more closely, safe in the knowledge that they would never notice me. I'd thought a lot about Lewis's compassion for the tourists who flocked through the gates every day, so desperate not to be disappointed. Since then I'd been looking at the park through new eyes. Now the families I saw seemed fractured by small disappointments. Children were not sweetly grateful for their special day out; they were tyrannical cyclones of self-entitlement, always wanting more. Parents did not look on in amused indulgence; they were simply too tired to resist all those shrill demands and too bored to fight with each other.

My childhood memories were quietly unspooling, slipping through my hands.

NATHAN, MEANWHILE, had decided to make the best of a bad job—quite literally. He resolved to become the best fryer of onions that had ever worked in the Fun-A-Lot kitchen. Every morning he put on a scuba mask and snorkel before peeling and slicing the hill of vegetables that awaited him. He made a peculiar sight as he wielded his knife, the rubber snorkel waving above his head like a naked flagpole in the wind, but he was able to chop quickly, uninterrupted by the sting of onion fumes. He worked the hot plate with care, piling up mountains of perfectly glistening, sweetly caramelized onions, garnishes for a thousand hot dogs and burgers. Through an act of sheer willpower, he actually began to enjoy his job. It helped that there was nowhere Nathan wanted to be more than in that awful, sweltering kitchen, because from where he worked he was able to look across the room and watch Faye smile at the waiting customers.

I think Nathan was hoping that Faye would notice the excellence of the fried condiments and turn around to see who had wrought such gastronomic wonders—*My goodness*, she would breathe, *that boy can certainly fry*—but she never did. Still, Nathan's ardor for her did not diminish. I had hoped that after a while some kind of instinct for self-preservation would kick in, but his infatuation still burned as hotly as ever.

There were other girls to look at, too, of course. None of them were as beautiful as Faye, but I still enjoyed watching them bustle through the park in their hokey medieval outfits. My gaze would linger surreptitiously over their satin-sheathed behinds as they sashayed along the gravel paths, but I knew better than to try to talk to any of them. Back then I was deeply conflicted about the opposite sex in general. I could still remember the night when I sat on Liam's bed and listened to him explain how babies were made in gruesome (if anatomically vague) terms. I knew my brother had to be telling the truth, because not even his warped imagination could have come up with something so disgusting. I finally buried my head under his pillow and begged him to stop. For days I couldn't look at my parents, I was so ashamed of them.

I was eight years old.

It seemed that I was the only one who had reservations about such things, however. That summer the park was a typhoon of teenage lust. Wherever I looked there were people necking and pawing at each other. In every corner I could detect the whiff of adolescent debauchery. After closing time, many of the older kids congregated outside the gates, smoking cigarettes and surreptitiously sharing cans of beer. This was when the riot of hormonal activity was at its most febrile. Boys showed off and smirked; girls preened and simpered. It was there that Nathan suffered most. He watched the older boys swarm hungrily around Faye while she played with her beautiful hair. To make things worse, Hollis Calhoun was one of the crowd vying for her attention. He was always cavorting about in front of her with a stupid grin on his face.

"I never thought we'd see *him* again," muttered Nathan.

I wasn't sure that you ever saw the last of people like Hollis Calhoun.

Nathan watched it all from a distance. Every fluttered eyelash was calibrated, each tinkling laugh measured and noted.

After a while the crowd would slowly drift away in twos and threes toward the beach. We could only imagine what went on down there. Nathan and I were never invited. Nathan would stare wordlessly after Faye as she sauntered off, her arm draped casually over someone's shoulder.

He was waiting to see if a favorite would emerge from the pack.

FOURTEEN

Once the older kids had left for the beach, Nathan and I needed something to do. Neither of us wanted to go home. I had no wish to return to my dying brother and my parents' baffled misery, and Nathan was always looking for reasons to postpone the long bike ride back to Sebbanquik Point. His mother spent every evening at her desk, hidden in a cloud of cigarette smoke. There was nothing for him there.

One June evening after the parking lot had emptied, the two of us cycled into Haverford. The center of town was heaving with people eating ice cream and wandering in and out of shops. The parking spaces were all occupied by cars with out-of-state license plates. We couldn't walk more than five yards down the sidewalk without having to circumnavigate another blackboard promising cut-price souvenirs.

By unspoken agreement we got back on our bikes. Half a mile up the town's main street, we turned onto Bridge Lane. It was a pretty street, its houses set well back from the road. At one point the road dipped in a steep incline; we freewheeled to the bottom of the hill, where a bridge crossed the river as it snaked inland from the sea. On the opposite bank stood the Haverford Paper Company. At one end of the vast brick building a tall chimney rose into the sky, solitary and bleak, and cold for years now.

We stopped on the bridge and listened to the steady pulse of the water beneath us. It was a beautiful evening.

"Have you ever been inside the mill?" asked Nathan.

I shook my head. "It's been locked up for years. There's no getting in."

"There's *always* a way in," said Nathan.

"Not here. People have tried."

"They haven't tried hard enough, then. Come on."

We rode across the bridge and left our bicycles in the deserted parking lot. Around the back of the building there was a pair of wide double doors, bound shut by a heavy, rusted padlock. We tugged at them but they did not budge an inch.

"You see?" I said.

Nathan stepped back and gazed up at the three stories of tall windows. "Look," he said, pointing. "See that top window, on the far right? The panes have been smashed."

I saw. The rest of the windows glowed orange in the warm reflection of the setting sun, but the one he was pointing at was a dark hole, swallowing the light.

"What good is that going to do?" I said. "We can't get up there."

Nathan walked toward the mill until he was standing beneath the broken window. "Look," he said with a grin.

A series of iron rungs had been hammered into the brickwork. They went in a vertical line up the wall, past the broken window, and then continued to the top of the chimney. It was some kind of maintenance ladder.

"I'm not climbing that," I said.

Nathan looked surprised. "Why not?"

"Who knows how long it's been since anyone's climbed it?" I replied. "Any one of these could come loose." I grabbed the lowest rung and shook it. It did not move.

"These things were built to last," said Nathan. He put one foot on the lowest rung.

"What if you fall?" I said. "You might slip."

"I might." Nathan climbed up another rung.

"There's nothing to catch you."

He peered down at me. "When is there *ever* anything to catch you, Robert?"

I had no answer to that. "Look," I said, "let's go and find somewhere else to explore."

"I want to see what's inside," said Nathan.

"Nathan, wait," I said. "There's a—"

He stopped. "There's a what?"

I took a deep breath. "There's a ghost."

To my relief Nathan came back down to the ground. When he was standing in front of me, his eyes were wide. "A ghost?" he said. "For real?"

I nodded. The story had been whispered across the town for generations. A delicious shiver of apprehension passed through me every time my father told it—which he had done often, at my eager request, throughout my childhood.

"For real," I said.

WILLA CAVICH BEGAN WORKING at the Haverford mill in 1927. She was a tall, thin girl—pretty enough, the story goes, but rather shy. She lived with her parents and her younger sister, Alice. Her job was to manage the inventory of chemicals that were used in the pulping process. She worked in a small office on the top floor of the mill. Willa liked to look out of the window and watch as the workers came and went at the end of their shifts. One man in particular caught her eye. His name was Jacques Durousillier, a recent immigrant from New Brunswick. While most of the men trudged in and out of the mill gates with their shoulders slumped in exhaustion, the Canadian carried himself with a swaggering brio. Twice a day he would step outside and smoke a cigarette, and Willa made sure to position herself near the window, just in case he might look up and see her there. One evening he was leaning against the mill doors as she left for the day, waiting for her.

Jacques Durousillier wooed Willa Cavich with an intensity that left her breathless and unstuck. He was ardent but also impatient. Willa did her best to resist. You'll have to marry me first, she told him night after night. He begged and pleaded, but, good Catholic girl that she was, she remained firm. There was nothing Willa wanted more than to hear a proposal of marriage from the man she adored, but it never came. Still, she decided that she was prepared to wait, if he was.

One Sunday after church Willa decided to surprise Jacques at the house he shared with four other millworkers. She walked across town, lunch packed in a small basket on her arm, her thoughts full of a romantic picnic by the ocean. When she pushed open the door to his room, at first Willa did not recognize the woman in the bed. Then she sat up, and Willa began to scream. Jacques Durousillier begged her to be quiet, but she did not, could not, stop. And then there was her sister, Alice, coming at her, sheets abandoned, her face a sour rictus of contempt. The slap caught Willa by surprise and sent her staggering sideways. She slipped, and as she fell her head hit the corner of the chest of drawers. Then there was no more screaming.

Jacques Durousillier and Alice Cavich stared in horror at the dead girl on the bedroom floor. They knew they had to get rid of the body. That night they wrapped Willa in a tarpaulin and dragged her to the empty mill. The first floor of the building was dominated by a giant pulping machine that chomped uncut timber by the yard, reducing hearty tree trunks to fibrous slurry in seconds. They hauled Willa Cavich onto the metal rollers in front of the machine's waiting steel teeth. When Jacques Durousillier switched on the machine, her body vanished instantly in a red mist of blood and splintered bone. No trace was left.

The next day the Canadian fled back across the border to New Brunswick. Alice Cavich, though, had nowhere to go and nothing but her guilt for company. Her confession, when it came, made headlines for a week or two. After her conviction she was remanded in custody to a mental institution in Bangor, where she lived for the rest of her life. Jacques Durousillier was never heard of again.

It was not long afterward that the sightings began.

From time to time workers would catch half a glimpse of a young, sad-looking woman standing next to the mouth of the pulping machine. When they looked again, she had vanished.

We all knew the real reason the mill had shut down. It wasn't economics; the place had been cursed. The ghost of Willa Cavich still haunted its vast, deserted spaces, alone in her sorrow and victorious in her revenge.

I LAID IT ON pretty thick, I admit. By the time I got to the part about the pulping machine, I was pleased to see that the color had drained from Nathan's face. We would be back on our bikes again soon enough. He shivered when I had finished. "That's a great story," he said. Then he turned back to the ladder and began climbing again.

"What are you doing?" I said.

Nathan turned and looked at me. "Don't you want to *see* the ghost?"

I stared up at him in disbelief. "*No*," I said.

"Are you scared?" asked Nathan.

"Of course I'm scared," I said.

He looked down at me and grinned. "Me, too."

And with that he began to climb again. I watched helplessly as he pulled himself higher and higher. Soon he was level with the broken window. There was a gap of about three feet between the ladder and the ledge. I watched anxiously as Nathan reached out a hand across the empty space. He stayed there without moving for a moment. Just as I'd begun to hope that he had realized he would never be able to make it safely across, he climbed two more rungs, so that he was higher than the window—and stretched out a foot. With one swift movement he let go of the iron rung and shifted his weight to the ledge. As he did so, he grabbed the window frame and hauled himself inside. The last thing I saw was the soles of his sneakers as he vanished through the hole.

For a moment there was complete silence. The awful thought occurred to me that the floors of the old mill had rotted away and that Nathan had crashed to the ground through an ancient forest of splintering timber. But then his face appeared, grinning down at me in triumph.

"Are you coming up?" he called.

I wasn't sure which scared me more—the thought of seeing Willa Cavich's ghost or jumping from the ladder to the window ledge. "Can't you come down and open a door?"

Nathan considered this. "Hang on," he said, and disappeared. Several minutes later a small door close to where I was standing opened. Nathan appeared and doffed an imaginary hat. "No ghosts so far," he reported.

We crept into a huge, high-ceilinged room that took up the entire ground floor of the mill. Pieces of disassembled machinery caked in orange rust filled the space like abandoned statues. The floor was mottled with faded shapes where the huge pieces of equipment had blocked out the sunlight for years. I tried to guess which discolored patch had been the pulping machine and squinted anxiously through the creeping twilight for Willa Cavich's ghost. There were pyramids of discarded turbines and cogs scattered around the room. We scavenged through these in an effort to distract ourselves from the fact that we were both terrified. Every few moments I thought I caught some movement out of the corner of my eye and would freeze, a scream already half bubbling up in my throat. But there was no ghost. After a while we summoned the courage to explore a little further. The second story of the building was divided by faded lines of white paint into hundreds of numbered bays. I guessed that this was where the paper was stored until it was ready to be shipped. There was a large hole in the floor so that palettes of paper could be lowered directly onto delivery trucks waiting below. A collection of hoists, pulleys, and hooks dangled over the double-height space, nooses with invisible bodies.

On the third floor we discovered a series of offices, home to old chairs and empty filing cabinets. There was a small laboratory, too, where we found ancient measuring scales, Bunsen burners, rubber tubes, and glass flasks of various shapes and sizes. I wondered which of these rooms Willa Cavich had worked in.

One thing I knew: ghost or no ghost, I did not want to be in the mill after the sun had gone down. We hurried through the rooms as darkness approached. When it was almost too dark to see, I stepped back out through the door Nathan had opened for me earlier. Nathan pulled the bolts back across and made his way up to the third floor. We had agreed that we wouldn't leave the place unlocked.

We wanted to keep our secret to ourselves.

NATHAN AND I BEGAN to visit the mill most evenings after the park had closed. Each night I watched him climb up the iron ladder to the broken window. Nathan never seemed to consider the possibility that he might miss his footing and fall as he stretched his leg across the void and stepped onto the ledge. The further away from the ground he was, the more carefree he appeared. He would whistle and fool about and pretend to slip on a rung or lose his grip, and then laugh at my terror-stricken face.

After the hurried thrill of that first night, we began to explore the place more thoroughly. Soon we couldn't wait to jump on our bikes and cycle to Bridge Lane at the end of each day. The summer stretched out ahead of us, and each evening now held the intoxicating promise of fresh discoveries.

It felt as if we had all the time in the world.

We even managed to stop worrying quite so much about Willa Cavich. For the first few nights the sour twist of fear lingered inside me as we moved between the massive fixtures on the ground floor. A lifetime of stories can take some shifting. I was still waiting to see the pale figure of a young woman standing in silence where her body had been pulverized.

One evening as we were nosing around on the second floor, Nathan gave a squawk of glee. "Robert!" he yelled. "Come and see this!" He was holding a long plastic paddle that was attached to the wall by a thick electric cord.

"What is it?" I asked.

"Watch," he said. He pressed a button on the paddle. A large iron hook that was suspended from the ceiling began to edge toward us, clanking noisily as it went. Nathan pressed another button. The pulley above the hook started to turn, unspooling a thick wire cable. We watched as the hook disappeared through the hole in the floor until it was almost touching the ground in the loading bay below. Nathan pressed another button and the cable stopped its descent. He ran downstairs and jumped onto the dangling hook, wedging a foot into its huge claw. "Make me fly, Robert!" he called.

For the next hour, Nathan flew across the second floor and through the hole between the warehouse and the loading bay. I sent him up and down and back and forth across the mill's vast, empty spaces. Nathan balanced on the hook and cackled with delight.

These flights became a regular part of our trips. Halfway through his second expedition, Nathan began to sing "Teenage Lust" by MC5 and followed this with a selection of other favorites from Liam's record collection. None of these songs lent themselves very well to a cappella vocal performance, being more or less devoid of anything that might be called a melody—besides, it was the loud, muddy guitar riffs that made the tunes memorable, not their nuanced and thoughtful lyrics. Still, Nathan kept belting out those songs. His voice echoed off the walls as he sang about drug overdoses, suicide, manic depression, and lousy sex. It was the purest expression of joy he could muster.

Nathan never asked me if I wanted to have a go on the hook, but that was fine with me. I enjoyed being the pilot. He couldn't operate the controls himself while he was flying. Just as I needed him to clamber up the iron ladder and let me into the building, now he needed me, too.

The old mill was every boy's dream. As we roamed its enormous rooms, we were confined only by our imaginations. Our games were grander, our ideas bigger, our sense of adventure never more joyfully fulfilled. There we found a refuge from all that plagued us. I could escape Liam's illness and the desperate heartbreak of my parents, and Nathan was able to forget about his father's death and his mother's slow unraveling behind her study door.

But no matter how much we relished our escape, the sanctuary offered by those redbrick walls wouldn't last forever.

FIFTEEN

Liam went back into the hospital over Labor Day weekend.
It had been several months since he'd been admitted with pneumonia, and I had begun to hope that the worst might be over. Maybe, I told myself, his body had become more resistant to the threat of infection.

Then there was my father's hand on my shoulder in the middle of the night, shaking me out of my sleep. The blue flash of the waiting ambulance lit up my bedroom wall. I stumbled downstairs in time to see my brother being carried out of the front door on a stretcher, my mother leaning over him. She climbed into the back of the ambulance with Liam, not looking back at us once. We followed behind in the station wagon. My father drove in silence, his face a mask of fear.

This time it took Liam five days to recover. I had been wrong, of course. His body wasn't getting stronger. It was weaker than ever. Doctors flocked around his bed more urgently than before. They took my mother and father to one side and talked to them in low voices. Liam lay there, his face obscured by the respirator mask, and pretended to be asleep. The moment the doctors bustled out of the room, he opened his eyes and gave us a tired smile. And I thought: My brother is too good for this.

Nathan came to the hospital every afternoon. He sat on the end of Liam's bed and the two of them talked about music. Sometimes Nathan performed his a cappella versions of their favorite punk songs, which always made Liam laugh so much that he ended up coughing into his respirator mask. I could feel my mother stiffen each time this happened, but she never said a word. Nathan told Liam all about Faye. We were about to start high school, and Nathan was thrilled at the prospect of seeing her every day. To my disbelief, Liam offered advice about how Nathan should behave when he and Faye started dating. Then he told Nathan about his college applications. Together they discussed different courses and debated the merits of various universities.

I listened to these conversations with increasing frustration. Liam and Nathan were both immersed in their own fantasies, speculating about futures that would never happen. Each of them was egging the other on.

Every night my father and I drove home while my mother stayed by Liam's bedside, holding his hand while he slept. By the time Liam was well enough to leave, she was so tired that she could barely speak. Our departure from the hospital looked like a victory parade. As we made our way toward the parking lot, doctors smiled their congratulations, nurses applauded, orderlies gave us high fives. We stumbled numbly on.

We all knew that we would be back before long.

LIAM'S HOSPITAL STAY eclipsed both the end of my first summer season at Fun-A-Lot and the start of my career at Haverford High School. I was apprehensive about starting somewhere new, with different rules and rituals to learn. Worse still, I would have Hollis

Calhoun to worry about again. I had kept out of his way all summer at the park, but there would be no avoiding him when the new term started. The prospect of creeping up and down school corridors once again made my stomach twist with bilious dread. I spent the first few days keeping a watchful eye on the crowds milling around ahead of me, on the lookout for Hollis's lumbering gait. When I finally saw him heading in my direction, I stopped and braced myself. But there was no slap on the head, no sly punch to the gut. Hollis walked right past me. When the same thing happened again, and then again, I cautiously allowed myself to believe that he really had decided to leave me alone. Gone was the cruel delight on his face whenever he saw me; now he seemed utterly indifferent to my existence.

I still had other things to worry about, of course. Within a couple of weeks of the start of school, Nathan's infatuation with Faye had mutated into a full-blown obsession. The knowledge that he was spending all day in the same building as her seemed to untether him. Thanks to an illegal raid of the school secretary's filing cabinets (which she unwisely left unlocked when she went to the staff room for her lunch), Nathan had acquired Faye's class schedule. He knew exactly where she was every minute of every day. At the end of each class I would see him checking his watch, calculating whether he had time to scamper halfway across the school to catch a glimpse of her as she walked from one classroom to the next. He always cut it perilously close, and collected a handful of tardy slips each week, but he didn't care. He became a poor lunchtime companion, distractedly scanning the lines in the cafeteria for Faye rather than listening to whatever it was I had to say. After school he would sit high up on the football bleachers with a dog-eared copy of an Albert Camus novel that he pretended to read while the cheerleading squad practiced. Faye danced and shook her pom-poms on the field below him, unaware of his surveillance. For all that his entire existence was now arranged around Faye's schedule, Nathan showed no desire to talk to her, and for that, at least, I was grateful.

I became nostalgic for the summer just gone, missing those long evenings that Nathan and I had spent at the mill. Things had seemed so much simpler back then. We had been inseparable, kings of the world, unconquerable heroes of our private domain. Now the rest of the world was crowding in, deftly picking apart everything that had bound us together.

My brother's illness was a reality that no amount of hopeful fantasy could avoid for very long, anyway. Moira tended to him every morning, and my mother kept the house as warm as an oven, but it was a battle that they would never win. In October Liam was admitted to the hospital again. We spent three days in the ICU, sitting around his bed, gazing down at this boy we loved. None of us had any words, so it was left to Liam to supply his own entertainment, and he always roped me in. Every so often he propped himself up on the pillows and raised a frail finger toward me. Leaving his respirator in place, he would start rasping and wheezing alarmingly, and then intone, "I've been waiting for you, Obi-Wan. We meet again, at last." *Star Wars* had been released that May. Over the course of the summer Liam had seen it eleven times. "The circle is now complete. When I left you, I was but the learner; now *I* am the master."

I knew my line. "Only a master of evil, Darth," I replied.

At this my brother settled back, satisfied. "The force is strong with this one," he declared.

My parents looked on, utterly baffled.

After that hospital stay, Liam's condition continued to deteriorate. Moira's visits took longer and longer. My mother lurked outside the bedroom door, glancing constantly at her watch. Every minute that she was kept outside was a minute with Liam that she would never have. Things were strictly finite now.

The Saturday morning before Thanksgiving, Moira came into the kitchen after she had performed her daily ministrations. My mother and I were sitting at the table.

"All done," she said. "He's in fine form today. Looking forward to the holiday."

My mother said nothing. Usually by then the house would have been a riot of Thanksgiving cheer, but the boxes of turkey decorations had not been taken down from the attic this year.

"I know you'll have a wonderful time," continued Moira. "Lots of memories to cherish."

"I don't want *memories*," said my mother.

"No, of course you don't. I understand."

"How can you possibly understand?"

"Mary," said Moira softly. "Do you mind if I tell you a little story?" She sat down at the table. "I left my family in Dublin during the war, when I was twenty-two years old. I went to train as a medical orderly in a military hospital about forty miles outside London. That was where I met Ted, my husband. He was an American infantryman. He'd been shot in the leg during the Normandy landings. He was lucky to survive. A lot of his friends didn't make it. He was so charming. All that American sass! And I never could resist a man in uniform." Moira smiled. "We got married while he was still on crutches. His war was over—he was given an honorable discharge. We came to America, newlyweds. More than thirty years later, and here we both still are. Ted went back to college on the GI Bill. He's a manager at a factory in South Portland. We've had a wonderful life together, but we were never blessed with children."

My mother looked up at her then.

"Ted's injury had made him sterile, you see. There was nothing to be done about it. It was just one of those things." Moira was silent for a moment. "There are still days when the sadness of it makes me want to curl up into a ball." She tucked a loose strand of gray hair behind her ear and smiled at my mother. "He's a good boy, your Liam. Brave as anything, that one. My point is, I would have given anything to have someone like that to love. Not for a lifetime. Just for five minutes."

"Not for a lifetime," echoed my mother.

"We only get the life we're given, Mary. Ted could have bled to death on that beach in Normandy and I would have had a different life—one far away from here, I don't doubt. Maybe one filled with children and grandchildren for me to adore. But that wasn't how it worked out." She was quiet for a moment. "So, if you can, be thankful for all the love in your heart."

"Even after Liam's gone?" whispered my mother.

"*Especially* after he's gone. You'll go on loving Liam just as much as you always have, and that will be a gift, believe me. That love will see you through an awful lot. It will give you such strength."

My mother had started to cry. "Even as it kills me?"

"But it won't kill you, not really," said Moira. "There'll be times when you might want to run out into the traffic and end it all. But love and pain are two sides of the same coin. You can't have one without the other. Sometimes that's how we know we're alive."

We sat in silence for some time then.

"I'm not ready," said my mother eventually.

"Of course you're not, dear. Nobody ever is."

"How am I supposed to let him go? How am I supposed to say good-bye?"

The nurse reached out across the table and took my mother's

hand in hers. I waited for her to respond—I had been wondering the same thing for years. But Moira knew there was no answer to that question. She just squeezed my mother's hand. "Five minutes," she said softly. "Five minutes of love. That was all I ever wanted."

I thought a lot about what Moira had said, but she never sat down at our kitchen table again. When we saw her the following week at St. Mary's she smiled at us and then looked away. Still, now there was a softness in my mother's eyes when she saw her. One day I heard her whisper something under her breath as she waved good-bye to Moira.

"That poor woman," she said.

ONE DAY IN EARLY DECEMBER, the school principal put his head around the classroom door and called my name during our weekly history quiz. I looked up in relief, and then I saw his face.

I packed away my books and scuttled past my classmates. In the principal's office I stared numbly at the backpack between my feet. I heard my father's hurried footsteps before I saw him.

In the ICU Liam was lying motionless in bed, half-hidden behind a jungle of machines. Two nurses were moving efficiently around him while my mother stood as close as she could. I recognized the nurses from our previous visits. One of them winked at me as she left the room.

As the door closed my mother turned to us. "The doctors say it's pneumonia again."

I heard the air escape from my father's mouth. It was the sound of hope dying.

"They want to do a tracheotomy," she said. "It will help him breathe." She looked at her sleeping son. His wasted body barely took up any of the bed. The respirator covered his nose and mouth. He seemed peaceful enough.

My father gazed down at him. "If that's what they say we should do, shouldn't we do it?"

"A hole in his throat," said my mother. "Once the tube goes in, it never comes out."

"But if it will make him more comfortable—"

My parents looked at each other in silence for a few moments.

"Mary, please," said my father.

I saw the agony on my mother's face. Her ruined son, punctured still further. "I don't know," she whispered.

"No hole," came a voice from the bed. As one we turned toward Liam.

"We thought you were asleep," said my father.

My brother reached up and pulled the mask away from his mouth. "I don't want them to put a hole in my neck," he said, quite loudly.

"But it'll be much easier for you to breathe," said my father.

"I don't want it," said Liam again. "No hole, okay? No hole."

"All right." My mother put her hand over his. "We'll tell the doctor."

Liam slumped back on the bed. My parents just stared at each other.

There was only room for one plastic chair on either side of the bed. There was a more comfortable armchair by the window. My mother never left Liam's side, but every so often my father and I swapped positions. We sometimes talked, but mostly we just watched my brother sleep. My mother gazed unblinkingly down at him, thirstily drinking him in. Sometimes my father had to look away. He spent a long time staring out of the window.

For the rest of the day my parents and I performed our sad minuet around the hospital bed. From time to time Liam would wake up, and then we all moved toward the bed, hungry for a piece of him. He lay propped up against the pillows and spoke haltingly, his words half-swallowed by the mask on his face.

Meanwhile the rest of the world continued without us. People wandered up and down the hospital's corridors at all hours of the day and night, befuddled by the never-changing, neon-bright gleam, like guests at a drab casino. It was a place where time had no purpose or significance. Sickness held to no schedule. The slow drag of hours and days was of no consequence to the profoundly ill. Either they would get better, or they would not. It was just a matter of waiting it out, seeing which way the thing would go. But no matter how slowly the minutes drained away, it was never slow enough for us.

Finally my father and I went home. It was almost midnight. My mother promised to telephone if there were any developments. We stopped for hamburgers and ate them in the car. I did not taste one mouthful. I climbed into bed, sure that I would never sleep. And then the next thing I knew my father was nudging me awake, promising eggs and bacon before we returned to the hospital. I crept downstairs into the new morning, ashamed of my sound and dreamless sleep.

When we pushed open the door to Liam's room, the first thing I saw was my mother, sitting up in her chair and leaning toward the bed. There were tears streaming down her face, and she was gasping for breath. I immediately assumed the worst, until I took another step into the room and saw that Liam was awake, and talking.

"And so the daddy air mattress says to the baby air mattress, 'Son, you've let me down, and you've let your mother down.'" My brother paused. "'But most of all, you've let *yourself* down.'"

My mother threw herself back against the chair, laughing so hard that she couldn't speak. Liam looked at my father and me and grinned. He had always been a wonderful joke teller.

It was another long day. Doctors came and went, but mostly we were left alone. Every so often I stepped out of the room and walked to the soda machine, grubby quarters warm between my fingers. Someone had taped scrawny lengths of silver tinsel along the corridors, and a miniature plastic Christmas tree stood on the counter of the nurses' station. I sat on a chair and sipped my drink. The cold bubbles bit deliciously at the back of my throat.

I knew the quiet rhythms of the ward by then. Doctors strode purposefully back and forth. Patients limped by in their bathrobes. And then there were those neither caring nor cared for—the families of the sick, hovering anxiously, locked in an eternity of waiting. I learned to calibrate the broken hope on the faces I saw. I watched as people came and went, happy to be just a spectator in other people's dramas.

As the day drew on, Liam began to fight for every breath. His oxygen saturation was low and had not moved upward since the previous day. He was stable but rarely conscious. As evening approached my father went downstairs to buy us some sandwiches from the cafeteria. While he was gone, my mother held Liam's hand tightly. Her eyes were shut, and she did not open them until my father stepped back inside the room.

Finally she spoke. "We should call Father Astor, Sam."

I saw the words slam into my father like bullets. "It's not time," he said. "It's too early."

"You don't know that." Her voice broke then. "We're close," she said. The words seemed to come from unimaginable depths within her.

My father glanced at me. I kept my eyes fixed on Liam's sleeping face, wanting no part of this. "Can't we wait a little longer?" he pleaded.

"But what if we leave it too late? I would never forgive myself."

"Mary, listen. We're through the worst of this, I can feel it." My father paused. I could see how badly he needed to believe it. "Liam's coming home," he said.

My mother could not speak for a while. "You're wrong," she finally whispered. "He's ready, Sam."

"No."

"He's ready, and so am I."

My father stared at her. "Mary." His voice was remote, an echo.

"I'm ready for him to go, Sam. I don't want to watch him suffer anymore." She gently brushed her fingers across my sleeping brother's hair. "He's been through enough."

"We're not giving up now."

"No, we're not giving up. We *never* gave up. We're letting go."

My father looked at her helplessly. "What's the difference?"

"There's all the difference in the world," said my mother. "Why do you think he refused the tracheotomy, Sam? He doesn't want to do this anymore. He's done."

My father turned to look at Liam.

"Call Father Astor," he said.

ONCE THE PRIEST HAD COME and gone, we agreed that nobody would be going home that night. My parents slumped in their chairs, keeping their vigil by Liam's bedside. We borrowed some blankets and fashioned them into a makeshift bed on the floor for me. I lay there, blinking in the half darkness. On the other side of the door, the hospital went about the noisy, messy business of saving people's lives. Inside the room, the four of us were completely silent. The only sounds were the dull whir of the respirator as it pumped air in and out of my brother's body and the raw wheeze of his laboring lungs. I did my best to keep my eyes open. There would be time for sleep later. But try as I might, I could feel oblivion wrap itself around me. As I was drifting into unconsciousness, my mother began to whisper under her breath—so softly that I could not make out her words, but I recognized their rhythm and cadences.

She was praying.

I remembered the conversation that I'd overheard through my parents' bedroom door last Christmas and thought of what my father had said then, in the middle of the night, when he thought nobody else was listening.

The answer to most prayers is no.

SIXTEEN

Liam died that night.

The end, when it came, was quick and violent. The room's silence was shattered by a hellacious squeal from one of the machines that surrounded the bed. It was joined by other warning buzzes and beeps, a deranged chorus of alarm, all of it too late. I had barely lifted my head off the floor when a team of nurses and doctors barreled through the door, and suddenly the room was a riot of light and movement. Liam disappeared behind a wall of white coats.

I struggled to my feet and stood next to my parents, a few steps from the scrum around the bed. My mother was covering her mouth with her hand. One of the doctors stepped away from the melee and approached us. "Liam's unresponsive," he said. "He's failing fast. A trach would really help him right now."

My mother leaned into my father but said nothing.

The doctor had no time to waste. "Please," he said. "Can we intubate?"

My mother closed her eyes and shook her head.

"Mary," said my father.

"He never asked for much," she said. "Let's at least give him this."

"But it's too—"

She turned on him. "Too what? Too soon? I thought that was the one thing we were never allowed to say! That Liam died too *soon!*"

"I was wrong." My father had begun to cry. "I can't let him go. Not yet. Please. Not yet."

My mother laid her fingers on his chest.

"There'll be no going back," my father whispered.

"Oh, Sam. I don't *want* to go back."

My father looked at the doctor. "No trach," he said.

The doctor's eyes darted between my parents. "You understand there's really no more—"

"We understand." The words barely escaped my father's lips.

The doctor nodded. "All right." He returned to Liam's bedside and spoke quietly to the other doctors and nurses. At once there was a collective dissipation of tension. People who had been hunched over the bed stood up straight and took a step or two back. I glanced up at the green neon digits. They were in freefall.

We moved forward as one. Acting as if the doctors and nurses were invisible, my mother climbed onto the bed and covered her dying son with her body. "Oh, Liam," she whispered. "You were the best boy there ever was." She kissed his cheek, breathing him in, baptizing him with her tears. But no matter how tightly she squeezed, how fiercely she clung, she could not hold on to him.

SOME TIME AFTER THAT, we stumbled out into the rest of our lives.

It was the middle of the night and freezing cold. My father somehow managed to drive us home. Nobody spoke a word. Liam and I had bickered and squabbled and laughed and cried for thousands of miles in the back of that station wagon. I stared at the empty space next to me.

When we arrived home, my mother walked into the kitchen and

looked around blankly, as if she didn't recognize the place. I climbed into my bed and switched off the light. I stared into the darkness.

Some hours later I went downstairs to the kitchen and drank a glass of milk. Then I tiptoed to Liam's bedroom. By force of habit I stopped outside for a moment and listened before I pushed open the door.

I half-expected to find my mother asleep on the bed, but the room was empty. Nothing had changed. The same posters were still on the walls. Liam's records were neatly arranged. On the window shelf was a half-drunk bottle of Gatorade and a paperback of *The Great Gatsby*. On the cover of the book there was a misty-looking photograph of Robert Redford and Mia Farrow. They seemed sad, remote. I flicked through the book until I found Liam's bookmark. He had only made it halfway through. I wondered whether he had given up on it or if he'd been planning to finish it when he returned home from the hospital.

There were unfinished stories everywhere.

I was filled with a terrible, wordless sadness then, and sat down on the edge of my brother's bed and began to cry. Liam was gone, and every day of the rest of my life, every single day, he would remain gone. I could miss him and love him, I could talk to him, shout at him, fight with him, but he was never coming back. I thought of all the questions I still wanted to ask him, all the jokes he still had to tell, all the songs we still had to argue about—but it was too late, too late now for everything.

Finally, my tears exhausted themselves. I picked up *Gatsby* again. The Haverford Public Library crest had been stamped on the title page. I thought of my mother making one final trip to return the book. I slipped it into the pocket of my bathrobe. I could spare her that pain at least. I lay down on Liam's bed and stared at the ceiling.

Sleep came for me in the end. When I woke up, the sun was streaming in through my brother's bedroom window. My parents were both in the kitchen. When I appeared in the doorway, my mother stepped toward me and wrapped me in her arms. I felt her squeeze my back and shoulders, as if she were checking I was really there. I cautiously put my arms around her.

"How are you, Robert?" she said.

It had been a long time since my mother had asked me that. Now it was the only question she had left.

My father put his coffee cup in the sink. "I have to go," he said.

I could not imagine anywhere he needed to be on this morning, except here, with us. "Where are you going?"

"The hospital," he said. He saw my baffled face. "There are forms to fill out, Robert. Things to take care of."

"Right now?"

He nodded. "Liam can't stay in the hospital," he said.

My brother's absence already felt so absolute that I hadn't considered that there were practical things to attend to, arrangements to be made. "I'll be back soon," said my father. He picked up the car keys off the kitchen table.

Once the front door had closed behind him, my mother looked at me. "I haven't slept yet," she said. "I'm going to bed for a while." She reached out and touched my shoulder. "Will you be all right on your own?"

"I'll be fine," I said.

"You could call Nathan."

I shook my head. Solitude was what I needed right then. It was the only way I could begin to fathom how lonely my brotherless life was going to be. I needed to confront my loss, not run away from it. I wanted to wade in with my eyes open and all my senses alert. I wanted to register everything, from giant waves of sorrow to the tiniest ripples of remorse. I didn't want to miss any of it.

As it turned out, I wasn't alone for long. My father must have called someone at St. Mary's with the news, because the morning was punctuated by the ringing of the doorbell, announcing a procession of church members bearing food and sympathy. I stood at the front door and numbly took delivery of a small mountain of Tupperware. My mother remained in the bedroom, the door firmly shut.

Every dinner came with written instructions for reheating and promises to pray for us. Some notes were decorated with hand-drawn hearts. The less appetizing meals—there were one or two pot roasts and a vegetarian ragout—I put straight into the freezer. Everything else I stuck in the fridge, arranging the ones that sounded tastiest at the front. By the time my father returned from the hospital, the shelves were full. I opened the door to show him. I had crammed boxes into every available inch of space. The fridge's neon glow illuminated every line on my father's tired face, as if he had stepped into the spotlight on a tiny stage. He stood in front of all that food, casting his eyes up and down the wall of plastic, and tears began to fall down his cheeks. I didn't know if he was overwhelmed by the kindness of others or dismayed at the futility of the gesture. No amount of homemade lasagna would ever bring Liam back.

Finally my father closed the refrigerator door and went upstairs. Minutes later he reappeared and sat at the kitchen table with a yellow folder I had never seen before. Inside the folder was a neatly typed list. I watched as he made one call after another. Funeral home, florist, newspaper. Hymns had already been chosen, the brief obituary composed, the tombstone selected. Just the date had needed to be filled in.

My parents had been ready for this for far, far too long.

Each time he picked up the receiver and dialed the next number, my father seemed to wilt a little more. After the practical arrangements had been made, he took a new piece of paper out of the folder. He stared at it for a moment and then shook his head. "I need a drink," he said. He went to the cupboard where the liquor was kept and poured himself a slug of bourbon. He sat back down and looked at the glass in front of him. Then he looked up at me. "Sometimes," he sighed, "bad news doesn't travel fast enough."

On the second piece of paper was a list of family and friends, and my father began to work his way down it. These conversations all had the same sad rhythm of regret. He did not bother with pleasantries. He reported the news, a sober recital of date, time, and place, and then waited in silence as the person on the other end of the line tried to articulate their sorrow, as if my father needed to be told how sad this all was. His eyes remained shut as he listened to these desperate condolences. There would be a few questions about how we were bearing up. Just fine, considering, he would reply, not looking at me, and then gave details of the funeral. After each call he took a sip of whiskey and waited for a few moments. Then he dialed the next number.

I watched him deliver the news over and over again. There were friends, acquaintances from church, members of the bridge club. So many people to tell, so many hearts to break. I could see my father willing himself on after each call. Sometimes nobody would pick up, and he let the unanswered phone ring on for longer than necessary, grateful for the temporary respite. That mechanical tone was easier to bear than the next chorus of well-meaning sympathy.

By the time he had finished, it was dark outside.

WHAT I REMEMBER MOST about the days after Liam's death is the silence that settled on our house. There was no more whirring of the motorized wheelchair as Liam between rooms, no more screeching guitar riffs so loud that the door frames rattled. My parents and I hardly spoke. Perhaps there simply wasn't anything to say. My brother's absence swamped us completely. When he left us, he stole all the words.

The funeral took place on a bitterly cold December morning. I sat between my parents in the front pew of St. Mary's. I don't remember much about the service itself. The incense made me sneeze, like it always did, although I found comfort in its familiarity even as it tickled the back of my nose.

Liam's coffin was carried out of the church on the shoulders of my father and five of his friends. It looked as if the whole town had shown up to pay its respects. As my mother and I followed the pallbearers down the aisle, I spotted both Lewis Jenks and Moira in the congregation.

The cemetery was blanketed in week-old snow. We stood in silence as the coffin was lowered into the ground and Father Astor said the final prayers for my dead brother. Before I knew it people were turning away, shivering and rubbing their hands together to stay warm. I watched the retreating tide of gray and black and envied these people the carefree existences they were returning to. They could drive away from all this, but we would be looking down on Liam's grave for the rest of our lives.

Just then I heard a familiar voice call my name. I turned and saw Lewis standing behind me. He was wearing a tattered overcoat, buttoned up high against the cold, and a dark brown fedora. It was the first time I'd ever seen him wearing anything other than his dungarees and work boots.

"Robert," he said. We shook hands. "I'm so sorry."

I wanted to hug him then. I wanted to tell him how much I missed my brother. I wanted to tell him that I couldn't wait for the summer season to start, that I was looking forward to working with him again. But I said none of that. Instead I just said, "Thanks, Lewis."

"Look." Lewis glanced across to where my parents were standing, staring down at the ground where Liam's coffin now lay. "There are times when there's so much sadness in a place, you can't hardly breathe. Am I right?"

I nodded.

"Yeah, I reckoned so. Well, listen. If you ever need to get away, come and see me." He reached into his pocket and handed me a small piece of paper. To my surprise, Lewis's handwriting was a neat, elegant cursive. I did not recognize the address. "It's fine if you never come by," he said. "But the offer's there." Before I could respond, Lewis patted me on the shoulder and strolled away.

I hadn't seen Nathan before the service started, and now I scanned the thinning crowd, looking for him. Just then I saw a plume of smoke jet skyward from behind a group of mourners. I headed toward it. Sure enough, there was Nathan's mother, sucking on a cigarette. Nathan stood next to her, wearing the same suit he had worn to his own father's funeral. He raised a hand in silent greeting.

"Hello, Robert," said Mrs. Tilly, expelling a lungful of smoke as she spoke. "I'm so very sorry about your brother."

"Thanks, Mrs. Tilly," I said. I turned to Nathan. "Do you remember when we went back to your house and flew that kite on the beach? After your father's funeral?"

Nathan nodded.

"I want to do something like that for Liam."

"You want to fly a kite?"

"No. But I want to find my own way to say good-bye. I don't know if he would have enjoyed that funeral much. Come back home with me?"

"Mom?" said Nathan.

Mrs. Tilly had dropped her cigarette in the snow and was trying to extinguish it with the heel of her shoe. She looked up at us, distracted. "What?"

"Can I go back to Robert's house?"

She smiled at us vaguely. "Of course. You boys go and have some fun."

Nathan and I exchanged glances. "Fun," said Nathan drily. "All right, then."

The church was a five-minute walk from our house. I went back to my parents and told them that Nathan and I were leaving. I left them still standing by Liam's grave.

Back at home we went into Liam's bedroom. Nathan sat down on the bed and looked at me. "Well?" he said.

"Maybe we should play his favorite records as a final send-off."

"Good idea," said Nathan.

"I know the perfect song to start with." I squatted down in front of Liam's albums and scanned the spines until I saw what I was looking for. I pulled out the record and put it on the turntable.

The song was "(I Live for) Cars and Girls" by the Dictators. Liam had loved the breezy, high-pitched harmonies, unashamed Beach Boys rip-offs, and frenetic, chugging guitar line that powered the song along. He used to rock back and forth in his wheelchair, singing along with the chorus:

There's nothing else in this crazy world
Except for cars and good, good, good girls

We listened to the song twice, and then Nathan chose the next record, something by Iggy and the Stooges. He lay on the bed and I stretched out on the carpet as we listened. The music was loud and fast and relentless. I let the waves of noise wash over me. When the song finished, I remained where I was, grateful for the silence.

"I wonder where Liam is now," I said.

"That depends," said Nathan.

"On what?"

"On what you believe."

"Why should it matter what *I* believe?" I said. "I'm not the one who's dead."

"Of course it matters!" exclaimed Nathan. "How can you believe Liam is in heaven if you don't think heaven exists?"

"But I *do* believe in heaven," I said quickly.

"And what about Liam?" asked Nathan.

I realized that I didn't know what Liam believed. He had always come to church with the rest of us, but even when his mortality was on all of our minds, he and I had never talked about what might happen after he died. If he'd had any doubts, he probably would have kept them to himself—my mother was always alert for the faintest whiff of heresy within the family. "I guess he did," I said after a moment, almost obliterated by remorse that guesswork was all I had left.

"Hey, look," said Nathan. He was holding an envelope in one hand, the Ramones' debut record in the other. "This was tucked inside the sleeve. It's got your name on it."

I grabbed the envelope and tore it open. My brother's messy handwriting was unmistakable.

Robbie:

If you've found this letter, that means that you've been looking through my records. Good for you. Maybe you've even played a few.

You always liked the hippies with their acoustic guitars more, but I still think there's hope for you. I want you to have my records when I'm gone.

And, Robbie, wherever I am now, it's a long way away, so do me a favor and play them LOUD.

Liam

I silently handed the letter to Nathan. While he was reading I slipped the Ramones record out of its sleeve. I was going to play "Now I Wanna Sniff Some Glue," ninety seconds of high-tempo anarchy with lyrics that always made Liam laugh. But instead I dropped the needle at the first track of side one, "Blitzkrieg Bop." I knew that Liam's decision to leave his letter where he did was significant. He adored all of his bands, but he loved the Ramones most of all. He had died wearing a T-shirt with their name on it. In honor of that, I decided to play the whole album, just in case he really was listening somewhere. As the opening riff blasted into the room, I remembered his request. I turned the music up as loud as it would go.

We were pummeled by the waves of sound that shrieked into the room. The songs were all short and frenetic, squalling riots of energy. It seemed like a perfect epitaph, a noisy counterpoint to the quiet grief of the funeral service. I knew Liam would have approved.

Buffeted by an onslaught of pile-driving guitar riffs, I lay on the floor and reread my brother's letter, over and over again. Liam had listened to these records to escape from his illness. Now they offered a means of retreat for me as well—just as he had known they would. That blistering eruption of sound cauterized my hurt, numbed me into oblivion, and, just for a while, made everything feel not quite so bad.

The music was so loud that we never heard the front door.

I only knew my parents were home when the bedroom door was flung open. Before I could scramble to my feet, my father had stormed across the room and yanked the needle off the record with a sickening scratch that was even more abrasive than Johnny Ramone's distorted guitar. In the silence that followed I could hear my ears ringing.

"Liam's body is barely in the ground and you're already playing his records!" shouted my father. He had removed his jacket and tie, but his shirt was still buttoned up to the neck, which made him look like a forgetful schoolboy who had mislaid part of his uniform. He stood in front of me, breathing heavily.

"We just wanted to say good-bye in our own way," I said.

My father's gaze fell on Nathan, who was sitting very still on the bed, and then turned back to me. "A church service not good enough for you?"

"Liam wouldn't have enjoyed all those hymns, Dad. This was more his thing."

My father looked at me for a moment. "I never, *ever* want to hear another of his records again," he said.

"Actually," I said, "they're *my* records." I gave him Liam's letter.

"Where did you find this?" he asked.

"Liam tucked it inside a record sleeve for me to find," I said, more defiantly than I felt. "The Ramones. They were his favorite."

But my father wasn't listening. He was staring at the letter, clutching the paper so tightly that it shook between his fingers. I glanced across at Nathan, who gave me the tiniest nod of encouragement. "So you see," I said, "Liam's records belong to me now."

My father handed the letter back to me. "You're welcome to the damn things," he said. "But you won't play them in my house."

"Dad—"

"Listen to me, Robert. If I hear so much as a single one of these songs again then I swear I'll break every one of those records over my knee, one by one."

He turned and walked out of the bedroom.

1978

SEVENTEEN

The weeks following Liam's death felt like waking from a long sleep. A black knot of loss remained inside me. Thoughts of my brother slammed into me the moment I awoke, fracturing the morning before my still-groggy brain could marshal its defenses. I couldn't remember a time when I didn't know that Liam was going to die, but still his absence shocked me, day after day. Pain lurked around every corner, ready to ambush me when I was least expecting it.

We barely noticed Christmas.

I watched my parents for clues about how they were feeling, but they were giving nothing away. They packed up their feelings, out of sight and beyond harm's reach. We politely went about things as if there were nothing amiss, but we were silent reservoirs of sorrow, each of us filling up with unspoken sadness. I climbed into my bed each night exhausted by the day's charades and masquerades but knowing that I would be awake for hours yet. My grief would not relinquish me; it gripped me tight, suffocating me. Images and memories of Liam crashed through my consciousness, an unrelenting kaleidoscope of everything that was lost. As I stared wide-eyed into the darkness, I heard my father sobbing through the walls and my mother murmuring softly as she tried to comfort him. I listened to their sorrow and wished that they would share it with me. But when I went down to breakfast the following morning their masks were back in place. All I wanted to do was talk about Liam. It was the one thing that seemed utterly impossible.

And so we each continued to negotiate separate courses through our heartbreak, tacking away from one another when our paths ran too close. My father spent more and more time at the park, and my mother disappeared in a storm of good deeds. She put herself on the church cleaning roster so often that the odor of industrial disinfectant began to cling to her. She volunteered to ferry elderly members of the St. Mary's congregation to and from Mass every morning. On weekends she escaped into a maelstrom of culinary industry, producing delicious-smelling items for a never-ending fiesta of church bake sales and raffles. She would swat away my hungry fingers whenever I tried to help myself to a slice of cake or a freshly baked cookie. *Not for you*, she would admonish me.

Nothing was ever for me.

JANUARY BROUGHT a brutal arctic front from the north. I couldn't remember its ever being so cold. The frozen air settled deep in my chest, heavy and malignant, and seemed to slow the world down to a lethargic crawl.

One bitter Saturday afternoon, Mrs. Tilly drove Nathan over to our house. My father was working at the park and my mother was organizing a winter coat drive at St. Mary's. Having the house to myself meant that, for once, I could play Liam's records as loud as I liked without fear of angry paternal sanction. Nathan and I spent several hours listening to music at a volume so loud that it made my head throb.

Nathan sat by the window and gazed out at the yard while the records played. It was only his second winter in Maine, and he still couldn't get over the snow. "I could look at this all day," he said, hugging his knees.

I walked across the room and looked out of the window. The snow hid everything. It made the world perfect and unblemished, and I knew that wasn't right. Suddenly I needed to be out in it, kicking up a storm, obliterating all those smooth lines. "Let's go outside," I said.

"But it's freezing," said Nathan.

"So we'll run around," I said. "Or we could build a snowman and dress him up." I opened the door to Liam's closet, looking for suitable snowman clothes.

"Hey, look at that," said Nathan. My brother's old wheelchair nestled at the back of the closet. Liam hadn't used it in years—not since the hospital had delivered the gleaming motorized model that trundled about the house with a nudge of its rubber joystick. The sides of the wheelchair were pushed together so that the gray leather seat creased upward. Nathan hauled it into the middle of the room and opened it so that the metal frame locked into place with two heavy clicks. "Interesting," he said.

"Interesting how?" I asked.

He looked at me thoughtfully. "Is your pond frozen?"

"Solid. Has been for weeks."

"Then I can think of something more fun than building snowmen."

We put on snowsuits, boots, hats, gloves, and scarves, and hauled the wheelchair out of the back door. Nobody had stepped into the yard for weeks, and the snow came up over our knees. We carried the wheelchair down to the pond on our shoulders, like the ceremonial throne of an invisible African prince. I glanced behind me and was pleased to see the messy trenches we had made, gratified by the violence we had inflicted on all that flawless white.

The frozen surface of the pond was flinty in the pale afternoon light. Nathan stepped out onto the ice and jumped up and down several times. Once he was satisfied that it was safe, he began to make his way across the pond, testing for weaknesses. The ice was the color of cold bone, the freeze a deep one. Nathan turned and beckoned to me. I pushed the wheelchair in front of me.

"Sit down," said Nathan when I joined him in the middle. I lowered myself into the seat. He pushed the wheelchair to the far side of the pond and then turned it around.

"Where are the brakes on this thing?" I asked.

"You won't need brakes," said Nathan as he started to push. Once we had gained some momentum he gave me a final shove and sent me careening over the ice. The sensation of unbound velocity was thrilling. It felt as if I were floating, free of friction and gravity. When the wheelchair hit the bank of snow on the far edge of the pond, I was catapulted out of the seat and landed facedown in the snow. As I lay there I felt a sudden rush of happiness.

Nathan hurried across the pond and helped me to my feet. We hauled the wheelchair upright and lifted it back onto the ice.

"My turn," he said.

As I launched him back across the pond, Nathan flung his arms in the air and let out a shriek of glee. By the time the wheelchair hit the opposite snowbank, he was laughing wildly.

And so, with Liam's old wheelchair as our getaway vehicle, we staged another escape. For the next hour we sent each other back and forth across the pond, cackling with delight as we flew across the ice. We were two dark points of constant motion in that vast, silent stillness of white. We barely noticed the cold. We knelt, we squatted, we stood—we rode that wheelchair every way we could. One time Nathan hopped onto the back of it, and we sailed across the ice together. Our shouts rose up into the winter air.

Finally we returned to the house, happy and exhausted, the wheelchair borne triumphantly aloft on our shoulders once again.

My mother was waiting for us in the kitchen.

She was standing by the window, still wearing her coat. Nathan and I froze at the back door.

"I made you some cocoa," she said. She pointed to two steaming mugs on the kitchen table. "You must be freezing. You've been out there for a long time. Take off your suits and warm up."

We did as we were told. We sat at the kitchen table in silence while my mother bustled around and told us about the coat drive at church. Nathan and I looked at each other over the rims of our mugs while she talked. Apologies and explanations formed on my lips but faded away as quickly as they came. The wheelchair stood by the back door, dripping tiny pools of melted snow onto the linoleum. My mother did not look at it once.

Later that afternoon, after we had driven Nathan back to Sebbanquik Point, I wiped off the wheelchair with a rag. I folded it up and put it back in Liam's closet. My mother didn't comment on its disappearance. I waited for her stinging rebuke, but it never came. There were no angry words of admonition, not one.

THE FOLLOWING MONDAY, when I got home from school, I went into Liam's bedroom, as I always did. I liked to spend a little time in there each day. I found comfort in being surrounded by his stuff. Those familiar things would never bring my brother back, but they made him feel less far away.

That day, though, the sheets had been removed from his bed, the trash had been emptied, and his mess had been picked up off the carpet. I walked over to the closet and opened the door.

The wheelchair was gone.

EIGHTEEN

After the incident with the wheelchair, my mother stopped volunteering at church. She became a constant, furtive presence in the house; I could feel her lurking, silently monitoring me. She spent hours gazing out the window, lost in thought. A stillness settled on her. She had been waiting for Liam to die for so long, and a terrible, fretful waiting it had been. His death had wrung out every last piece of her, and now there was nothing for her to do but sit quietly until her strength returned. Within that new calm I thought I could also detect a new resilience. She knew that she had survived the worst of it.

My father, in contrast, could not stop moving. He ricocheted between our home and the park, filling his days with a never-ending circus of chores and distractions. He was always stepping out the door, escaping to somewhere else. There was no stopping him, but that was the point. That riot of perpetual forward motion gave him no time to think. It was only late at night, when he had no choice but to stop moving, that the tears came.

Between my mother's quiet surveillance and my father's frenetic activity, home began to suffocate me. Now that I was no longer allowed to stay in the house alone, I could never play Liam's records.

They remained in his bedroom, silent, gathering dust. I thought about my brother's letter to me, his plea to keep playing the music loud, and felt another twinge of betrayal, one more reason to feel bad about everything. Then one morning I remembered the invitation that Lewis had made at the funeral. The piece of paper that he had given me was still in my suit pocket. I dialed the phone number he'd written down and listened to the ringtone in my ear. Just as I was about to hang up, there was a rattle and I heard Lewis speak gruffly.

"Who is this?"

"Lewis? This is Robert Carter."

"Robert! How are you?"

"Uh, okay, I guess," I said. "Although I had a question."

"Shoot."

"Do you have a record player?"

"Sure I do," said Lewis. "I even have some records to play on it. Do you want to stop by sometime for a listen? You missing all that bebop from last summer?"

"Actually," I said, "I was wondering if I could bring some records of my own."

There was a pause. "What kind of records?" asked Lewis.

"They used to belong to my brother," I said, carefully avoiding the question. "And now they're mine. Only I'm not allowed to play them in the house anymore. So I was wondering if I could listen to them at your place."

"You should come over," said Lewis.

THE NEXT AFTERNOON Nathan and I walked to Lewis's house after school. He lived in a small single-story house on the west side of town. We walked up the narrow path that led to his front door and rang the bell. When the door opened, Lewis stood there in a pair of corduroy trousers, a faded plaid shirt, and an immense cardigan with leather patches on the elbows.

Lewis clapped me fondly on the back. "It's good to see you, Robert," he said. "And you must be Nathan." Lewis shook Nathan's hand. Nathan's eyes grew big as he peered down at Lewis's toe. An old black Labrador wandered over. The fur around the dog's mouth was mostly white, and his pale brown eyes were fogged by the milky sheath of old age. He blinked up at me and wagged his tail.

"This is Dizzy," said Lewis. "As in Gillespie." He saw my blank face. "Trumpet player?" I shook my head. Lewis sighed. "You had a whole summer of jazz, Robert, and you got nothing to show for it. Between them Diz and Bird pretty much invented bebop," he told us. He paused. "I had a Bird, too, but he died. Diz here is getting along, too. He doesn't see too good."

Nathan finally spoke. "You had a dog called Bird?"

"Yes I did," said Lewis. "You ever heard of Mr. Charles Parker, Nathan?" he asked. "The greatest saxophonist that ever lived?"

"Nope," said Nathan cheerfully.

"No," muttered Lewis. "I didn't think so. Well, come on in." There was a large couch in the middle of the living room. It looked worn and faded, gently hillocked by years of use. Dizzy clambered up and curled himself against one of the armrests. He closed his eyes and let out a small sigh. "Did you bring your records?" asked Lewis.

I reached into my backpack and handed him the albums I'd brought. He fanned them out in his enormous hands as if they were playing cards. He held up the cover of *Back in the USA* by MC5.

"Are those people men or women?" he asked.

"Men," I said.

"Huh," said Lewis. He handed the album back to me and led me over to the record player. "All right, then," he said. "Let's have a listen."

I took the record out of its sleeve and placed it on the turntable. A few seconds later came the first notes of the opening track, a bright and raucous cover version of "Tutti-Frutti." It was much quieter than we were used to, but it seemed rude to turn the volume up. The three of us sat on the old couch and listened to the music. Lewis thoughtfully scratched the grizzled fur beneath Dizzy's chin. After a few minutes he asked, "How long does this go on for?"

"The whole album? Maybe half an hour," I said.

Lewis stood up. "I think I'll see you in about half an hour, then," he said.

"Where are you going?" I asked.

"I just remembered, the dog needs his walk." Lewis tapped the side of his head. "And my ears have started to bleed. Oh, and my brain is rotting, too. But you boys go ahead and enjoy yourselves."

With a backward wave Lewis left the room, his dog trotting behind him. We heard him in the hallway, pulling on his boots and coat. "Come on, Diz," he said, "let's go sing ourselves some real tunes."

The front door opened and then closed again. Nathan and I looked at each other.

"Now what?" I said.

Nathan walked over to the stereo and turned up the volume.

I'D NEVER LOVED LIAM'S music while he was alive, but now it offered me a way back to him. I was greedy for every unpolished note, each raw crash of the cymbals and messy guitar chord. As the music poured into Lewis's living room I thought of my brother rocking back and forth in his wheelchair. Those familiar three-chord frenzies filled up a hole inside me. Rather than being submerged by my usual sense of loss, I found myself grateful that I had such a happy image to remember him by.

When the record finished we sat in silence. A few moments later I heard the front door open, and then Dizzy padded back into the room and took up his old post on the couch. "Is it safe?" called Lewis from the hallway. I wondered guiltily if he had been standing outside, waiting for the music to stop.

"Don't worry," I said. "The coast is clear."

Lewis reappeared. "You didn't put on another record?" he asked.

"One was enough." I pointed at the albums I'd brought. "Can I leave those here?" I asked. "And is it all right if I bring more next time?"

"You have *more?*" Lewis looked appalled.

"We don't have to listen to them," I said, hurt.

"Tell you what," said Lewis. "For every album of yours that we play, I get to play you one of mine."

"Would that be Dizzy and Bird?" asked Nathan.

"Oh yes," said Lewis, beaming.

"He made me listen to that stuff all last summer," I warned Nathan.

"Come on, Robert," said Nathan. "I want to hear Charlie Parker play." He grinned. "I want to hear Bird take flight."

"We're going to have ourselves a *barrelful* of fun," said Lewis, rubbing his hands together.

The thought of having to suffer through yet more saxophone solos dimmed my enthusiasm for future trips to Lewis's house, but it was a price I was willing to pay.

"How's your father doing, Robert?" asked Lewis.

"He seems sad. But he keeps it to himself."

Lewis nodded. "I wouldn't expect anything else from a good

Mainer like him. He'll bottle it all up and soldier on. Don't know that it's healthy, but it's what we do."

"Maybe things will get better once the season starts," I said hopefully.

"Maybe so," said Lewis. "Are you looking forward to the summer?"

"As long as you won't make me listen to any more jazz," I said.

Lewis looked at me. "We won't be working together this year, Robert," he said.

"What? Why not?"

"It's time for you to learn new things. You need to know everything about the place, work each job. Your father's grooming you for greatness, you know."

"I don't want greatness," I said. "I want to work with you."

"Oh, I think I've taught you all I can."

We both knew this wasn't true. "What's he going to have me do?" I asked. I glanced at Nathan. "Not the kitchen," I whispered.

"No, not the kitchen," said Lewis. "The Ferris wheel."

"Really?"

Lewis nodded. "It's what we in the trade call a signature attraction."

"I suppose I'd better start practicing my English accent," I said.

"No more a pixie," sighed Lewis.

"What about me?" asked Nathan.

"You, Nathan," said Lewis, "are going to be the park mascot."

"The dragon?" Nathan was unable to hide his delight. He turned to me. "How did your dad know I wanted that job?"

"Because you told him about a million times," I said, grinning.

"I'm sure you'll be a fine dragon," said Lewis.

Nathan looked pleased. "I can go wherever I like in the dragon suit, right?"

Lewis nodded. "Where the crowds are, you follow."

"This is going to change everything," said Nathan.

"What do you mean?" I said.

"Faye spent all last summer with her back to me while I worked the grill. At school I only ever see her for a few seconds at a time. But in the dragon suit I'll be able to go and see her whenever I want." He grinned. "And you know what's best of all?"

"What?" I said grumpily. I already knew that I wouldn't hear about anything else until Memorial Day.

"What's best of *all*," he said, "is that she'll never know that I'm watching her. She won't see me at all. She'll just see the dragon."

Lewis snorted. "Being able to look at this girl all day won't help you much if she doesn't know it's you in there," he said.

"I don't *want* her to know it's me," said Nathan.

Lewis frowned. "But if you're keen on this girl, you need to—"

"You know, Nathan has a plan, and he's going to stick to it," I interrupted. I didn't want Lewis putting suicidal ideas into his head. I looked at Nathan. "Right?"

"Right," he said.

I sat back, satisfied. Nathan had no business talking to a girl like Faye. No good could ever come of it. The longer he stayed hidden inside the dragon costume, the better.

NINETEEN

For the rest of that spring, Nathan and I returned to Lewis's house once a week. Each time I brought another of Liam's records. Every visit followed the same routine. I would put on the record I'd brought; after the first track, Lewis would stand up and whistle at Dizzy, and the two of them would escape for a walk, leaving Nathan and me to turn up the volume as loud as we liked. When Lewis returned, he would bend down in front of his record collection and trace his fingers along the spines of the cardboard sleeves until he found what he was looking for. Each visit we listened to a different musician. Clifford Brown, Max Roach, Bud Powell, Miles Davis, Sonny Stitt—to my dismay, there were far more than just Dizzy Gillespie and Charlie Parker to contend with.

The music Lewis played made no sense to me, but Nathan was listening carefully. He read the liner notes on the backs of the record sleeves—long, abstruse essays full of strange hipster jive. I scoffed at these. What sort of music, I demanded, needs all those words to explain itself? At least the Ramones could say what they needed to say in three minutes, with no further elaboration necessary.

Even I had to admit that the jazz albums *looked* more elegant than Liam's records. They had abstract designs in muted colors, hip winks to those in the know. The photographs of the musicians were monochrome studies of cool. Men with saxophones slung low around their necks stared away from the camera, calm and remote. As the music played, Lewis showed us old programs he had saved from jazz clubs on Fifty-Second Street in Manhattan, from just after the war— Jimmy Ryan's, the Three Deuces, the Onyx. He had seen many of the legends in their heyday, he said, and he told us stories of those long-ago New York nights. Thelonious Monk at the Five Spot, quitting his post at the piano to dance in front of the audience while the band played on. Dexter Gordon, strung out on heroin, hustling up to the bar between sets and hitting up star-struck customers for drinks. Kenny Clarke, hungrily eyeing the passing waitresses from behind his drum kit. Nathan listened to these tales, rapt. Just as I had sat unnoticed on Liam's bed for evenings on end, now Lewis and Nathan forgot I was there.

It was sometime during that spring that Nathan began to smoke. We were walking out of school one afternoon when he produced a pack of Winstons from his pocket. I watched in astonishment as he struck a match.

"What are you doing?" I asked him.

"What does it look like I'm doing?"

"Where did you get those?"

Nathan blew smoke into the air. "My mom buys cigarettes by the crate. She won't notice if a few disappear." He took another puff.

"Oh, I get it," I said. "The jazz musicians."

Nathan looked at me. "What about them?"

"They all smoke. Those photos."

"You think I started smoking because of *those* guys?"

"Well, didn't you?"

"Robert," said Nathan, waving his cigarette at me. "This is *work*."

"What do you mean?"

"I'm going to be a dragon, right? And you know what they say. There's no smoke without fire."

I frowned. "So?"

"So I'm going to blow smoke out of the dragon's nostrils."

"Tell me you're joking," I said.

"It would be kind of a neat effect, don't you think? Realistic."

"Nathan, you're going to be walking around in a crummy dragon costume made of fur. Nobody's going to think you're *real*."

He pursed his lips and exhaled a long, thin plume of smoke. "That was a better one," he said. "More dragonlike."

Of course, it wasn't Nathan's way to go at things in any mode other than full tilt. He began to experiment with different exhalation techniques. He was particularly delighted when he worked out how to blow smoke out of his nose—just like a real dragon, he told me jubilantly. (I let that one go.) As the weeks passed, he began to smoke with a roguish panache, carelessly flicking ash behind him as he walked and inhaling lungfuls of smoke with relish. He no longer looked apprehensive when he pulled the pack of cigarettes from his pocket. Instead I saw a needful glint in his eye. He became restless in class toward the end of each school day. He couldn't get out of the gates fast enough to light up. His fumbling hands betrayed his craving. By April Nathan had become as much of an addict as his mother.

OUR HOME HAD BECOME a museum of unwanted memories. My brother lived on in the tiniest nooks and crannies; he lingered in the shadows. Every time I walked into a room, I couldn't escape the sensation that his wheelchair had rolled out just moments before. I was caught in a macabre game of hide-and-go-seek, hunting a ghostly quarry I could never catch. Liam was everywhere, yet always remained tantalizingly out of reach.

Then, a few weeks after Easter, the mailbox began to fill with responses to the college applications that Liam had sent off the previous fall. My parents had forgotten to tell the universities that he was dead. The heavy, grandly embossed envelopes sat in a pile on the kitchen counter. One morning when I came downstairs for breakfast my mother was sitting at the table with a cup of coffee in her hands. She had spread out the envelopes in front of her. I sat down.

"Pick a card, any card," she said.

I pointed to a cream-colored envelope edged in gold. My mother pulled it out of the stack. I did not recognize the name of the school. The return address was somewhere in California. I couldn't imagine anything being further away.

"Look at them all, Robert," she sighed. She held the envelope I'd chosen up to the light. "I wonder what this one says. Is it a yes or a no? What would Liam have studied? Who would he have met?"

"You should open it," I said.

My mother shook her head. "There's beauty in the unknown, Robert. Beauty and hope." She tapped the envelope with her fingertips. "If I open this and discover that Liam was accepted, or won a scholarship, or something else wonderful—well." She was silent for a moment. "Sometimes life can be a little more bearable if you don't know all there is to know. I'm not sure if I have room inside me for any more regret. Not right now." She smiled at me sadly. "All these different futures," she said, "and Liam isn't going to get to choose even one of them."

As the weeks passed, the stack of envelopes grew. I would have hidden them away, tucked them out of sight, but my mother kept them in full view. Sometimes I saw her gaze drift toward them while she stirred a pot on the stove. Every day she could have opened those envelopes, and every day she chose to turn away from whatever information might be inside. Each act of denial was also an act of self-preservation. My mother was reasserting control over a life that had spiraled out of her clutches, and she was getting stronger every day.

And then everything started to go wrong.

TWENTY

One afternoon in early May I arrived home from school and saw my father's station wagon in the driveway. It was unusual for him to return from the park so early. I slipped my backpack off my shoulder and opened the front door, wondering what was going on. As I approached the kitchen I heard my mother speaking.

"You should be ashamed of yourself," she said.

"Well, I'm not," answered my father. "I'm not ashamed at all. Those things were piling up like a *tombstone*, Mary. It was morbid. It was another damn grave, right here in our kitchen."

"There was no need to throw them out." My mother sounded disappointed rather than angry.

"No, that's exactly what was needed. I don't want to be reminded that our son is dead every time I get a cup of coffee."

"It was just some envelopes."

"But they weren't just envelopes. They were a reminder of all the things Liam won't ever learn, of the future he won't ever have. Every time I looked at those letters all I could think was, Well, that's a terrific waste of postage. And anyway, you didn't open a single one of them!"

"I was going to. I just wasn't ready. And now I can't."

They were silent for a moment.

"Why would you want to know? This fall thousands of kids will go off on new adventures at those splendid educational establishments. They'll read a bunch of books, make new friends, drink too much, sleep with unsuitable people, and have the time of their lives." I heard my father's voice catch. "But Liam won't be one of them. And nothing that any of those letters say will change that."

"But couldn't you have talked to me first before throwing them all away? Couldn't you have asked me what I thought?"

"Talking to you is a tall order these days, Mary."

"A tall order?" My mother sounded surprised. "What do you mean?"

"I don't know you anymore," said my father. "I don't know where you went."

"I'm still here, Sam."

"But how can you be so calm?"

My mother was silent for a moment. "Do you remember what you said to me last Christmas? About whether Liam's life was too short?"

"Mary—"

"You said that age was just a number. Do you remember? I've never forgotten it. I hated you for saying it. I wanted to wring your neck. I wanted you to stop being so accepting of this awful thing that was happening to us. I wanted you to shout and scream and yell."

"Why are you telling me this now?"

"Because I was wrong, Sam. People mourn differently; I see that now. Just because you weren't behaving like me didn't mean you weren't sad. You were just coping in your own way. That's all I'm doing now." My mother paused. "If you want to know why I'm so calm, it's because I've been praying."

"Praying? Do you really—"

"You told me before that it was useless. Well, it isn't now. I know that Liam is in heaven, and that helps."

"I don't want Liam to be in heaven. I want him in his bedroom, playing those lousy records."

"Yes, and you told me all the wanting in the world won't change a thing. You told me we have to accept things as they are. But throwing away those letters feels like you're hiding from the truth."

"I was trying to help us move on, that's all."

"Liam's only been dead a few months!"

"But don't you want the pain to stop?"

"You can't hurry grief, Sam. It'll leave when it's ready."

"Well, I don't need to go out looking for it. I certainly didn't need to see those letters every damn day." I heard the scraping of a kitchen chair. "I see Liam everywhere I turn, Mary. I see him in your face. I see him in Robert's eyes. I can't escape."

"Oh, there's no escape. Why would you ever think that?"

"Is it really so terrible to want to forget?" asked my father. "I want to wake up in the morning without this sadness pressing the life out of me. I'd love to feel nothing, just for a little while. Wouldn't you?"

I thought of Moira, then, and her quiet wish for just five minutes of love. I didn't want to listen to my parents anymore. I stepped back outside and closed the front door behind me. There was an old Adirondack chair on the front porch. Years ago, before the wheelchair, my mother would sit in it and watch as Liam and I played together in the front yard. I remembered that chair as smooth and beautiful, but now the paint had cracked with age and the wood was mottled with tiny, dark fissures. I sat down. There was no movement in front of me, except for an orange tabby cat strolling languidly across the street. I slid into the chair until my spine was pressing up against the slats. I put my hands palm-down on the wide wooden armrests, and suddenly I was Captain Kirk on the bridge of the starship *Enterprise*, in command and ready for adventure. I closed my eyes and imagined melting into that old chair until we were one and the same. Then I marshaled my crew, barked orders, and *whoosh!* Warp factor nine! I made my escape.

THE FOLLOWING DAY I arrived home in good spirits. That afternoon after school Nathan and I had bicycled over to see Lewis. He had baked us cupcakes, which we had devoured as we listened first to the Sex Pistols, then to Lester Young. Nathan and I had made plans for a trip to the paper mill over the weekend. It would be our first visit there since the fall, and I was looking forward to losing myself again in the dusty adventures we created within those walls.

I had managed not to think too much about the conversation between my parents that I had overheard the previous afternoon. But my mother was right. In the end, there was no escape.

I leaned my bike up against the side of the house and went inside, cheerfully whistling "Pretty Vacant." The kitchen was empty. Usually by then my mother would have been cooking supper, but the stove was cold.

"Mom?" I called.

There was no reply. I went upstairs to my bedroom. My mother was sitting on my bed.

"There you are," I said.

"Here I am," she agreed.

"Is everything all right?"

"Not really, no." She patted the covers next to her. "Sit down."

I sat. She turned to me and without another word wrapped her arms around me and held me tight.

"Mom? What is it? What's happened?"

"Your father's gone, Robert."

"Gone? Gone where?"

She let go of me. "It doesn't matter where."

"I don't understand," I said.

"Dad says he can't live here anymore."

"Not ever?"

She shrugged.

"But what about us?"

"We're going to be fine." She sighed. "Dad will always love you, Robert. But for now he's too sad to be here."

I thought back to their conversation the day before. My father, wanting to escape. I felt as if I had been punched in the stomach. I hadn't realized he wanted to escape from *me*.

"Where is he?"

My mother looked at me for a long minute. "At the park," she said finally.

"I want to go and see him," I said.

She shook her head. "You need to leave him be, Robert."

"The least he could do is tell me that he's leaving to my face."

My mother suddenly looked very tired. "Let me drive you there," she said.

"I'd rather go on my own." I didn't want her to see me cry.

"All right. But, Robert? Don't expect your father to change his mind. He needs time to think things through."

"What about what *I* need?"

My mother looked pained. "I'm just warning you."

I turned and ran down the stairs. The seat of my bike was still warm. I set off, pumping my legs as fast as I could. I bent down low over the handlebars and leaned into corners, clicking through the gears. Before long my calf muscles were burning, but still I rose off the seat and worked the pedals with everything I had, determined not to slow down. There was nothing but me, the bike, and the road. I left everything else behind. I would have kept going forever.

As I turned down the last stretch of road toward the park, I caught an acrid stench on the early-evening breeze and looked up. Half a mile in the distance a tower of black smoke was rising into the sky. It looked as if it was coming from the park grounds. At once a sour flood of terror rose in my throat. *Not a fire,* I thought. *Not now.* Then I was off again, flying toward the blaze.

From a distance the smoke had seemed eerily motionless, but as I got closer I could see dark ash eddying upward in restless, billowing clouds. At the front gates of the park I realized that there were no fire engines screaming down the road, no flashing lights or sirens. There was no crowd of curious onlookers. This disaster was a purely private affair. I raced into the parking lot.

My father was standing with his back to me, his hands on his hips, quite still. By his feet were three red plastic canisters. In front of him was a blazing pyre. Flames roared and spat, a roiling, hellish sheath of fire. Even from where I stood, the heat was ferocious. Then I realized what was burning.

It was the old carousel horses.

My father had hauled the ancient steeds out from the corner of his workshop and had piled them high in the middle of the parking lot, and then he had set the fire. Now the tangled pyramid of equine body parts burned fiercely. Each time a charred limb disintegrated, a brilliant typhoon of sparks flew into the evening air. The bodies of the horses were blackened by the fire, the paint long since burned away. In the middle of the inferno I saw a beautiful carved head, caught in stark silhouette against the flames. The horse's lips were pulled back, its teeth bared. For many summers it had been an expression of prancing joy and pride, but now it looked like a silent scream of agony.

"Dad!" I called out.

My father turned toward me. His face and arms were covered in grime and soot. He looked at me and then turned back to watch the fire without a word. I left my bike on the ground and walked toward him. The heat was searing.

"I called the fire department," he said. "I told them not to come."

We stood in silence and watched.

Finally my father spoke again. "I started carving horses for the carousel the year before Liam was born," he said, staring into the fire. "But I realized today that I had no idea why I was keeping the old ones." He paused. "I'm a sentimental fool, Robert. Always trying to hold on to what's already gone. But what's the point? We can't turn back time." He gestured toward the burning horses. "These old beauties were relics. They were just old memories."

"What's wrong with old memories?" I asked.

"Sometimes they stop you from moving forward."

"Forward? To where?"

"Somewhere else. Anywhere else."

"But sometimes memories are all we have!"

"Maybe. But I just want to feel nothing for a while."

I wrapped my arms around his torso, burying my head in his shirt. His clothes reeked of gasoline. His body was hot from the fire. "Please come home," I whispered.

"Oh, Robert. Sometimes things are so broken that there's just no way in the world you can ever put them back together."

After that, there was no more talking. We stood and watched the horses burn until there was just a pile of gray ashes on the ground.

THREE WEEKS LATER, Fun-A-Lot opened for the season.

TWENTY-ONE

Memorial Day weekend was unseasonably warm that year.

On the park's opening day I stood at the bottom of the Ferris wheel, shepherding guests onto the ride. Now that I was to be interacting with the public all day, I qualified for a different costume, although it wasn't much of an improvement on last year's outfit. My father told me I was some kind of monk, although he was vague with the details. Like Friar Tuck, he'd said, but that would have put me several centuries adrift from the rest of my colleagues. I had been issued a long brown tunic, complete with matching cowl and plastic crucifix. The outfit appeared to have been sewn together out of heavy burlap sacks.

Despite my discomfort, I was happy to be there. All the sights and sounds and smells of the park were just as they had always been. After all that had happened since last summer, after everything that had been lost, the place was reassuringly familiar in a world that had changed beyond all recognition. Liam was dead. My father had not come home. But as I looked out across the park drenched in early-summer sunshine, I found myself wondering whether everything might be okay. I was learning what my father already knew—that coming to work every day was precisely the kind of balm that my put-upon heart required.

THERE WERE TWENTY METAL PODS dotted around the Ferris wheel's circumference. Each time one of the cabins came in to dock at the bottom of the wheel, it was my job to usher one set of passengers out and get the next group settled in with the door securely fastened. This needed to be done quickly. I had to hurry to the control console and crank the wheel back to life for another fractional rotation until the next pod came in to land. There was never time for a break—any interruption would have left scores of people stranded in the air. I learned to go for hours without needing the restroom.

My job was an education in other ways, too. There was no end to what people thought they could get away with in those pods, high up in the sky and out of sight of the rest of the world. It was not uncommon to find beer cans and cigarette butts on the floor. I watched a lot of young couples climb into the pods wearing self-conscious grins. I stared at the bottoms of the cabins as they passed overhead and wondered what was going on above me.

Misbehavior was not limited to consenting adults, however. I also had to watch for families with small children who had misjudged their bathroom stops. I lost count of the puddles of pee that I mopped up. Once I even discovered a small turd steaming in the corner of a pod. The family who had left this behind had smiled at me as they disembarked, as if nothing in the world were amiss.

Lewis was right; the Ferris wheel was a signature attraction. There was always a long line, which meant that Nathan was often there in the dragon suit, cavorting in front of the waiting crowds. After just a few days he seemed to inhabit the costume like a second skin. He lived the role absolutely and without compromise. Once he had pulled on the dragon's fiberglass head, he always remained in character. He threw himself into each performance with everything he had. He learned to convey the entire spectrum of dragon emotion—from joy to sorrow, from ferocity to gentleness—all without the benefit of words (because dragons do not talk) or a changing facial expression (the dragon's friendly grin was as fixed as the bared teeth of the carousel horses). Nathan's performance was pure physicality. He leapt about, he performed little dance routines, and, when the occasion called for it, he would shake his ass to make the dragon's tail wiggle and bounce. The guests loved it.

Every so often Nathan would stop for a cigarette and blow smoke out of the dragon's nose. The outfit was roomy enough that he could extricate one arm from the suit and hold his cigarette between puffs, although this left one of the dragon's wings drooping and motionless, as if it had suffered a small stroke. I did see some parents wrinkle their noses when they smelled the tobacco, but overall people appreciated the effect.

Nathan was supposed to wander through the whole park, but when he wasn't at the Ferris wheel, he spent most of his time in front of the concession stand. It was, he explained, where the longest lines were, but we both knew the real reason. Everything he did was designed to attract Faye's attention. I would sometimes walk past the food area on my breaks to watch him in action. He barged ahead of people in the line, pretended to steal French fries, and generally goofed around. I was probably the only person who noticed how, after each joke, the dragon turned its head toward the concession stand window.

We met up by the gates each evening when the park closed. Nathan changed into fresh clothes after he had finished work—it was so hot inside the dragon suit that by the end of the day he was drenched in sweat. Just like last year, Nathan would tell me about Faye's inexhaustible charms. And, just like last year, we would watch as the older boys tried to impress her.

One night Hollis Calhoun was hitting on her pretty hard. Nathan watched him, a forgotten cigarette smoldering between his fingers.

"That guy," he muttered.

"Hollis is a piece of work," I agreed.

"He's working the mini golf this season," said Nathan. I knew this, of course. I had slipped into my father's office one afternoon and looked at the employee roster to see where Hollis would be working. He had left me alone for the entire school year, but I was taking nothing for granted. I still wanted to avoid him if I could. "He sits in that wooden shack all day and hands out putters and golf balls," continued Nathan. "And he checks out every female who comes within twenty feet of him."

I pictured Hollis surrounded by the fake cacti and cowboy paraphernalia, eyeing the passing girls and making artless overtures to the pretty ones. "I bet that's a bust," I chuckled.

"That's the weird thing," said Nathan. "A lot of the girls ignore him, but some actually seem to *like* it." He shook his head in bewilderment. "I don't understand it." His gaze drifted across to where Hollis was whispering something in Faye's ear. "And then he comes here and does *that*."

I understood. For Hollis, Faye was just another girl, one more potential conquest. That was what offended Nathan the most.

Just then Faye burst out laughing and placed a hand on Hollis's arm. Nathan looked at his shoes and said nothing.

WORKING THE FERRIS WHEEL meant that I was rooted to one spot, and I envied both Nathan and Lewis, who spent their days roaming the park. I always kept an eye out for Lewis as he stomped from one job to the next. Sometimes he was whistling a bebop solo, but more often than not he was muttering under his breath. There was a slump to his shoulders that hadn't been there last year. He walked a little more slowly, stood a little less tall. I told myself that it was because he was missing me. I was certainly missing him. I began hoping that something would go wrong with the Ferris wheel, just so Lewis could come by and fix it. I missed his little hut, the tinny radio, even the briny stink of those awful sardine sandwiches. My visits to his house with Nathan were fun, but they weren't the same. I missed having Lewis to myself.

Maybe he could tell. He stopped by my booth every day, ostensibly to check that everything was running smoothly, but really just because he wanted to see that I was all right. I could never talk for long—those cabins never stopped arriving and departing, and the line never got any shorter—but I was always happy to see him.

In contrast, I hardly saw my father at all. Occasionally I spotted him hurrying by, but he never glanced in my direction. Those sightings were difficult for me. My father had not come home. He bought his breakfast, lunch, and dinner from the concession stand. I imagined him washing in the men's restrooms early in the mornings and sleeping on the sofa in his office beneath a haphazard collection of too-small blankets. He presented his best face to the world while the park was open for business, but there were small clues that hinted at a slow unraveling within. Not many noticed the absence of military creases down the front of his slacks, but I did. Not many spotted the occasional shadow of silver bristles on his chin, but I did. And not many looked behind his mask of brisk efficiency and saw the absence of hope in his eyes. But I did.

AT THE END OF most days I would climb onto my bike and ride home, although sometimes my mother would come and collect me.

She sat in the car, ready with a bright smile and a wave when I came out of the gates.

"How come you never go and see Dad when you pick me up?" I asked her one evening as I shoved my bike into the trunk.

She shrugged. "No need. I know where he is."

"Don't you miss him?"

"I miss him like crazy, Robert."

"So you could go and talk to him."

My mother looked straight ahead as she put the car in gear and pulled out into the stream of vehicles crawling toward the exit. "Yes, well," she said. "I want to give him the time he needs to work things out."

"What is there to work out?"

"While your brother was alive, Dad always insisted that Liam's life wasn't too short—that it was exactly the length it should be. But when we were in the hospital that last time, he realized he had been wrong. I think that made everything much worse for him. God gave me the strength to cope with the pain, but I don't think your father was ready for it. So try not to be mad at him. He misses Liam, that's all."

"What about me? Doesn't he miss me, too?"

My mother was silent for a moment. "Dad's heart is broken right now," she said. "He's just trying to mend it."

"Is your heart broken, too?" I asked.

"Oh, Robert. All these questions."

We drove in silence for a while. Finally my mother started to talk again.

"There was nothing your father could do to stop Liam from dying," she said. "Not one thing. That was almost impossible for him to live with. He had to watch him get sicker and sicker, and then die."

"We all did."

"Yes, but it was especially hard for him. He wanted to protect his son. He thought that was his job. And when he couldn't, he felt like it was his fault."

"Of course it wasn't his fault."

"No, it wasn't. But sometimes that can be hard to see. You'll be a father one day, Robert, and then you'll understand." My mother paused. "Dad used to talk about being a superhero, about putting on a cape and battling the forces of evil to protect his family."

"What was his superpower?"

She looked at me and smiled. "Love, of course. Nothing in the world is stronger than that."

THE FOLLOWING EVENING Nathan and I lingered in the parking lot, watching Faye as she milled around with her friends. That night, for the first time, she was carrying a guitar case. Nathan groaned in bewitched anguish.

"I bet she's going to play it on the beach," he breathed. "We have to go and listen!"

"Those kids aren't going to want us around," I said.

"We won't go *with* them," said Nathan. "We can just follow them and watch from a distance."

I shook my head. "Let's go and do something else." We had always stayed away from the nightly beach parties—we were too young to hope for an invitation. Besides, I wasn't sure that either of us really wanted to know what went on down there.

"But what if she never brings her guitar again?" said Nathan.

I sighed. It was the night of my mother's weekly Bible study class, and she would not be getting back until late. I had no reason to hurry home.

We took a circuitous route to the beach that involved elaborate detours and much doubling back. The parties always happened at the same spot, close to the path that led through the sand dunes from the beach parking lot. The place was easily identified by the charred embers of nightly bonfires, the scattered army of cigarette ends half-buried in the sand, and the occasional empty can of Pabst that somebody had left behind. We found a sand dune some thirty yards away and hunkered down, out of sight.

By the time we arrived, the sun had vanished behind the trees to the west, and the night's festivities had already begun. We peered cautiously over the top of the sand dune. A small fire had been lit, and we could see the happy faces of the partygoers glowing in the flickering flames. Most of the kids were sitting cross-legged on the sand, smoking cigarettes and passing around a bottle. Faye sat in the middle of the crowd, languidly strumming her guitar as she chatted to the girl next to her. The chords floated into the air, clear and pretty. Nathan did not take his eyes off Faye, but I was watching Hollis Calhoun, who was sitting with his back to us. He was his usual brutish self, shouting and laughing too loudly.

After fifteen minutes, I was starting to get cold. The wind had begun to whip in off the ocean. Nothing much was happening on the beach. I don't know quite what I had been expecting, but I was disappointed to discover how boring it was to watch teenagers smoke and drink.

"Let's go," I whispered.

Before Nathan could reply there was a smattering of whoops and applause. Everyone turned toward Faye and grew quiet. She gave her audience a shy grin and then began to play. I recognized the picked arpeggios of the introduction to "Scarborough Fair." When she began to sing, her voice was breathy, low, and beautiful. Some of her audience swayed gently in time to the music, but neither Nathan nor I moved a muscle. We were both hypnotized. When she sang,

Remember me to one who lives there
He once was a true love of mine

Nathan closed his eyes and let out a small groan of helpless desire. At the end of the song the group around the fire cheered and clapped while Faye lowered her eyes modestly to the ground. I turned toward Nathan. He looked thunderstruck.

"Nathan? Are you all right?"

He stared back at me. "We should go now," he said.

We made our way back to our bikes without saying another word.

WHEN I ARRIVED HOME, my father's station wagon was parked in its usual spot in the driveway.

"Dad!" I yelled as I unlocked the front door. "Are you home? It's me!"

The house was completely quiet.

"Dad?" I called out.

Finally I heard the slow thud of footsteps, and then my father appeared in the doorway to the sitting room. He was carrying a pile of six or seven books.

"Hello, Robert," he said.

"Are you looking for Mom?" I said. "Because she's not here. She's—"

"At Bible study," said my father. "Yes, I know."

Whatever vague hopes had been swirling around inside me evaporated in an instant. Of course my father had known that my mother wouldn't be there. That was precisely why he had come. He hovered awkwardly in the doorway, not looking at me. "I really just came to get some books to read," he said.

I took the top book off the pile he was carrying. On the cover was a picture of a woman in a purple crinoline dress. She was standing alone in the middle of a cornfield. Her face was turned away, and she appeared to be gazing at something just beyond the horizon. The title was printed in a dramatic, curlicued font across the stormy sky.

"*Desires of the Duchess*," I said. It was by one of my mother's favorite authors, V. V. St. Cloud. I turned the book over and read the synopsis on the back cover. There were passionate lady aristocrats, swarthy plebeian heroes, and lashings of unspeakable villainy. "Doesn't seem like your usual thing," I said. When my father picked up a book, which wasn't often, they tended to be blockbusters as fat and heavy as bricks, usually by James Clavell or Harold Robbins.

"It's not," agreed my father. "But there's not much to do in the office late at night, so I thought I would expand my literary horizons."

"You could always come home," I said. "That way you wouldn't have to sneak in and out of your own house, stealing Mom's books."

My father's face looked pained. "Don't be mad at me, Robert," he said.

He opened the front door. I numbly watched him go and then wandered into Liam's room and lay on the bed with the lights off. I struggled to make sense of my father's clandestine visit. What could he possibly want with all those trashy romance novels?

I climbed off Liam's bed and walked into the living room. There were still several V. V. St. Cloud novels on the shelves. The books all appeared to be similar to *Desires of the Duchess*, in that they were historical romances set in England, although the time period varied. One took place during the Blitz in London—*love flourished among the ruins as enemy bombs rained down on the devastated city*, the book jacket screeched—and the earliest I found told of the tempestuous affair between one of the knights of the Round Table and a buxom serving wench. I finally picked one called *Star-Crossed*. I'd hoped it might be a tale of intergalactic romance, but on the cover there was a picture of a woman standing in the middle of a deserted stage. I took it back to my room and started to read.

I didn't move for the next six hours.

TWENTY-TWO

Star-Crossed begins in a remote part of Northern England in 1821. The heroine, Betsy Cribbins, is nineteen years old. She works as a scullery maid in a large country house. Not even the ugly uniform that she wears every day can hide her ravishing beauty, which V. V. St. Cloud took several pages to describe in rapturous, overwrought prose. It's hardly surprising that she attracts a lot of unwanted attention. She has to fend off everyone from the chauffeur to visiting viscounts who have been at the port bottle after dinner. Luckily she is quick on her feet and can outrun most of her assailants, especially the drunk ones. While Betsy works long hours in the kitchen and keeps an eye out for horny footmen and dukes, she is quietly nurturing a secret dream: she longs to find fame and fortune on the stage in London. Sometimes she creeps into the library late at night and borrows leather-bound volumes of plays by Shakespeare, Sheridan, and Marlowe, which she reads hungrily, imagining herself playing the female leads. These fantasies sustain her as she scours the kitchen flagstones.

Enter Roger Fortescue-Pemberton, the eldest (and very handsome) son of the family, who has returned to the estate from London, where he is a successful lawyer. One night, after the rest of the household has gone to bed, Roger discovers Betsy in the library, pulling a copy of *The School for Scandal* off the shelves. The scene that followed was gripping and tense, all the more so because I didn't have the slightest idea what was going on. The prose was so bafflingly opaque that it was only several pages after Betsy had been left on the floor with her maid's uniform torn in several places that I realized what had happened. Betsy creeps back to her room, packs her belongings into a small bag, and quietly leaves the house. Her shame pursues her out the door.

Betsy uses the last of her savings to travel to London and makes her way to Drury Lane, home of the city's most famous theater. There she auditions for a part in a new production of *Romeo and Juliet* and—improbably, in my opinion—wins the role of Juliet. The theater owner, a man called Collins, finds a place for Betsy to stay in Shoreditch. Rehearsals begin. Things are looking up.

And then disaster strikes. Betsy falls hopelessly in love with Percy Rylance, the actor playing Romeo. Percy has eyes of dazzling blue and a roguishly strong chin (whatever *that* meant). Betsy longs for Percy but is too scared to tell him how she feels. Instead she hides her feelings behind frosty indifference. And she is right to be cautious: Percy clearly dislikes her as much as she adores him. At the end of each scene they rehearse, he coldly turns away from her.

Betsy forges bravely on, her broken heart heavy inside her. The opening night of the play is a stunning success. The audience loves her. There are multiple curtain calls. Flowers are thrown onto the stage. As the curtain descends for the final time, Percy storms off the stage. In what should be her moment of triumph, Betsy is desolate. She is weeping in her dressing room when Mr. Collins knocks on the door. He strokes her hand and offers to drive her back to Shoreditch in his carriage. Betsy gratefully accepts.

I was as naïve as Betsy. Only when Collins pushes her through the door of her lodgings and throws her down onto the bed did I realize what was going to happen next.

When Betsy arrives at the theater the following day, she is dead inside. That night her performance is more spellbinding than ever. As she stares into Percy's eyes, she can still feel Collins's sour breath on her neck, his knuckles against her skin.

Afterward Collins comes into her dressing room again. With an ugly leer, he explains how things are going to be from now on. Betsy will do whatever he demands of her, or he will throw her back out onto the street. She has no choice but to comply with his disgusting demands. And so she shuttles between the adoration of the public and the humiliations that Collins inflicts upon her in private. (By this stage I was getting more adept at parsing V. V. St. Cloud's elaborate circumlocutions, but there were still times when I was left scratching my head.)

Some weeks later, Betsy is waiting in the wings for her opening scene when, to her horror, she sees none other than Roger Fortescue-Pemberton sitting in one of the theater's boxes. She can feel his eyes on her throughout the play. After the final curtain Betsy returns backstage and waits for Collins. When she hears the knock on the door, Betsy braces herself—but it is not Collins! It is Roger Fortescue-Pemberton! He is warm and charming, showering her with compliments, and of course he is as handsome as ever. Betsy realizes that Roger does not recognize her as the lowly scullery maid he so casually took advantage of months earlier. Just then, the door opens and Collins stands at the threshold, staring in fury at the unexpected intruder. The two men face off against each other. Collins is growling and ferocious, a bulldog. Fortescue-Pemberton is arrogant and aloof. Words are exchanged. Insults are hurled. Before Betsy can stop them, they are marching outside to the alleyway behind the theater to settle their fight. It's a duel!

(By now I was turning the pages so fast that I didn't stop to consider the improbability of all this. Where, for example, had the guns come from?)

Death, at least, was rendered in more straightforward prose than sex. Two pages later, the evil Collins is lying in the gutter, a crimson bullet hole in the middle of his forehead. It turns out that Fortescue-Pemberton is a marvelous shot. He dusts off his evening dress, bows deeply toward Betsy, and hands her the gun before he turns to go. Betsy is left alone in the alleyway, the corpse of her tormentor at her feet.

Moments later (wouldn't you know it) a policeman walks by. He sees the dead man and Betsy with the gun in her hand. She is arrested and locked up in Pentonville prison and charged with murder. The newspapers are full of the scandal.

The day of the trial arrives. Betsy sits in the dock, her hands shackled. Imagine her horror (and mine) when the counsel for the prosecution walks into the courtroom—it's none other than Roger Fortescue-Pemberton! Betsy watches numbly as the man who murdered Collins constructs the case against her for that very crime. She knows that if she shouts out the truth, nobody will believe her in a million years.

It takes the jury less than an hour to reach its verdict. The foreman declares her guilty, and then the judge gravely sentences her to death by hanging. Then a most peculiar thing happens. As Betsy is lifted to her feet by the prison warders, Roger Fortescue-Pemberton jumps to his feet and announces that his conscience will not allow him to watch an innocent woman go to the scaffold in his place. In front of an electrified courtroom, he confesses to the murder!

A week later, Betsy is a free woman, but she is unable to stop thinking about Roger Fortescue-Pemberton. Finally she goes to visit him in prison. Betsy sees the remorse in his face and decides that this man is not so bad.

By this stage even I could see what was going to happen next.

In the weeks leading up to Fortescue-Pemberton's execution, Betsy visits him every day. They sit surrounded by villains and brigands, aware that their time together is impossibly short. Their love is fierce and uncomplicated, seasoned by the tragedy that they both know lies ahead. Nothing will stop the slow march of days toward the hangman's noose.

Betsy attends the execution. She can barely watch as Roger climbs the wooden stairs of the scaffold. Just before the canvas hood is pulled down over his head, he looks at her and gives her a brave smile. It is the memory of that smile that she treasures the most. It is all that she has left.

But in fact it is not quite all. A week later Betsy learns that Roger has left her enough money to buy a small house and to provide a decent income for the rest of her life. She moves to a small market town in Kent, mercifully far from the public eye. There is a degree of solace in the unchanging peace of her days, and her broken heart slowly heals. Her sadness is sweetened by the knowledge that she has been deeply and ardently adored.

As I turned the final page I let out a sigh of relief. The book was a symphony of powerful human emotion and I was wrung out, overcome, exhausted. Then I saw a single word on the next page: EPILOGUE.

V. V. St. Cloud had saved the best for last.

Many, many years later, Betsy receives a letter from Percy Rylance. Percy has become one of the most famous actors in England, thanks in no small part to the notoriety caused by Collins's murder behind the Drury Lane theater all those years before. Percy begs her to come and visit him in London. There is, he writes, something he must tell her.

Betsy is intrigued but apprehensive. She takes a coach into the city. Percy lives in a large town house in Bloomsbury. When she sees him, Betsy is unable to hide her shock. He has become an old man. His hair has fallen out, his skin is lined and gray.

Percy tells her that he is dying. And death, he says, makes you understand that there's no time left for regret. Now that I'm too ill to work, he says, my head is no longer full of other people's lines. And I realize that I have my own story that needs to be told.

On I read, cursing V. V. St. Cloud as I turned each page.

Percy Rylance makes his confession. He tells Betsy that he has loved her from the very first time he saw her. She, though, was so manifestly uninterested in him that he barricaded himself behind a fortress of chilly disdain. But his love for her never faltered, not for one moment. He stayed true to Betsy through the years. He never married, never took advantage of the legion of admiring ladies who flocked to be by his side. And he never again played the role of Romeo. Percy always promised himself that he would bear his suffering in silence, but now that the end is near, he finds that he does not want the greatest drama of his life to go unremarked.

Betsy allows her tears to fall. Percy pats her hand and tells her that it is not her fault. But he doesn't understand—she is weeping not for him, but for her. The truth both dazzles and crucifies her: Betsy and Percy loved each other fiercely but in treacherous silence. Each night they declared their passion in front of a theater of strangers, but neither was able to confess their feelings in private. Percy loved her! Betsy looks back and sees another, sweeter life that was hers for the taking, if only she'd had the courage to follow her heart.

Betsy returns to her cottage, ready to live out the rest of her life alone. But as she watches the hedgerows of the English countryside pass by the coach window, she discovers that her heart is not heavy. Despite everything, the final line in the book is bursting with hope, for Betsy tells herself:

There's just so much to live for.

IT WAS FOUR O'CLOCK in the morning. I switched off the lamp on my bedside table and stared into the darkness.

Was this a happy ending? Betsy Cribbins had been denied a life with either of the men she had adored. Her love affair with Roger Fortescue-Pemberton was tragic, but it was Percy Rylance's dying confession that really got me. They had loved each other all along! Poor Betsy had been so close to happiness and yet so very far. But she remained unbowed to the end. *I* might have been devastated by the epilogue's revelations, but Betsy discovered a quiet joy in Percy Rylance's secret. She was loved! That would have to be enough. Betsy navigated past her regret and found new peace in her heart.

Maybe that's the answer, I thought. If you're still standing on the final page, then that's enough of a happy ending. A little heartbreak could be survived. I thought about my father, my mother, and me. I wondered if we would all still be standing when our story was done.

TWENTY-THREE

I yawned my way through the next day, struggling to stay awake. As I shepherded people on and off the Ferris wheel, I couldn't stop thinking about Betsy Cribbins and Percy Rylance. The book's finale had killed me. A lifetime of happiness with her first true love had been there for Betsy to claim all along; all it would have taken was a few simple words. And yet she had lost everything, simply by remaining silent.

Halfway through the afternoon, Nathan appeared and began doing an elaborate dance in front of the line for the Ferris wheel. This had become one of his favorite routines and always went over well with the crowd. The dragon shimmied and spun, moving from elegant ballet poses to groovy disco moves. Sometimes Nathan just jumped up and down, shaking his head from side to side and waving his wings about. I was sure when he did this he had one of Liam's punk songs going through his head. At other times he would take a small child by the hands and lead them in a formal ballroom waltz, which got the most laughs of all. The dragon slowly made its way up the line of customers. Finally it wandered over to where I was standing and flapped a wing at me in greeting.

"Nice work back there," I said.

I heard the rough click of a cigarette lighter. Seconds later two thin columns of smoke emerged from the dragon's nostrils.

"Tough day?" I yawned.

"It's a hard job, spreading joy to the masses," said Nathan. His voice echoed down the dragon's fiberglass snout. I knew at once that something was up. It was one of Nathan's cardinal rules that the dragon never, ever talked.

"You're a trouper," I told him. "A real pro."

Nathan nodded and turned to one side so that his limp, non-functioning wing was hidden from the view of the guests. "I have a favor to ask."

"Hold on." I hitched up my cassock and went to usher one family out of the lowest pod and help another one climb in. Nathan waited patiently for me to return to the booth.

"My mom has gone away for a while," he told me.

"Oh yeah? Where did she go?"

"I don't know," said Nathan. "She does this every so often—just disappears for a week or two. Of course, Dad was always around before."

"Do you want to stay with us while she's gone?"

"Actually no." The dragon shook his head. "But thank you."

"What, then?"

Nathan pointed at the Ferris wheel. "I want to sleep up there."

I blinked. "Why?"

"All you would have to do is to meet me here each night and send me up to the top," said Nathan. "When I get to the highest point, you stop the wheel and go home."

"And?"

"And then you come back in the morning and bring me down again."

"You're crazy," I said.

The dragon turned and waved to a little girl who was walking close by. "Think of it as aerial camping," said Nathan. "I could start a whole new fad. It could be a big moneymaker for you."

"Why don't you just come and stay with us instead?"

"Because I want to be up in the air," said Nathan.

"But what will you do all night?"

He shrugged. "Sleep, I guess. Maybe I'll bring a book to read."

And that was when it hit me: Nathan needed to read *Star-Crossed*. I thought of him the previous evening, gazing devotedly across the sand at Faye as she played her guitar. Just like Betsy Cribbins, he was hamstrung by desire, tongue-tied by adoration. For a long time I'd believed that Nathan's lovelorn silence was for the best, but now V. V. St. Cloud's story had me wondering if that was really true. Betsy had suffered a tragic, lonely fate because she was too timid to tell Percy Rylance how she felt. I didn't want Nathan to make the same mistake. He had been trapped in petrified limbo for too long; perhaps it would be worth risking a little heartbreak. *Star-Crossed* would be the key that would set him free.

"All right," I said. "Meet me in the parking lot at ten o'clock tonight."

The dragon straightened up. "Cool," he said, and then he sauntered off, flapping his tattered wings as he went.

AFTER SUPPER THAT EVENING I yawned ostentatiously and told my mother I was going upstairs for an early night. When I heard the low drone of the television from the living room, I knew it was safe to make my escape. (My mother had taken to sitting in front of the television until she fell asleep. Once that happened, nothing short of an earthquake could disturb her. I often came downstairs in the morning to find her snoring peacefully on the couch, the set still on.) I crept downstairs, climbed onto my bike, and set off for the park.

In my basket was my mother's copy of *Star-Crossed*.

Nathan was waiting for me in the parking lot, a backpack slung over his shoulder. He stubbed out a cigarette as I approached.

"What's in the backpack?" I asked him.

"A sweater, a blanket, a flashlight, a bottle of water, two apples, a box of matches, and a pack of cigarettes. I come prepared."

"You would have made an excellent Boy Scout," I told him. "Except maybe for the cigarettes." I handed him the book. "One more thing for you."

"V. V. St. Cloud?" said Nathan. "My mom's got some of these novels."

"Here's the deal," I said. "I'll send you up in the Ferris wheel, but you have to promise me that you'll read this book."

Nathan turned the book over and read the back cover. "Why?"

"You'll see."

Nathan weighed the book thoughtfully in his hand. "All right, then," he said.

We slipped through the side gate that the park employees used. At night the edges of the paths were illuminated by a series of barely glowing emergency lamps, just bright enough that we could see where we were going without a flashlight. Beyond them, there was nothing but dark shadow. It was eerie, moving through those spaces usually so full of blaring spectacle when every noise was silenced, every movement stilled.

Rather than going directly to the Ferris wheel, first we sneaked around the side of the office. I wanted to check on my father. I peered in through the window, unsure what I would see. Perhaps he would be staggering around the room wailing in wordless misery, or he might be curled up in a fetal position on the carpet with an empty bottle of whiskey by his side. In fact he was sitting on the couch, immersed in *Desires of the Duchess*. As we watched, my father turned a page and then took a sip from a cup of coffee. It was not the picture of emotional unraveling that I had been expecting. I found myself a little disappointed that he seemed so *normal*. Given that he was pulling our family apart, I thought he should look more distraught.

Nathan and I watched him through the window for several minutes and then set off through the park. The only sound was the crunch of our footsteps on the gravel. Suddenly Nathan grabbed my arm. "Wait," he whispered. "Can you hear something?" We stood still and listened. From out of the darkness somebody appeared to be talking, but it was too quiet for me to make out any words.

"We should leave," I said nervously.

Nathan looked at me, mystified. "What do you mean?"

We had stopped by the entrance to the miniature golf course. "There's somebody over there," I said. "Let's go."

"Why?"

"Because I don't want to get *caught*."

"But whoever that is, it's not your father. So that means they shouldn't be here, either."

"I don't care," I hissed.

While we had been talking the whispering had gotten a little louder, and then we both heard, very distinctly, two words.

Oh, Faye.

We stared at each other.

"We really should go," I said weakly.

Oh, baby, whispered the voice. *Oh yes.*

In an instant Nathan had turned and disappeared into the darkness of the golf course. After a moment's hesitation, I followed him. I crept from one wigwam to the next until I caught up with him, crouching behind a large plastic cactus. Nathan pointed furiously around it. I stuck my head out to look.

The centerpiece of the mini golf course was the sixth hole, which featured a life-size statue of a kneeling Pocahontas. Players had to knock their ball up an incline and into a hole on top of the statue's head. The ball would disappear down a tunnel and moments later it would fly out of the beautiful Indian princess's mouth and land on the putting green. Pocahontas wore a perpetually astonished expression, her mouth a perfect O of surprise as golf balls shot out of it all day long. It wasn't very dignified or regal, but what I saw when I peered around the cactus was far worse.

Hollis Calhoun was standing in front of the kneeling squaw. His groin was directly level with the princess's open mouth. He was clutching the back of her head with his left hand and moving his hips gently back and forth. As he did so, he continued to whisper to himself.

Oh yeah. Oh baby. Just like that. Oh yeah.

I stared in mute astonishment for a few seconds and then retreated back behind the cactus. Next to me Nathan was staring blindly into space.

I coughed. "Is he—?"

Nathan nodded. He looked as if he might throw up.

Oh, Faye, groaned Hollis again.

"Come on," hissed Nathan, his face dark with fury. We set off back the way we had come. Hollis was unaware that he had been spied upon. Once we regained the path, Nathan stormed off toward the Ferris wheel, muttering to himself.

"Nathan!" I whispered. I had to hurry to keep up with him. "Come on, Nathan, don't be mad."

He turned to me. *"He was saying Faye's name!"* he hissed.

"At least she wasn't actually there."

Nathan shuddered at this.

We arrived at the Ferris wheel. Nathan checked through his bag while I unlocked the control panel and turned the motor on. The thrum as the engine creaked into life sounded as if it would wake up half of Maine. I wanted to get Nathan up in the air as quickly as possible. Now there wasn't just my father to worry about—Hollis Calhoun might also hear something. Nathan climbed into the lowest pod and immediately lit a cigarette, which he pulled on angrily. I closed the metal door and secured the latch. "I'll be back first thing in the morning," I said. "Enjoy the book." I went to the booth and eased the wheel into motion, trying not to think about the loudly cranking gears as the massive arms began to move. I stared up into the night sky. When Nathan's pod reached the top of the wheel, I switched off the engine. The silence that followed was absolute.

Nathan was trapped in a small metal cage, suspended a hundred feet above the ground with no way of getting down again until I came back in the morning. I wanted to call out and check that he was not having second thoughts. But Nathan never had second thoughts about anything.

I climbed back onto my bicycle and set off for home, wondering if my plan was going to work.

TWENTY-FOUR

I couldn't sleep that night.

Exhausted as I was after staying up so late the previous evening, I couldn't stop thinking about Nathan, alone in the metal pod with the wind whipping in off the ocean. It was also difficult to dispel the vision of Hollis Calhoun thrusting himself at Pocahontas, Faye's name on his lips. I had never seen Nathan so angry. I took my mind off it all by opening the copy of *The Great Gatsby* that I had found in Liam's bedroom. I was soon bewitched by the beautiful debauchery of Fitzgerald's universe. Elegant creatures talked in sentences as crisp and as dry as a glass of vintage champagne, but nobody was listening to what anyone else was saying. Floating above the fray of all that ravishing self-absorption stood Gatsby, watching and waiting for Daisy Buchanan.

I didn't like Daisy, though, not one bit. From the moment she first appeared, dressed in white and perched on the enormous couch in her sitting room, I could tell that she was a phony. Gatsby was too good for her; anyone could see that. I turned the pages, captivated by the exquisite train wreck of it all. Oh, the careless violence of that hot Long Island summer! Once again, I read late into the night. Fitzgerald's quietly devastating truths chilled me.

I did not want Faye to be another Daisy Buchanan, so careless with other people's hearts. Nathan deserved better than that. But his dreams, I realized, were just as grand and impossible as Gatsby's had been. They had no business in this world.

It occurred to me then that I had given Nathan the wrong book.

As THE FIRST LIGHT of the new morning began to peep through my bedroom window, I got dressed and left a note for my mother on the kitchen table. I climbed onto my bike and sped down the deserted roads, watching the sun rise over the horizon in front of me. At the park I opened the side gate and ran to the Ferris wheel.

"Nathan!" I called out softly.

There was no reply.

I called again, more loudly this time. There was still no answer. I went to the booth and cranked the Ferris wheel into life. When Nathan's pod reached the docking station I hurried over.

Nathan was sitting up, his blanket around his shoulders, reading. As I swung the metal door open, he held up his finger. He was on the final page of *Star-Crossed*. I stood there and watched him. Finally he lowered his finger and closed the book. Then he looked up at me.

"This," he said, "is a great book. But such a tragic ending. Poor Betsy!"

I thought of Gatsby lying facedown in his swimming pool with a bullet in his back. *That* was a tragic ending. "It's a good read," I said neutrally.

"A *good read?*" said Nathan. "It's amazing! To think that Betsy's whole life could have been different if she'd just said a few words to Percy. All the happiness she had ever wanted could have been hers!"

This, of course, was precisely what I had been hoping Nathan would glean from V. V. St. Cloud's story, but now I was regretting having given him the book. I was starting to see that no good could possibly come from this. Gatsby had adored Daisy, and look where it had gotten him.

"It's just a silly romance novel," I said. "You shouldn't read too much into it."

Nathan stood up and stepped out of the pod. He arched his back and extended his palms out toward the rising sun. Then he turned to me. His eyes were shining. "Poor Betsy!" he said again.

THROUGHOUT THE DAY I caught glimpses of Nathan as he strolled through the park in the dragon suit. He must have been exhausted after his sleepless night on the Ferris wheel, but I thought I could detect an extra bounce in his step, an additional swish to his tail.

It was a Friday. Many visitors to Maine arrived and departed over the weekend, so there was a valedictory feel to Fridays at Fun-A-Lot. I saw quiet desperation in the faces of some of the parents, as if this visit to the park at the end of their week away was one last throw of the dice, a final bid for some happy memories to take back home. When my break came I walked through the park toward the concession stand. It was the height of the lunch rush. There were two long lines snaking back across the concrete. Nathan was parading up and down, provoking squeals of delight from the watching children. Every so often he would stop and put his arm around a kid's shoulders to pose for a photograph. When Nathan saw me he raised his arm for a high five. Embarrassed, I put my hand in the air and slapped the tip of his wing with my open palm. (He might have been hiding inside the dragon suit, but everyone could see me.) Nathan put his arms around me and forced me into an awkward foxtrot. We pranced up and down the line of laughing guests and I tried not to tread on his huge dragon feet.

"You're in an excellent mood," I said.

Nathan did not reply. He took a step away from me and lifted my arm into the air. I dutifully pirouetted under his wing, beaming for the watching crowd. Soon after that Nathan released me, our impromptu dance done. He bowed deeply; I lifted up my cassock and curtseyed back. The crowd applauded good-naturedly. As I walked back to the Ferris wheel, I wondered what was going through Nathan's head. He had gripped me and spun me and danced with a silent joy that was palpable even from within all that fake green fur. But I had no idea what it meant.

THAT EVENING WE MET as usual by the park gates.

"Let's go to the beach," said Nathan at once.

"Again?" I said.

"She's got her guitar," whispered Nathan. I glanced across to where Faye was standing. Her guitar case was slung across her back. Her hair was gleaming in the evening sun.

"How about the mill instead?" I said.

"I don't want to go to the mill."

"Come on. I'll send you flying on the hook."

Nathan shook his head. "I want to go to the beach."

"But we don't go to the beach, do we?" I said. "We hide behind a sand dune and spy on people who *actually* go to the beach."

Nathan looked at me, his eyes walls.

"We don't have to go to the mill," I said. "We could go to my house and watch some TV."

Nathan reached out and gripped my arm.

"Robert," he said. "*Please.*"

And that was it. We would go to the beach.

When we finally arrived at the sand dune where we had hidden before, Faye was already playing her guitar. There were shallow troughs in the ground where we had lain two nights previously, and we settled back into position. I stared up at the sky while Nathan crept forward and peeked over the crest of the dune.

"There are more people than last time," he reported. "Hollis Calhoun is there, of course." He fell silent, and I knew he was thinking about Hollis's whispered croon as he had his filthy way with Pocahontas the previous night.

Nathan stood up.

"Where are you going?" I said.

"Where do you think?" He bent down and brushed the sand off his knees. "I'm going to talk to Faye."

"What?" I said.

"This is what you wanted, isn't it?" said Nathan. "That's why you gave me the book to read."

"Well, yes, but—"

"You think I'm going to make the same mistake as Betsy Cribbins, don't you? You think I'm too scared to tell Faye how I feel."

"Well actually, now that I've had more—"

"You're going to get your way, Robert. I'm going to walk over there right now."

I grabbed his arm and hauled him back down to the sand. "Stop fooling around," I hissed. "Somebody might see you."

"I'm not fooling around." Nathan got to his feet again. "Remember Betsy," he said. "There's no time to lose."

"Nathan, you can't make decisions based on a stupid book!"

He looked down at me. "Why did you give it to me, then?"

Just then Faye began to play "Annie's Song." Under Liam's tutelage, Nathan had learned to hate John Denver with a near-religious fervor, but to my dismay, when Faye sang the opening lines he hummed right along with her.

"Wouldn't it be better to wait until there aren't so many people around?" I said.

Nathan laughed. "I've waited too long already! I see that now."

I thought of Gatsby again, facedown in the swimming pool. "This is an incredibly bad idea," I said.

Faye's lovely voice was floating through the air. I saw a new serenity in Nathan's eyes, and I knew that it was too late. "Sorry, Robert," he said. "I'm not going to be another Betsy Cribbins. No more hiding in the sand dune for me."

With that he began to walk toward the music.

TWENTY-FIVE

My brother used to tell me stories about the musicians who played at CBGB, the grimy club on Manhattan's Lower East Side that was the birthplace of punk rock. A small roster of bands played there, pummeling audiences with their raw energy and sloppy three-chord progressions. The presiding spirit of the place was Iggy Pop. Smashed out of his head on whatever barbarous cocktail of drugs he'd scored backstage, he clung to the microphone stand for dear life, long haired, bare chested, and whippet thin, so wasted he couldn't remember his own lyrics. Members of the crowd hurled beer bottles at him in disgust; he smashed them beneath his boots and rolled around on the broken glass. When he climbed to his feet, shards remained stuck in his back, his punctured skin a tapestry of feral derangement. When the Stooges were on the bill, people came just to watch Iggy's torrid whiplash of self-destruction. He would wade into the crowd, looking for a fight. Sometimes the fight came to him—people would get up onstage and kick the shit out of him, leaving him sprawled motionless in a pool of his own vomit while the band played on.

When my brother told me these stories, I liked to imagine that I was there myself, but watching from a safe distance. In my mind those scenes always unspooled in total silence, like an old black-and-white movie, which gave Iggy's manic disintegration an almost formal, mournful inevitability.

I think about what happened on the evening that Nathan finally spoke to Faye in a similar way. Once he had made up his mind, there was nothing I could do to stop any of it. I just had to watch.

I SCRAMBLED UP the sand dune as Nathan strode across the beach. If I'd given him *Gatsby* instead of V. V. St. Cloud's stupid book, he would have realized what a disastrous mistake he was making. But Nathan was going large, doubling down, and in front of an audience, to boot.

Just then another question occurred to me: What if his plan actually worked?

Nathan and Faye!

Even contemplating the possibility of the two of them together made my stomach lurch in envy. As I watched Nathan approach the group, I realized that whatever happened next, there would be no good outcome for me. I didn't want Nathan to be hurt. But if by some miracle his gambit paid off, I would be so lacerated by jealousy that I wouldn't be able to be pleased for him, either.

I followed Nathan across the sand. I reasoned that nobody was going to notice me if I stayed in the shadows, especially not with the floor show that was about to start.

Nathan walked into the middle of the group until he was standing a few feet in front of Faye. After a few moments she stopped singing, her fingers resting uncertainly on the guitar strings. There was no noise except the distant pulse of the waves. She looked up at Nathan with a quizzical expression.

"Please don't stop," said Nathan. "That was beautiful."

"Hey, I remember you," said Hollis Calhoun.

Nathan didn't even glance in his direction. "Do you know the problem with John Denver?" he asked Faye.

"No," she said. "What is the problem with John Denver?"

"The problem," said Nathan, "is that every song is a fucking question."

I closed my eyes.

"Oh, really," said Faye. She peered at Nathan more closely. "What do you think I should do about that?"

"You should play some songs with answers," said Nathan.

"What's your name?" asked Faye.

"Nathan Tilly."

Faye inclined her head to one side. "Hello, Nathan Tilly," she said. "I haven't seen you around before."

"I work at Fun-A-Lot," Nathan said coolly, as if there weren't a group of people hanging on every word he said. "This is actually my second season there. Last year I was in the kitchen. I was in charge of onions."

There was a pause.

"Uh-huh," said Faye.

"Maybe you noticed them. The onions."

Oh, Nathan, no, I thought.

Faye shrugged. "I don't think so."

"They were always perfectly caramelized," said Nathan.

"Sorry," said Faye.

"Well anyway," said Nathan, recovering gamely, "this year I'm the park mascot."

"Really? You're the dragon?"

Nathan beamed. "That's me," he said.

"I've seen you dancing," said Faye. "You do a nice job. People are always laughing at you."

"You should get to know me better," said Nathan. "I'm a pretty funny guy."

By then some of the other girls in the circle were leaning toward one another, whispering. Hollis was glaring at Nathan with undisguised hostility. But Nathan did not take his eyes off Faye, and Faye did not take her eyes off Nathan.

"What do you want, Nathan Tilly?" asked Faye. "You don't want to talk about John Denver, do you?"

"No," agreed Nathan, "I don't." He was silent for a moment. I circled quietly around the group so I could get a better view. Nathan pulled a pack of cigarettes out of his pocket. He took two and bent down to light them from the fire. He handed one to Faye, who took it hesitantly.

"Thanks," she said.

The two of them smoked in silence for a moment. All those months of stealing his mother's cigarettes were paying dividends now. After Nathan drew the smoke into his mouth he opened his lips and let the smoke linger there for a second before languidly pulling it into his lungs. Each time this maneuver was accompanied by a sultry little twist of his head, but even then he did not relinquish eye contact with Faye. Nathan was smoking like a movie star.

"I've been thinking about you since last year," he said.

"Wait, I know where I've seen this guy before," said one of the other girls. "He was always hanging around in the hallways at school."

"Maybe you do look familiar," said Faye.

"It's been a great summer, so far," said Nathan. "Mainly because I can walk over to the concession stand and see you whenever I want. That's made me pretty happy."

Faye was completely still. "Okay," she said.

"Then I read a book," said Nathan. My stomach performed a

somersault. "And this book made me realize that life is not a dress rehearsal." I recognized the line. Unable to resist such an obvious theatrical metaphor, V. V. St. Cloud had used it more than once in *Star-Crossed*.

Faye said nothing.

"And so, since life *isn't* a dress rehearsal," continued Nathan, "I wanted to invite you for a trip on my dad's lobster boat."

Hollis Calhoun began to laugh—a high-pitched, ugly noise that reminded me of the whinnies of the park's Shetland ponies.

Nathan still didn't take his eyes off Faye. "That's the other thing," he said. "I've been watching these baboons who prance around in front of you every night."

"Oh yes?" said Faye.

"Baboons?" said Hollis.

"They like to show off, but it's just a dumb act," said Nathan. "They want to impress you because you're pretty, that's all. They don't care about you."

Faye looked at him steadily. "But you're different, I suppose."

"I am," agreed Nathan.

"He just called me a *baboon*," said Hollis.

Faye sat back. "You don't know me, Nathan Tilly." I could hear the warning in her voice. "You don't know me at all."

"Sure I do." Nathan was so focused on maintaining eye contact with Faye that he didn't notice that Hollis Calhoun had clambered to his feet and was coming at him, low and hard and fast.

"Nathan!" I yelled, just as Hollis rammed his shoulder into Nathan's ribs. Nathan's head twisted sideways as his body hit the sand. A second later, Hollis landed on top of him. He leaned forward, his face so close to Nathan's that it looked like they were about to kiss. It was a move I knew well.

"Stay there," hissed Hollis. And then, to my horror, he raised his head and looked in my direction. Nathan hadn't heard my warning shout, but Hollis had. "Who's out there?" he yelled.

I've never wanted to run further or faster than I did just then, but I wasn't going to abandon Nathan. I took a deep breath and slowly walked out of the shadows. "Hello, Hollis," I said.

"I might have guessed," said Hollis with a sneer.

"Hey," said Faye. "You're Sam's kid."

I blinked in astonishment. Faye knew who I was!

"It's Robert, right?" she said.

She even knew my name! I nodded dumbly.

Hollis had climbed off Nathan, who was stretched out on the sand, gasping to pull air back into his lungs. Now he approached me, that familiar glint of malice in his eye. "Are you two clowns in on this together?"

"In on what?" I asked.

"Whatever stupid stunt your friend is trying to pull," said Hollis. "Interrupting our party and bothering people with his dumb pickup lines." He pulled his lips back in an ugly grin. "Is there anything *you* want to say?" He grabbed my arm and squeezed it hard.

"Let him go, Hollis," said Faye.

Hollis knew that all eyes were on him. "That little prick called me a baboon." He nodded at Nathan, who had rolled away from us, his face half-buried in the sand.

"So?" said Faye. "Just forget it."

Hollis let go of my arm and idly cuffed me on the back of the head. "Hey, Tommy," he said. Another kid got to his feet. I recognized him from school. He was one of the goons Hollis hung out with. "Here," said Hollis, shoving me toward him. I collided with the boy's chest. It felt as if I had been thrown against a brick wall. "Let's take these boys for a swim."

I looked toward Faye for help, but she was staring at the sand in front of her. She did not look up as Nathan and I were hauled away.

Moments later we were moving down the beach toward the ocean. The kid called Tommy had me in a fierce arm lock, which he twisted a little tighter every couple of steps. Hollis had wrapped an enormous arm around Nathan's body and was dragging him across the sand. It was astonishing how quickly it became cold and dark as we left the warmth of the fire behind. I glanced back at the flickering light. The other kids were still sitting around the flames. None of them had moved.

We scuttled awkwardly across the sand in our ungainly twosomes.

"Some people just don't ever learn," grunted Hollis as he hauled Nathan toward the water's edge. "That stunt you pulled in the locker room got me out of being held back in middle school, so I left you alone last year. You know, as a reward. But this?" He cuffed the back of Nathan's head. "It's like you *want* the attention. You came looking for it."

I could hear the ocean grow louder, and when the waves lapped over my feet for the first time I caught my breath in surprise at how cold the water was. Tommy twisted my arm until I fell forward onto my knees, just as another wave rolled in. The water crashed against me, soaking me up to my chest.

Tommy looked across at Hollis. "Now what?" he shouted.

Nathan was kneeling in the water, where Hollis had dropped him.

"We should wash out their filthy little mouths," said Hollis. He lifted Nathan up by his shirt and dragged him a few steps further forward into the surf. Nathan's arms dangled limply beneath him. As the next big wave rolled in, Hollis grabbed Nathan's hair and yanked his head back so that the water hit him full in the face. Nathan began to cough, but Hollis held him steady and waited for the

ALEX GEORGE

next wave. When it came, he pulled Nathan's head back again and another wall of freezing seawater smashed into him.

Tommy dragged me further into the waves. As we moved forward I began to struggle. His fingers were in my hair and he pushed me down. My ears filled with the roar of the ocean, and then the water hit me.

The shock of the wave's impact obliterated everything else. The back of my nose erupted with the power of a well-executed uppercut. Ice-cold saltwater filled my mouth. It flushed through my ears and filled up my eyes. I could not breathe. In my panic I inhaled some of the ocean into my lungs. I struggled and fought, but Tommy's hands remained on the back of my neck, holding me down. Beneath the waves, the ocean was eerily silent. Then I was hauled out of the water. I gasped as I pulled air into my lungs. My whole body was shaking with cold.

"Having fun yet?" shouted Tommy. When the next wave rolled in, he plunged my head back beneath the water again.

I tried to escape, but he was too strong for me. I twisted my head toward Nathan and Hollis. Hollis was holding Nathan's head beneath the waves, that familiar smirk on his face. Nathan hadn't made a sound from the moment that Hollis had first hit him.

As the submersions continued, the cold crept deeper into my bones. My teeth had begun to chatter ferociously. Just as I was starting to wonder whether Tommy and Hollis would ever get bored of their vicious little game, there was a yell from somewhere behind us.

"Hey!"

Tommy straightened up warily, pulling me up with him. Faye was striding across the sand toward us.

"What are you doing?" she demanded.

Hollis grinned at her. "Quick swimming lesson."

"Jesus, Hollis, you're drowning them." Faye ran a hand through her hair. "What is *wrong* with you?"

"They asked for it," said Hollis.

"But they're just kids, for God's sake."

"So?" said Hollis.

"So there's no need to be a *complete* asshole."

At this Hollis shrugged and dropped Nathan into the water. Nathan slowly got to his feet. Tommy let go of my shirt. The four of us stood there with the freezing surf washing over our ankles, all watching Faye. She looked at me and then at Nathan. "Are you guys all right?" she asked.

I glanced at Nathan. "We're fine," I said.

"Faye—" began Nathan, but she held up her hand.

"No," she said quickly. "No more from you." She turned back to Hollis. "You need to leave them alone now," she told him. "Come back to the fire."

Hollis took a step away from Nathan, as if the half-drowned boy on the sand were nothing to do with him. "We were done, anyway," he yawned.

Faye turned and began to walk back up the beach. Hollis and Tommy followed. Nathan and I watched them go. Neither of us said a word. Only once they had reached the fire—we could hear the distant cheering and whooping—did Nathan turn and look at me. He was bedraggled and soaked to the skin.

To my stupefaction, he smiled at me.

"She came to save us," he said.

TWENTY-SIX

We slowly made our way along the beach, our sodden clothes clinging to our skin. More than anything in the world, I wanted to be warm. I told Nathan that he would die of pneumonia if he spent the night on the Ferris wheel in his wet clothes. He didn't argue. We climbed onto our bikes and pedaled back to my house in silence. My fingers were so cold that I could barely hold on to the handlebars. To my relief, my mother was asleep on the couch in front of *The Rockford Files*, and we managed to creep upstairs without disturbing her. We set up the cot in my bedroom, just as we had done two winters ago. It had never felt so good to climb into a warm bed. I switched off the light, and we lay there in the dark.

"So," said Nathan. "How do you think that went?"

"Let's see," I said. "Hollis used you as a punching bag, I almost got my arm twisted off, and we nearly drowned. Apart from that, it was perfect."

"Always with the negative," said Nathan.

"And you invited her for a ride in the *lobster boat!*"

"What's wrong with that?"

I sighed. "Did you ever go out in it with your father?"

Nathan shook his head. "We never got around to it," he admitted.

"Yeah, I didn't think so." Lobster boats were stark and utilitarian, designed for hard work and rough seas, not amorous excursions. "It was a strange choice for a first date, that's all."

"It was the first thing that popped into my head," said Nathan.

"Admit it, the whole thing was humiliating." I was also worried that the evening had put me firmly back on Hollis Calhoun's radar. The last thing I wanted was for him to hunt me down again when the school year began and resume old hostilities. The only good to have come from our misadventure on the beach was that Nathan's obsession with Faye had reached its inevitable conclusion. I admired the way he had marched up to her and fearlessly made his play, but I was also relieved that the charade was finally over.

"I think Faye likes me," said Nathan.

I was momentarily lost for words. "What makes you say that?" I asked.

"She came to rescue us."

"Only after we'd nearly drowned!"

"But she came. That means something."

I took a deep breath. "Nathan, look. I heard the conversation around the fire."

He was silent for a long time. "All of it?" he said eventually.

"Onions, John Denver, all of it."

"Huh," said Nathan.

"You did your best. But face it. She's not interested in you."

"You're wrong," said Nathan. "There was a definite spark between us."

He was so desperately in love with Faye that he was unwilling, or unable, to contemplate the idea that she might not like him back. He was going to marshal his considerable willpower to make himself believe that his courage would be rewarded and that everything was going to work out all right.

It didn't help that Faye had been kind to Nathan. At first I was shocked when she had let Hollis and his goon drag us away from the group, but now I saw it as an act of mercy on her part: she had spared Nathan the agony of being humiliated in front of that crowd. But even such a small kindness was liable to complicate things. *No more from you*, she had told Nathan at the water's edge, but it had not been enough. He was absolutely determined not to take a hint.

"But Faye didn't hang around on the beach with you," I said. "She went back to the fire with Hollis."

"She called Hollis an asshole," said Nathan.

"Well, Hollis *is* an asshole."

"She didn't call *me* an asshole."

"And you think that means she likes you more?"

"Obviously," said Nathan.

I switched the light back on and looked at him. "Maybe you've forgotten what else she said."

"What?"

"She said: *They're just kids, for God's sake.*"

We stared at each other in silence.

"Oh, I get it," said Nathan.

"What?"

Nathan rolled over so that his back was toward me. "You're jealous," he said over his shoulder.

"Don't be stupid."

"You are. You're jealous."

"How can I be jealous of something that doesn't exist?"

"It exists, Robert. You just don't want to believe it."

I switched off the light and pulled the bedcovers over my head.

ALEX GEORGE

———

THE FOLLOWING MORNING Nathan and I got dressed and ate breakfast without looking at each other. The jagged shards of the argument the night before lay between us, raw and treacherous. The new
morning had not diminished their capacity to hurt. I was still smart-
ing from Nathan's accusations of jealousy, largely because he was
right, even if not in the way that he imagined.

I *was* jealous—but of Faye, not Nathan. I was bored of listening
to him talk about her all the time. I wanted to go back to the old
days when we used to have lunch in the school cafeteria and just
talk, when his gaze was not always drifting over my shoulder in
search of her. I wanted to hang out at the mill again, to be friends
together. I didn't want to spend evenings hiding behind a sand dune,
watching Nathan wish for impossible things.

We cycled to the park in silence.

That day on my lunch break I walked over to the concession
stand. I knew Nathan would be there working the crowds, and I
wanted to see how Faye reacted to his antics now. I pulled the hood
of my monk's costume low over my head and loitered just out of her
line of vision. She was at the cash register, taking orders and smiling at customers, looking as ravishing as ever. Nathan was there
too, entertaining the customers and glancing toward the front of
the line.

Faye did not look in his direction once.

Still the dragon danced on.

WHEN I ARRIVED AT the Ferris wheel that evening to send Nathan
off for another night lofted high in the air, he was nowhere to be
seen. I sat in the lowest pod and wondered if our fight that morning

meant that he wasn't going to show up. Perhaps he had noticed Faye's muted reaction to his performance that afternoon, and he'd gone back to Sebbanquik Point to lick his wounds. I stared up at the stars.

It didn't seem likely.

Sure enough, after a few minutes he appeared, whistling cheerfully.

"All ready?" I asked.

"I brought my cassette deck," said Nathan. "I'm going to have a little party."

"Something to celebrate?"

"I think so. Even if you don't."

"Listen, Nathan. I watched Faye this afternoon while you worked the line at the concession stand. She didn't look at you. She never even cracked a smile."

"You'd like that, wouldn't you?"

I shook my head. "I know what I saw."

"Why can't you just be happy for me, Robert?"

"I'm trying to *help*," I said.

"If you want to help, just get me into the sky and then go home."

"Fine," I hissed.

Nathan slung his backpack over his shoulder and climbed on board. I stormed back to the control booth. After half a rotation of the wheel, I switched off the engine.

I looked up and saw the flicker of Nathan's flashlight high above me. A long stretch of the coastline was visible from the Ferris wheel's highest point. I realized that Nathan would be able to see the distant glow of Faye's bonfire on the beach. I thought of Gatsby standing on the lawn of his mansion, gazing out across the water toward East Egg and that green light at the end of Daisy Buchanan's dock. Like Gatsby, Nathan was watching and vigilant, alone with his dreams.

Just then Karen Carpenter's voice filled the air.

Such a feeling's coming over me
There is wonder in most everything I see

I stared up at the Ferris wheel. The pod began to rock back and forth as Nathan joined in the chorus.

I'm on top of the world
Looking down on creation

I doubted whether the hinges that connected the pod to the wheel itself were designed to withstand that kind of movement.

"Nathan!" I called out. "Stop it! You're going to break something!"

The pod kept on swinging, as regular as a metronome. I guessed Nathan couldn't hear me over the music. Either that, or he was ignoring me. I turned to leave, furious with him. As I was making my way back to the parking lot, a scream of uncut fear ripped through the night air.

It was the sort of noise that I had previously heard only during the Saturday night horror double features in the Haverford cinema. In the safety and comfort of a dark movie theater, with a carton of popcorn by my side and people all around me, the sound of human terror always made my skin crawl deliciously. It was another matter to hear the same full-throated scream in a deserted amusement park.

I guessed that one of the hinges on Nathan's pod must have snapped. I pictured it dangling precariously in midair and began to run back toward the Ferris wheel as fast as I could. As I pelted down the gravel paths the scream came again, and I realized with a cold jolt that the noise hadn't come from the Ferris wheel at all. I stopped in the darkness, too scared to move. Then a low, keening wail began, fattened by terror. I had never heard anything like it in my life. Whoever was making that noise needed help. Swallowing my fear, I moved toward the sound. The moaning grew louder. I quickened my pace and peeled off the path into the teepees and plastic cacti of the miniature golf course. I heard a hysterical sobbing and then the unmistakable sound of someone being violently sick.

I spotted movement a few yards ahead of me and stopped. I squinted into the darkness.

Hollis Calhoun was stumbling back and forth on the putting green of the sixth hole. His trousers were around his ankles. One hand was covering his eyes, the other was clutching his groin.

"Hollis! Hollis, it's me," I called out. "It's Robert Carter. What's the matter? What happened?"

At the sound of my voice, Hollis turned and began to lumber toward me, his eyes wild and unfocused.

"What's wrong?" I said.

Hollis's mouth opened and closed wordlessly. All he could manage was a small whimper of distress.

"Did you see something?" I asked.

Finally he pointed toward Pocahontas.

"The statue?" I said.

He nodded. A tiny bubble of spittle emerged out of one side of his mouth and then popped. I looked toward the Indian princess but couldn't see anything wrong. "Pull your pants up," I said. "I'll go and take a look."

Hollis bent down and did as he was told. Once he had rebuckled his belt, I walked over to the statue. My heart clattered against my chest. Hollis did not take his eyes off me. Standing a safe distance away, I bent down to peer inside Pocahontas's mouth.

A familiar face stared back at me.

———

IT HAD BEEN NEARLY two years since I'd first encountered Nathan's dead mongoose in the Tillys' kitchen, and Philippe now looked decidedly the worse for wear. Most of his fur had fallen out, and he had lost an eyeball; the one that remained was mottled and discolored and was glaring ferociously at me. His mouth was open and his teeth were bared. They appeared to be glistening darkly with blood. Hollis must have unzipped in front of Pocahontas's mouth, as usual; discovered that there was something already in the hole; bent down to see what it was; and come face-to-face with Nathan's dead, one-eyed pet.

I reached into Pocahontas's mouth and tugged the mongoose out. My fingers were covered in a sticky red substance. It was ketchup. I held Philippe at arm's length. The stench of putrefaction was unspeakable. I dropped the body on the ground. Hollis took a step backward and began to sob loudly.

"Hollis?" He hadn't heard me. "*Hollis.*" I shook his arm. "We need to go now, okay? And, Hollis? It's really important that we're *super quiet.*"

He looked at me then.

"My dad is still in the office," I explained. "You don't want to have to explain what you're doing here this late, do you?" Hollis blinked and then shook his head. "Come on, then." Without letting go of his arm, I steered him onto the path and we made our way back toward the front of the park. Hollis stumbled occasionally in the dark, but he kept up with me. His breathing was labored, and he emitted an occasional sob of bewilderment, but otherwise he was quiet. His right hand clutched involuntarily at his groin from time to time. Finally we arrived at the side gate. I turned to him.

"You okay?"

A fat tear emerged from his left eye and began to roll down his cheek. He shook his head.

I patted him on the arm. "Go home, get some sleep." This was asking the impossible, I realized. I knew if I put my penis into the mouth of an Indian princess and unexpectedly encountered the fangs of a rotting mongoose, I would never sleep again.

Hollis began to cry in earnest then, big, heaving sobs of distress.

"Go home," I said again, glancing anxiously in the direction of the office. I helped him onto his bike and watched as he wobbled off across the asphalt. At the front entrance to the parking lot he paused for a moment, and then, to my dismay, turned around and began to pedal back toward me. He pulled up in front of me and looked me in the eye. That was when he spoke for the first time.

"If you tell anyone about this," he said thickly, "anyone at all, *ever*, I will hunt you down and I will kill you."

He pushed off again. I watched until he disappeared out of the parking lot. I wondered if Hollis had any idea what had happened to him.

Nathan Tilly had just exacted a very precise revenge.

THE FOLLOWING MORNING, I got to the park earlier than usual. As soon as Nathan's pod reached the ground I threw back the security bolt and flung open the door. "What kind of a stunt was that?" I demanded.

"Stunt?" yawned Nathan.

"Last night Hollis was stumbling around the mini golf course, screaming his head off."

"Ah." Nathan's eyes flashed in satisfaction.

"I'm surprised you didn't hear him yelling."

"I wish I had," said Nathan.

"Look, Nathan," I said. "What Hollis did at the beach—that was bad. And what he was doing to the Pocahontas statue—well, that was bad, too."

"It was *very* bad," said Nathan.

"So, I get it, okay? But *what you did*, Nathan! It's not right. He won't ever be the same."

"Good," sniffed Nathan.

"And the ketchup!"

Nathan looked pleased. "The little touch that means so much."

"It's not right," I said again. "And what if he guesses you're behind it? Have you thought about that?"

"Don't worry. Hollis may have suspicions, but that will be all. He'll never know for sure, because he'll never want to talk about it." Nathan grinned at me. "It's going to drive him crazy."

He was probably right. There was no way Hollis Calhoun was ever going to start asking questions about what had happened. Still, I worried that my own presence in the park so late might incriminate me in some way. I spent the morning wondering whether I was going to regret helping him the night before.

When my break came, I walked over to the mini golf course. I wanted to see Hollis for myself. I stopped a safe distance away and watched him for several minutes.

Hollis was not doing well. The obnoxious, arrogant bully I knew had vanished overnight. Now he meekly handed over the putters and golf balls, unwilling to look anyone in the eye. Once or twice he glanced nervously over his shoulder. There were dark rings of exhaustion beneath his eyes. He probably hadn't slept.

I walked up to the hut. Hollis stiffened as I approached.

"Hey, Hollis," I said.

"What do you want?" he mumbled.

"Just checking in." I beamed at him. "I wanted to see how you were doing."

He looked at me sourly. "I'm fine."

"Really? Okay, then." I turned to go.

"Wait." There were clouds of doubt behind his eyes. "I did have one question," he said, so quietly I could hardly hear him.

"Shoot," I said.

"Where do you think that thing came from?"

I shrugged affably. "No idea," I said.

Hollis eyed me suspiciously. The beast had not appeared by accident, he knew that much. All those glances behind him suggested that he was afraid something else unpleasant might happen.

I thought about all the misery that Hollis Calhoun had inflicted on me over the years. Watching his discomfort felt like a small but hard-earned reward.

I sauntered off, whistling as I went.

TWENTY-SEVEN

N ine years earlier, a hill on the western side of the park grounds had been cleared of trees and a large sign appeared: **YOUR NEXT FUN-FILLED ATTRACTION COMING SOON!** My father had spent months designing a forest of interconnected tree houses linked with rope bridges. He had visions of children clambering over one another, breathing in the fresh Maine air as they played. There would be slides, ladders, trampolines, lookout posts, old-fashioned adventures—and not a single motor or electrical circuit that could break down. The attraction's crowning glory would be two zip lines that sent people flying from the summit of the hill down to the bottom in a glorious whoosh of adrenaline.

The season the sign went up was the wettest summer in Maine on record. My father looked out of his office window at the deserted park, trying not to think about all the money he was losing and wondering if he would be able to open again the following year. He was, just, but that one ruinous summer had scuppered his dreams of ever building those tree houses. He decided to leave the sign where it was, a reminder to himself of the perils of betting on the Maine weather.

My father had had plenty of practice at making the best of a bad situation, and he realized that the newly cleared hill made a perfect outdoor amphitheater. From that year on, after the close of normal business on the Fourth of July, the gates of Fun-A-Lot reopened and welcomed the public for a giant fireworks display, free of charge. Rockets were launched into the sky from the top of the hill at a safe distance from the spectators watching below.

My father loved to plan the fireworks. He spent hours looking at catalogs, choosing rockets. During the show he scurried around in the darkness, clipboard in one hand and stopwatch in the other, moving between the marked and numbered fireworks. Lewis followed him with a huge box of matches, waiting for my father's nod before lighting each fuse.

Liam rarely visited the park after he became too sick to work there, but he always came to see the fireworks. July 4, 1978, was his birthday, and he liked to joke that the display was all for him. He sat in his wheelchair, his face turned upward to the night sky, an expression of pure joy on his face. I knew that when my father sat down to plan each year's fireworks, he had only one spectator in mind. But without Liam to delight, he had lost his appetite for the job. That summer he asked Lewis to arrange the display, and Lewis had co-opted me as his assistant.

July 4 dawned bright and beautiful. When I woke, I lay in my bed and watched the morning sun stream through the window. As a million tiny dust motes tangoed restlessly above me, I thought about my brother. Like Christmas, our Independence Day celebrations had always been freighted with unspoken grief as we all privately wondered if this birthday would be Liam's last. Now that he was gone, I discovered that the pain had not diminished; there was just a change in the flavor of my sorrow, a sideways shift from fearful speculation to numb regret.

Liam loved his birthdays more than anything. He savored every minute of the day, exulting in his own specialness. Such self-obsession in anyone else would have been insufferable, but Liam's enthusiasm was so good-natured, so infectious, that it was impossible not to go along with his idea that, actually, for those twenty-four hours he really *was* the most important person on the planet. Every birthday morning that I could remember had begun with a shockingly loud blast of something fast and fractious from Liam's bedroom. Last year it had been "I Wanna Be Sedated" by the Ramones. My mother had stood at the top of the stairs, wincing as she listened to Joey Ramone sing. She turned to look at my father. "Well," she had sighed, "at least that's finally one of Liam's songs I can agree with."

I glanced at my alarm clock. Usually by now we would have been watching Liam open his presents—which he always did with unabashed glee, loving everything. But today the house was silent and still, and the absence of joy was absolute and heartbreaking. There was nothing I would have liked more than to vaporize my regret with a few blasts of demented, thrashing guitar, but there would be no more early-morning punk anthems, no more hoots of delight at unexpected gifts. Last year there had been four of us in the house; now it was just my mother and me. I climbed out of bed and tiptoed along the hall. I reached out and twisted the handle of my parents' bedroom door, but it was locked.

"Mom?" I whispered.

There was no answer.

I went downstairs and fixed myself breakfast. Soon after that I climbed on my bike and set off for work.

My father had rearranged the work roster so that I could spend the day helping Lewis get ready for the fireworks display. An hour before the gates opened, Lewis pulled into the parking lot in his battered pickup. There was a mountain of unmarked cardboard boxes piled up high in the back.

"Those are the fireworks?" I asked.

"Those are the fireworks," grunted Lewis as he hauled one of the boxes off the bed of the pickup.

"Shouldn't they be in proper packaging? With instructions and everything?"

"Most likely," agreed Lewis. "Here, take that one, will you?"

As I picked up the box he was pointing at, the smell of cordite hit the back of my nostrils. "Are you sure these are safe?" I said, wrinkling my nose.

"The only thing dangerous about these," said Lewis, "is that they might give me a heart attack carrying them to the top of that damn hill. Come on."

By ten o'clock the park was bathed in sunshine, as if the weather were trying to do the patriotic thing by us all. Lewis and I spent the day hauling the fireworks up to the launching site and arranging them for that night's show. Lewis had sketched out diagrams and made a timetable for when each rocket should be lit. By the time we had finished, the top of the hill was carpeted with multicolored warheads. Lewis was going to light the fuses while I carried the clipboard and the stopwatch. It was also my job to wield the flashlight, so Lewis had both hands free.

As the day went on I found myself thinking about my family, what was left of it. I wished, more than anything in the world, that my father would quit the couch in his office and come home. It was my bad luck that he couldn't be thankful for his one remaining son. Instead I was just a reminder to him of the future that Liam would never have.

Every year on Liam's birthday my mother had given me a small gift—"something to open," she called it, a little treat to cheer me up in case I was despondent about all the attention that my brother was getting. (It had apparently never occurred to her that my feelings of fraternal insignificance might not be limited to Liam's birthday.) There had been no gift this year, of course, so I felt more invisible than ever. My mother had not answered my knock on her bedroom door, and my father was nowhere to be seen. But it was Liam's birthday, and I needed to talk about him, to remember him. Once Lewis and I had finished setting up the fireworks, I walked down the hill to my father's office and pushed open the door.

My father was sitting at his desk, staring into space. His fingers were resting on the rim of an empty glass. Even though he had been living there for several weeks, the office looked just the same as it always did. There was a large fortification of filing cabinets along one side of the room. (My father was a born bureaucrat, a meticulous keeper of records. Every piece of paper that passed across his desk was date-stamped, Xeroxed several times, and then filed in different places in a complex data-retrieval system of his own devising.) The walls were adorned with dusty plaques from the local chamber of commerce. The insincerity of those abbreviated, price-per-word tributes was obvious even to me. Pressed behind a sheet of glass on the wall above the desk there was a yellowing, two-page profile of my father that had run in the *Haverford Gazette* in June 1960 to mark his first year in charge. There was a photograph of my parents standing proudly in front of the park gates. My father was holding a plastic sword above his head, a goofy grin on his face. My mother was wearing a short dress with a large floral-print design. She looked pretty and was smiling, her hands resting contentedly on her extravagantly swollen belly. Liam was born a month later.

"Hey, Dad," I said.

My father took his hand away from the glass. "Robert," he said. "Is something wrong?"

"It's Liam's birthday," I said. "So I wanted to see you."

He gave a short nod but said nothing.

I looked out of the window. "Quiet today."

"Ah, yes. People prefer to celebrate their independence at home, being driven crazy by their families. But we'll be busy tonight."

"Lewis has enough explosives to blow up half of Maine."

"I'm pleased to hear it," said my father.

"Are you going to be there?"

"I don't know, Robert," he sighed. "I don't know if I can."

"Liam always loved the fireworks," I said. "He'd want you to be there."

"It doesn't much matter what Liam wants anymore, does it?"

I stared at him. "Of course it matters. That's how we'll keep his memory alive."

"Oh, Robert, you and your memories."

"Today is *still* his birthday," I said stubbornly.

My father sighed and reached for the glass in front of him. He spun it around his index finger, caught it, and then twirled it again. Each time the glass landed back on the desk with a heavy thump. "You want a memory?" he said. "I'll give you a memory. The day Liam was born was the happiest and most terrifying day of my life. Your mother was two weeks overdue. She was as big as a barn, and miserable. She made me drive her to the hospital. She marched into the maternity ward and *demanded* that they take that baby out, right there and then. And the doctors did what they were told. They found her a bed and induced labor. But Liam wasn't budging without a fight." He paused. "We went in on July second. By the time the doctors finally got him out, it was Independence Day. I should have known then that he was going to be trouble. To be honest, I'm not sure your mother ever quite forgave him for it." He paused. "She was amazing, though. She was in a world of pain, Robert, but you never would have known it. I was by her side all the way through, and she never complained once. Just squeezed my hand a little harder when it really hurt. She was so brave and so beautiful."

I closed my eyes. *So come home*, I wanted to say.

"And when Liam finally appeared—well. He was *furious*. He yelled so loud that he got a bubble on his lung. They kept him in the intensive care unit for three days, just to keep an eye on him. They put him in a plastic box. There were all these tubes going in and out of him, a machine that monitored his heartbeat, the works. He was so tightly wrapped up in blankets that you could hardly see him." My father smiled. "The nurses kept waking him up every couple of hours to check he was all right and to stick another needle into his leg. Your mother was about ready to kill them all by the end. But Liam was strong. The other babies in the ICU had all been born prematurely. Your brother was twice as big as they were. He was just there as a precaution, but the rest of them were fighting for their lives." He paused. "It taught me that there are always people worse off than you. I remember looking at those other parents and seeing the terror on their faces. I felt guilty that Liam was so healthy. But grateful, too, of course." He looked away. "It all came back to me when we were in the hospital last winter. I tried to be thankful that at least he didn't die when he was a newborn, in the ICU, before we could get to know him."

"Did it work?"

"The being thankful?" My father sighed. "Not really."

When I closed the office door a few moments later, he was still sitting at his desk, staring into space, remembering his baby boy.

TWENTY-EIGHT

Lewis had put me in charge of keeping watch over the fireworks until that night. I patrolled my turf diligently, went over the checklist, and made sure each rocket was correctly numbered and in the right place. I checked the batteries in my flashlight five or six times.

On the far side of the park, the highest point of the roller coaster was visible above the treetops. The contours of its vast, lopsided parabola reminded me of a giant, landlocked whale. Every eight minutes I watched the convoy of carriages trundle slowly up to the crest of the ride, pause for the briefest moment, and then plummet toward the ground. The screams of the riders marked the passing of the day as regularly as any clock.

As the evening approached, people began to congregate around the picnic tables at the bottom of the hill. Multicolored coolers were lugged onto the grass and prodigious quantities of food and drink were produced. By the time the sky had begun to darken, every square inch of grass was covered by tarpaulins. There was laughter from somewhere below me. I looked down to see the dragon dancing through the maze of picnicking families, waving an American flag. People cheered as he made his way through the crowd.

"That boy sure loves his job."

Lewis was standing beside me. We watched as Nathan borrowed a guest's rolled-up umbrella and pretended that it was a rifle. He marched up and down in front of the crowd, goose-stepping crazily and saluting as he went.

"He does," I agreed.

"Go grab something to eat," said Lewis. "I'll man the fort here."

I set off gratefully down the hill. There was a relaxed atmosphere in the park, quite different from the usual frenetic daytime pace. I kept my eyes open for my father as I walked through the crowds. Usually on these evenings he liked to stand by the front gate and welcome guests as they arrived, enjoying his role as generous host, but tonight he was nowhere to be seen. I tried not to feel too disappointed.

As always, the concession stand was doing excellent business. My stomach rumbled as I waited in line to order food. I realized that I hadn't eaten all day. When I got to the window, Faye was looking down at me. It was the first time I'd come face-to-face with her since the night on the beach.

"How's it going, Faye?" I asked. "Remember me?"

"Sure, Robert Carter, I remember you," she said.

"Could I get a hot dog? With extra onions?"

"Ah, the famous onions." As I handed over my money, she said, "Can I ask you something about your friend Nathan?"

"Sure," I said.

She gave me my change. "What's his deal?" she asked. "He's been hanging around here more than ever."

"The thing about Nathan," I said, "is that he's a very optimistic person."

Those pretty blue eyes looked down at me appraisingly. "Uh-huh."

"This may sound crazy," I said, "but he thinks you like him."

"He's a funny little guy, huh," said Faye after a moment.

I took a deep breath. "Will you tell him he's wrong? Please? I've tried, but he won't listen to me."

Faye gave me a small smile. "My shift ends when the fireworks start. Tell him to come and find me then."

"Only please be kind," I said.

Her eyes softened. "Here's your hot dog. With extra onions."

I walked through the park. I didn't taste a bite of my hot dog. Guilt had left me dry-mouthed. I told myself that I'd done Nathan a favor. I told myself that now there would be no more humiliating encounters on the beach, no more dunkings in the freezing ocean. But it was a lie. I hadn't done it for Nathan. I'd done it for me. I wanted my friend back.

Just then I saw Nathan ambling toward me. He was still carrying the American flag I'd seen him with earlier.

"There you are," I said, hoping that I didn't look as guilty as I felt. "How's it going?"

The dragon gave me two thumbs up.

"You're having a busy night."

This time I got a happy nod and a small dance step.

"Nobody's listening, Nathan," I said. "You can talk to me, you know."

The dragon shook its head and wagged a finger at me.

"Just for the record," I said stiffly, "you're being incredibly annoying."

Nathan put his fists up to his eyes and pretended to cry, swaying from side to side. Behind him, his tail swung back and forth.

"If you're finished, I have a message for you. From Faye."

Nathan went very still.

"She wants you to go and find her at the concession stand when the fireworks begin. She has something she wants to talk to you about." I clapped him on the back. "You'll go and see her?"

The dragon nodded vigorously.

"All right, then," I said. I looked at my watch. "I have to get back to Lewis."

Nathan nodded again, and then turned and took off down the path, a spring of excitement in his step. I hurried up the hill, hoping that Faye would be gentle with him.

A HALF HOUR LATER we were ready to begin. Lewis took a box of extra-long matches from his overalls and checked his watch. "Right," he said. "Let's give these folks a fireworks display we can all be proud of. God bless America, and all that jazz." With that he squatted down and struck the first match. His face was illuminated briefly in its sulfuric glow. Then he touched the match to the base of the first rocket and scuttled backward as the fuse caught. The flame hissed up the dangling string, and then the firework launched into the night air with a satisfying whoosh. After a couple of seconds there was a loud bang over our heads, and the night sky exploded into a thousand glittering pinpoints of light. The crowd at the bottom of the hill broke into excited applause. Almost at once, the firework faded away into nothingness. I was still staring into the sky when Lewis snapped at me.

"Robert! Flashlight!"

He was squatting down by the adjacent rocket, ready with the next match. As soon as I pointed the beam of light at him, he lit the fuse. I stopped looking upward after that. We soon developed a rhythm as we worked our way along the lines of fireworks. I ticked the rockets off my checklist and called out the seconds between each launch. Lewis inched his way along, igniting fuses and then retreating to a safe distance, leaving a trail of spent matches in his wake. The sky was a rainbow of color. Beneath us, the watching crowd gasped as each new rocket exploded overhead.

We had set the fireworks out in parallel ranks across the hilltop. The final phase would, Lewis had promised me, set the sky alight in a blaze of red, white, and blue—a suitably patriotic finale. As we turned to address the last line of rockets, out of the corner of my eye I caught some movement in the shadows to my right. The far side of the hill, out of sight from where the crowds were sitting, was untouched woodland. It was on the periphery of those trees that I saw something move. I wanted to shine my flashlight down there, but I couldn't leave Lewis scrabbling around in the dark. Seconds later, the next rocket exploded high above us and illuminated the sky in shimmering cyclones of brilliant white. I glanced back down toward the edge of the forest. There, captured in the fleeting light as clearly as if it were the middle of a summer afternoon, I saw Faye walking backward, her arms stretched out in front of her.

Advancing toward her with sinister, lumbering intent was the dragon.

At that moment the sky returned to darkness and Faye and Nathan vanished back into the shadows. I stood staring at the spot where they had been.

"Robert!" called Lewis sharply.

The flashlight was hanging limply in my hand, forgotten. I directed the beam back at Lewis. He struck another match. Seconds later the next rocket shot into the sky. My eyes were already fixed on the edge of the woods. When the explosion came, Faye and Nathan were caught in the flickering constellation of light, their bodies casting faint shadows across the grass in every direction.

Nathan had caught up with Faye. He was standing in front of her, his wings raised toward her in supplication. Then, to my horror, he stepped forward and tried to grab her. Faye pushed Nathan away with both hands, and he staggered back under the force of her shove. Then the two of them disappeared again into darkness.

I pointed the flashlight at Lewis. "Keep that beam on my hands!" he called. "I can't see a damn thing!"

"Sorry," I muttered. I clutched the flashlight tightly, trying to make sense of what I had just seen.

When the next firework exploded high above us, I looked down toward the forest again. Faye had disappeared, and Nathan had fallen to his knees. The dragon's snout was pressed into the ground. It looked as if he was praying, but it was too late for that.

"Damn," muttered Lewis. He was glaring at the next rocket in line. "Nothing's happening." He began to move back toward it.

"Shouldn't you wait?" I asked. Lewis had told me countless times never to return to a firework once it had been lit.

"We don't have time!" he said. "Come closer, will you, and shine the light over here." I directed the flashlight at the base of the inert rocket. Lewis squinted at it. "I think we got ourselves a dud," he sighed. He pulled out another match and struck it. "Let me see if I can—"

He never finished his sentence. The rocket exploded with an enormous bang, snapping Lewis's head back as if he had been punched on the chin. It missed his face by inches. His instinctive recoil caused him to stagger backward, and as he tried to regain his balance, his fingers let go of the burning match. The naked flame arced through the air until it landed inside a cardboard box that lay a few feet behind where we were standing.

The box was full of extra fireworks.

"Aw, shit," said Lewis.

There was a noise like a very loud cough, accompanied by a muted flash. Then the air was filled with a furious screaming sound as a rocket tried to launch itself out of the box. A second later there was a brilliant eruption of white light.

"Move back!" cried Lewis.

But I could not move. I watched, hypnotized, as the chain reaction of detonations continued to rage, pummeling the insides of the box. Within seconds the cardboard was obliterated. Without the box to contain them, rockets began to explode in every direction. They had been stacked horizontally, and so shot out a few inches above the ground, rather than flying into the sky. Some scudded harmlessly into the nearby grass, but one or two disappeared over the side of the hill and exploded just above the heads of the watching crowd, dangerously close. There was a chorus of frightened shouts as parents dove to protect their children. More rockets escaped from the box and flew in unpredictable trajectories over the crowd. People began to scatter, heading for the safety of the trees as coruscating whirlwinds of fire showered down on them.

"What should we do?" I yelled to Lewis.

But Lewis didn't seem to have heard me. He was standing very still, and then his right hand shot up to his chest. He frowned, tilting his head to one side. He opened his mouth as if to say something, but no sound came out. Then he fell to his knees.

"Lewis!" I shouted.

He turned toward me, an expression of untold sadness on his face. Then his eyes rolled back in his head and he collapsed forward onto the grass.

TWENTY-NINE

It was the same hospital.

On my last visit we had exited slowly through the front entrance, blinking into the cold winter night. No more could be done for us. This time, though, there was still a life to save.

A phalanx of orderlies in green scrubs was waiting for the ambulance as it squealed to a halt in front of the ER. I watched as Lewis was slid onto a waiting gurney. He was gone within seconds, and I was left alone in the harsh neon glare of the ambulance's interior, staring numbly at the space where my friend had just been.

AFTER LEWIS COLLAPSED on the grass I tried to revive him. I rolled him onto his back and began shouting his name and shaking his shoulders. Fireworks were still shooting haphazardly out of the cardboard box. I tried to haul Lewis away from the danger area, but he was too heavy for me to shift. As I swatted helplessly at his chest, yelling at him to wake up, I remembered squatting down next to Nathan's father after his fall from the Tillys' roof. I was determined not to let life slip away from Lewis in the same way.

"Lewis!" I shouted. "I'm going to get some help, okay? I'll be right back, I promise." I put my hand in front of his mouth and could feel the faintest breath on my fingers. He was still alive, at least. I stood up. My nose was running and my eyes had filled with tears. I ran down the hill. The crowds were still scurrying to safety, away from the rockets that were exploding just over their heads. The air was thick with the cries of frightened children. Staff were trying to usher people safely toward the exit. My father should have been directing operations and reassuring anxious guests, but he was nowhere to be seen. I tore through them all and flung open the door to his office. The number for the Haverford Fire Department and Rescue Squad was taped to the wall immediately above the telephone. My voice cracked as I explained what had happened.

Next to the side entrance that Nathan and I used at night there was a bigger gate for delivery trucks. I grabbed the ring of keys that my father kept in the top drawer of his desk and ran there. It took me seven tries to find the key that opened the padlock. I hauled the gate open so the ambulance could drive right in.

By then all the fireworks in the box had finally detonated. Crowds were moving toward the parking lot, grumbling and confused. I ran against the current of people, back up the hill to where Lewis was lying. He hadn't moved. I knelt down beside his body and put my hand on his chest. He was still breathing. I suddenly knew with absolute certainty that as long as I kept talking, Lewis would stay alive. My words would be his life support. And so I began to babble. I told him that he was going to be all right, that the ambulance would be there soon, that I wouldn't leave him. I told him about the panicked crowds at the bottom of the hill. I told him about the silent confrontation I had just witnessed between Faye and Nathan. Words spilled out of me, jumbled by fear. I couldn't tell if Lewis could hear me. I watched his face as I spoke.

Occasionally his lips moved a fraction but he let out no more than a faint sigh.

Finally I heard the wail of a siren, and moments later blue lights were flashing at the bottom of the hill. Then there were people swarming around Lewis's body. A paramedic hurried over to me and asked me what had happened. I did my best to explain. By then Lewis had been strapped onto a stretcher, his mouth hidden beneath a plastic mask. I looked down at him and thought of Liam. My brother's body had been so tiny and frail by the end. Lewis must have weighed five times as much, but size didn't matter when you were fighting for your life. The men hoisted Lewis off the ground and set off toward the ambulance.

"Is he going to be all right?" I asked.

"We'll see," said the paramedic.

"What happened to him?"

"Looks like your friend had a heart attack."

Lewis had predicted that he'd have a heart attack that morning, as we had carried the fireworks up the hill. Maybe he had known more than he was letting on. The paramedics let me climb into the back of the ambulance with them. As we pulled out of the parking lot, I didn't take my eyes off Lewis. I wanted to remember every last contour of his face, each well-worn wrinkle.

AFTER LEWIS HAD BEEN bustled through the doors of the ER, I leaned back against the wall of the ambulance. Abandoned on the floor of the vehicle lay Lewis's enormous boots. I picked them up. The cracked leather was gnarled, the thick brown laces stiff with mud and dust. Their weight was astonishing. No wonder Lewis huffed as he marched through the park, I thought. It must have been like walking with a block of concrete attached to each foot.

Just then a face appeared at the back door of the ambulance. A woman in medical scrubs was smiling at me. "Hey, mister," she said. "How are you doing?"

"Is Lewis going to be all right?" I asked her.

"He's in the best hands," she answered. "They'll scoot him in, fix him up, and he'll be right as rain before you know it. Your friend looks as tough as those old boots you've got there." She pointed at Lewis's footwear.

I smiled at her gratefully. "He is."

She looked at me. "Does your family know you're here, honey?"

I shook my head.

"You'd better come inside," she said. "Let's find a telephone so you can call home. It's late."

"I'm staying here until Lewis is feeling better," I told her.

"Well, okay. But we still need to let your mom and dad know where you are."

I followed the woman into the hospital. She led me down a corridor to a small office.

"Here you go," she said. "Call your folks, okay?"

I picked up the telephone and called the park. After a few moments there was a click, and I heard my father clear his throat and start to talk, relentlessly upbeat. He thanked me for calling Fun-A-Lot, explained that the park was presently closed, and asked me to leave a message. Just before the machine beeped, he urged me to have a *wonderful, fun-der-ful day!* Tongue-tied, I let the tape run for a few moments. Finally, cautiously, I began to speak. I explained what had happened and told him we were at the hospital. Then I called home. After several rings I heard my mother's voice, breathless and confused.

"Who is this?" she demanded. In the background I could hear the low drone of voices on the television. I'd woken her up.

"Mom, it's me."

"Robert. What time is it? Where are you?"

"I'm at the hospital."

My mother had suffered through her share of medical emergencies in the middle of the night, and her old instincts kicked right back in. "What's happened?" she asked, instantly awake. "Are you all right?"

"I'm fine," I said.

"Is it Dad?" I heard the catch in her voice.

"No, it's Lewis. He's had a heart attack. We came here in an ambulance."

"Oh no," said my mother. "Poor Lewis."

I felt tears spring to my eyes. "Nobody's told me how he's doing."

"Where's your father? Is he there with you?"

"He's not here. I don't know where he is."

"What about Nathan?"

The last time I'd seen Nathan, he had been facedown on the grass in his dragon costume. "He's not here, either," I said.

"You're all on your own," said my mother. "I'm coming to get you."

"I'm staying here until I know Lewis is going to be all right," I told her.

There was a pause on the other end of the line. "All right, then," she said. "We'll wait together."

When my mother appeared in the waiting room a half hour later she was laden down with blankets, magazines, and bags of food. "We don't know how long we might be here for," she explained, offering me a bar of chocolate. I devoured the candy hungrily. As I watched her lay out provisions, it occurred to me that my mother had already spent far too much time in this hospital. And yet here she was, settling down for another long haul without comment or complaint. I reached out and held her hand tightly.

"Thanks, Mom," I said. She smiled at me and handed me a blanket.

"Here," she said. "You're going to need this."

I suppose at some point I must have fallen asleep, because the next thing I felt was a hand on my shoulder. It was my mother. A man in a white coat stood next to her.

"Robert," said my mother. "This is Dr. Paxley."

I struggled to my feet, shaking the stiffness out of my bones. "Is Lewis going to be all right?" I asked.

The doctor smiled. "It looks like he's going to be fine."

It felt as if I had been waiting to hear those words for my entire life. I stood in front of this kind stranger and began to cry.

Dr. Paxley watched me for a few moments. "Robert, what you did was very brave," he told me. "You saved Mr. Jenks's life. If you hadn't reacted as quickly as you did, we might not have gotten to him in time. You should be proud of yourself."

"Can I see him?" I asked.

"Well, he's asleep right now," said Dr. Paxley. "But he'll be awake in the morning. I think you should go home with your mother and get some rest until then."

I shook my head. "I want to be here when he wakes up."

Dr. Paxley looked at his watch. "You must be exhausted."

"Can I stay by his bed?" I turned to my mother. "Can I, Mom? Like we used to with Liam?"

My mother and the doctor exchanged glances. "We *are* used to sleeping in those hospital chairs," she said.

Ten minutes later we were ushered into a small, dimly lit room. The bed could barely contain Lewis. He lay in an ungainly sprawl beneath the sheets. His face had the same restful look that I had seen in the ambulance. We settled down beside him.

I watched the minute hand of the clock above the door, silently marking off time with each slow sweep of the dial. Now that Lewis was out of immediate danger, I had plenty of things to think about. I looked at my mother, asleep in the chair next to me, and wondered where my father was. He should have been there, not her. With every hour that passed without him, twin knots of shame and disappointment grew, thorny and entangled, in my chest.

And Nathan, where was he?

THIRTY

At about six o'clock in the morning, the silence of the hospital room was broken by a wet, rasping cough. I turned toward the bed and saw Lewis watching me.

"Lewis," I said softly.

"Robert. What the hell are you doing here?" he asked. Then he saw my mother, who was still asleep in her chair. "And what the hell is she doing here?" He paused for a moment. "Scratch those two questions," he told me. "I've got a better one. What the hell am *I* doing here?"

"You had a heart attack," I said. "Don't you remember?"

"That was a heart attack?" said Lewis.

"The doctor says you're going to be okay."

Lewis winced. "The last thing I remember, I was standing on top of the hill. That box of rockets—"

"Everything's fine," I said. "Nobody was hurt. Well, except for you."

Lewis lay back in his pillows and sighed. "I should know better than to drop a burning match around fireworks," he said, and then he erupted into another fit of coughing, loud enough to wake my mother.

"Lewis," she yawned, "how are you feeling?"

"A little beaten up, to be honest, Mrs. Carter," said Lewis. He coughed again, grimacing as he did so. "There was no need for you to stay."

She smiled. "Robert wanted to be here when you woke up. I was happy to keep him company."

Lewis's eyes fell back on me. "Thanks, Robert," he said.

I beamed at him. "I'm just glad you're all right."

My mother got to her feet. "I'll go and tell someone you're awake." She pushed open the door and was gone.

"I guess they'll keep me in here for a little bit," said Lewis, looking around him. "Can you do something for me?"

"Sure," I said.

"Dizzy will be busting for a pee and wondering where the hell I am. Could you take him for a walk and feed him? There's dog food in the basement."

Just then the door opened. I turned, expecting Dr. Paxley, but it was my father who stumbled in. He looked ten years older than when I'd seen him the previous afternoon. He was wearing the same clothes he'd worn the day before, and there were streaks of dirt across his forehead and cheeks. Most of all, he stank. A pungent cocktail of sweat and stale alcohol rolled off him. He sat down heavily in the chair my mother had slept in. "Jesus Christ, Lewis," he breathed. "What happened?"

"I could ask you the same thing," said Lewis.

My father looked down. "It was a rough night."

"For both of us, it looks like."

My father reached out and took Lewis's hand. "Everything is going to be just fine, Lewis. Don't you worry about a thing."

"All I'm really worried about right now is getting my dog fed," said

Lewis. He gently took his hand back and slipped it under the blanket. "And Robert's going to take care of that for me."

The door opened and my mother walked back in. I realized from the startled look on her face that she hadn't seen my father in weeks. "Good God, Sam," she said. "You look awful."

"How are you, Mary?" he asked.

"Better than you, apparently. What happened to you?"

"I was up half the night," said my father. "I couldn't sleep. Every time I closed my eyes, Liam was there, right in front of me. I finally went for a walk." He paused. "When I got to the bumper cars, there was one car sitting alone in the middle of the rink. I walked out to it and climbed in. I sat there for ages." He looked up at my mother with exhausted eyes. "I was thinking about all the kids who work at the park every day. They're all going to grow up and get married, have kids of their own. And the more I thought about that, the angrier I got. I sat there, Mary, honest to God, I sat there and I thought: *Why couldn't it have been one of them who died?*"

"Oh, Sam," said my mother.

"Then, more than anything, I needed to smash that car into the wall. I needed to drive it as fast as it would go, ram it into whatever I could. I wanted to hit something so hard. I spun the wheel left, then right. I stamped on the pedal. But nothing happened."

"The power was off," said my mother.

He nodded. "I grabbed the steering wheel with both hands and just started shaking it. And the strange thing was, once I'd started, I couldn't stop. I kept at it, like a lunatic. The car was shuddering like it was going to fall apart. And then the steering wheel came off in my hands. I tore the thing right off its column." My father looked down at his filthy shirt. "After Liam died, it felt as if there was nothing left. But there was. You and Robert were there the whole time.

But I just couldn't see you." He looked at my mother and then at me. "I just couldn't see," he said sadly.

A LITTLE WHILE LATER, my mother drove me home. I rested my head against the car window and looked out at the streets I'd known my whole life. I was exhausted, but I had promised Lewis I would go and feed Dizzy. My thoughts drifted back to Nathan. The last time I'd seen him he'd been on his knees in the dragon suit, illuminated from above by the exploding fireworks. None of what I'd witnessed made any sense. If Faye had told Nathan she wasn't interested in him, why had he tried to grab her?

It was still early morning when we got home. I dialed Nathan's number. The phone rang for an age.

"Hello?" yawned Nathan.

"Nathan?" I said. "It's me."

"Robert," he said. "Where were you last night? I waited for you by the Ferris wheel but you didn't show up."

My fingers gripped the telephone tightly. "Lewis had a heart attack. I was at the hospital with him."

There was a long silence at the other end of the line. Finally Nathan spoke. "Is he okay?"

"Yeah. He's going to be fine." I paused. "Didn't you hear the ambulance arrive?"

"I guess I was distracted. It was a weird night."

I stared at the wall. "A weird night?" As the silence lengthened, disappointment and exhaustion threatened to overwhelm me. "Weird how?" I prompted.

There was another long pause. "I can't really explain it," said Nathan.

It wasn't good enough. I needed to hear him confess what he'd done. "Well look," I said. "I have to go to Lewis's house to feed Dizzy. He's been cooped up inside all night. Can you meet me there?"

A half hour later I climbed onto my bike and set off for Lewis's house. I would have given anything to collapse into my bed, but Dizzy was waiting, probably with his back legs crossed. Nathan was already there when I arrived. I took the key that Lewis had given me and unlocked the front door. Dizzy had begun yowling the moment he had heard us. As I pushed the door open, he scampered past me and squatted on his haunches in the middle of the front yard.

"Wow," I said after a moment. "He really had to go."

Dizzy gave me a reproachful look.

"So tell me about last night," I said.

"There's not much to tell."

"I saw what happened, Nathan."

"What do you mean?"

"I saw you during the fireworks," I said. "I saw you try to grab Faye."

"Faye?" Nathan looked mystified. "Robert, I would never—"

"But she pushed you over."

"What are you talking about?"

"Come *on*, Nathan, I saw you! Faye shoved you. You fell on your knees with your tail in the air!"

"My tail?"

"You were wearing the dragon suit."

Nathan went very still. "That wasn't me," he said.

"I *saw* you," I said.

"No, you didn't. Robert, listen. Remember I said it had been a weird night? That was what I was going to tell you. Someone took the dragon suit."

"Oh please." A sour laugh choked up from deep inside me.

"I swear it's true," said Nathan. "I wore the suit all day, as usual.

When the park closed, I hung it in my locker, just like I always do, and went out to the parking lot for a smoke. When I came back for the fireworks, it was gone."

The lie was so transparent that I felt sorry for him. "So you didn't chase Faye into the forest," I said. "You didn't try and grab her."

"Of course not."

"Then who was it?"

"Maybe it was Hollis."

"That doesn't make any sense," I said. "Why would he steal the costume?"

Nathan thought. "He must have wanted her to think it was me."

I shook my head. "He doesn't care about you."

"Perhaps he does," said Nathan. "Perhaps he's worried that Faye is going to choose me over him."

I closed my eyes. "Hollis is dumb, but he's not *that* dumb."

"Well, maybe he guessed that I put Philippe in Pocahontas's mouth."

"If that were true, he'd just beat the crap out of you. He's not going to try and *frame* you for something." I paused. "It wasn't Hollis in the dragon suit, was it?"

Nathan looked at me. "It wasn't me, Robert."

I sighed. "Why won't you just admit it?"

"Why won't *you* just believe me?"

We were both silent after that.

It was a warm morning. Nathan and I watched Dizzy pad around the front yard, methodically sniffing all the flower beds. Neither of us looked at the other. Finally the dog came up to me and nudged the side of my leg. He was hungry. He led us back inside and I went in search of dog food.

Lewis's basement floor was a mosaic of cracked concrete. Shelves ran along the far wall. They were overflowing with gardening equipment, old tins of paint, and dilapidated wooden crates. Halfway along I found the dog food. As I picked up the nearest tin, a large, misshapen piece of canvas on the next shelf down caught my eye. The name L. P. JENKS was stenciled onto the material in faded ink. I turned it over. On the underside there was a cat's cradle of heavy straps.

"Nathan!" I shouted. "Come and look at this!"

When he appeared I showed him what I had found. "What do you think it is?" I asked.

"It's some kind of harness," he said. He pointed to the straps. "Arms go through there. Legs there. And there's a buckle in the middle." He prodded it. "This looks old. Military issue. I bet it's for a parachute." He peered along the bottom shelf and pointed to a bag the size of a large, overstuffed pillow. It had a faded insignia printed on it, and beneath it the letters USAAF.

I had read enough pulpy wartime thrillers to recognize the acronym. "United States Army Air Force," I said.

"Lewis was a *pilot*," breathed Nathan.

WE CLIMBED BACK ONTO our bikes and cycled to the hospital. When we arrived Lewis was sitting up in bed, suspiciously eying a bowl of brown soup on a tray in front of him. His eyes lit up for a second when he saw us, and then the frown returned.

"If I'd known you were coming I'd have asked you to bring me a sardine sandwich," he said.

"How are you feeling?" asked Nathan.

"They tell me I'm going to make it," said Lewis. "But this hospital food may kill me yet." He pushed the bowl away.

"Hey, Lewis," I said. "Can I ask you a question?"

"Course you can."

"When I was in your basement looking for dog food, I found a weird thing. It looked like an old parachute."

"It had your name on it," added Nathan.

"Ah," said Lewis.

"And, well, we were wondering about that."

"Were you now," said Lewis.

There was an edgy silence.

"Is it yours?" prompted Nathan.

Lewis looked at him. "Like you said, it had my name on it."

"So were you a pilot, then? In the war?"

"I wasn't a pilot," said Lewis. "But I did fly in planes in the war."

"How come you've never mentioned that before?" I asked.

"I don't like to talk about it."

"Why not?"

Lewis closed his eyes for a moment. "What the hell," he said. "I nearly died yesterday. And this isn't something I want to take to my grave." He reached for his glass of water and took a sip. Then he began to speak.

THIRTY-ONE

I grew up in a small town up in Franklin County," began Lewis. "There wasn't much there except for the Otis mill on the banks of the Androscoggin River. It was one of the largest paper mills in the country back then. I knew from the time I was in grade school I'd get a job there one day. Everybody did. That was how it was. Sure enough, the week after I left school I started working in the warehouse, stacking boxes and sweeping floors. Two years after that, in 1939, war broke out. My daddy had fought in France during the Great War. He grew up in Nebraska but settled in Maine when he came back from the fighting. He'd been there at the very end, and the stories he told scared me stupid. One thing I knew: I didn't want to go and fight. But they began the draft again, and I didn't have no choice but to sign up. Every day I returned home from my shift at the mill, looking for the letter calling me up. But it didn't come. The draft was a lottery, you see, and I stayed lucky. Other boys in town got their letter, and I watched them go. Some came home, some didn't. You just never knew."

Lewis took another sip of water. "Five years later, my letter still hadn't come. In June 1944 the Allies landed in Normandy. By then we all knew the Germans weren't going to win, and I finally dared to hope that the war might be over before I had to fight. My father knew better, though. This won't end anytime soon, he warned me. The Germans will keep fighting until the very end. He told me about one of the men under his command who was killed by a German sniper just days before the armistice, in the fall of 1918. He was shot in the back of the head while he was untangling his coat from some barbed wire. He was no threat to anybody." Lewis paused. "A month later, my draft notice arrived. I was conscripted into the United States Army Air Force. I'd never even been on a plane before, and suddenly I was being flown to a military base in the Arizona desert."

"Were you excited?" asked Nathan.

"Yes and no. I liked to imagine returning home as a hero with medals on my chest and a big parade in my honor. But I was scared, too. Each night I prayed that the war would end before my training was done."

"What did you do in Arizona?" I asked.

"Bombardier training school."

I frowned. "What are bombardiers?"

"They drop bombs," said Lewis.

"So not a pilot," said Nathan.

Lewis looked at him. "Not a pilot." He paused. "There was a flight simulator on top of a tall scaffold. We took turns trying to hit cardboard targets while the rest of the class pushed the scaffold across a hangar. After weeks of that we did drills over the desert in Beech AT-11s. They were twin-propeller planes that had been fitted with bomb bays. The bombardiers sat inside a special nose made of Plexiglas at the front of the aircraft. I could see for miles in every direction. I'll never forget the sight of the ground falling away beneath me each time we took off."

Nathan leaned forward. "That must have been amazing."

Lewis nodded. "I used to pretend that the plane wasn't there, that it was just me, launching into the sky. On those flights the bomb bays were filled with bags of sand. There were target areas marked out in the desert, and we had to hit them. As high as we were flying, it was difficult. You needed instinct, a cool head, and some luck. Turned out I had all three.

"The bed next to mine in the barracks belonged to a boy from Kansas called Bolt. Bolt liked to read the newspaper reports out loud. By then the Luftwaffe was in tatters. The Allies were flying over Germany again, attacking munitions plants and factories. We assumed that we'd be going to Europe to join them, but when our training was finished, we got our orders for an island in the Pacific Ocean called Saipan. The air force was using it as a base for their bombing raids over Japan. We were using a new kind of airplane— the B-29 bomber. People called it the Superfortress.

"In Saipan I liked to watch the bombers leave on their missions. They flew in formations of a hundred or more, like a giant silver cloud stretching across the sky. Every sixty seconds another plane would thunder off the end of the runway, engines screaming. There was no point in talking. You couldn't hear anything.

"My first combat mission was December 1944. We attacked a factory in Nagoya. It took about six hours to reach the Japanese mainland from Saipan. I was so damn nervous. As we approached the target I ran through my pre-drop routine. I had done this hundreds of times in training, but my hands were slippery with sweat. There weren't sandbags in the bomb bays anymore." Lewis looked at us. "The other important difference between training exercises and actual engagement with the enemy was that in the desert, nobody ever shot back. At Nagoya the sky around us was exploding with antiaircraft fire. I kept waiting for a bullet to smash through the glass and kill me. It's a strange feeling, knowing that each breath you take might be your last. Just do your job, the crew leader yelled at me when the attacks began. I concentrated on my bombsight and tried to forget about the tracer shells streaking past the windows. When we flew over the target I opened the doors to the bomb bays and pulled back hard on the release. There were so many bombs falling, I couldn't tell which were mine."

I glanced at Nathan. He was staring at the floor.

"The following night, back on Saipan, I lay in bed and thought about how close we had come to getting shot out of the sky. I realized there wasn't much point worrying about it. Either I would survive, or I wouldn't. There was nothing I could do about it either way.

"By February 1945 there were rumors that high command was getting frustrated. Dropping bombs from high altitudes wasn't accurate enough. That changed in early March." He paused. "I remember the briefing. As the group commander marched into the room, I could tell from the look on his face that something was up. Colonel Stark, his name was. He walked up to the podium at the front of the room, saluted, and gestured to us to sit down. Then he told us that from now on things were going to be different. Raids would take place at night, instead of in daylight. And instead of flying at more than thirty thousand feet, the B-29s would fly low—somewhere between five thousand and seven thousand feet. Everyone was muttering to themselves, but Stark hadn't finished. To make room for more bombs, he announced, all guns except for the tail cannon will be removed from the aircraft. At this, all hell broke loose. Men started yelling. Bolt was the loudest of all. He stood up and shouted, No guns? At that altitude? That's suicide! Colonel Stark waited for the ruckus to calm down. The next target, he told us, was Tokyo.

"It was going to be the biggest attack yet. The first planes would carry pathfinder bombs, five-hundred-pound monsters filled with napalm, designed to explode a hundred feet above the ground. The napalm would blast outward and thousands of fires would start at once. That would create a giant target for the rest of the squadron to aim at. We would be low to the ground, and the fires would be easy to see in the dark. The area of Tokyo that we were targeting, Colonel Stark said, was especially vulnerable to this kind of attack. The blaze would spread fast. Streets were narrow, and most of the buildings were flimsy and flammable."

"Doesn't sound like factories," said Nathan.

"It wasn't. We were going to be bombing people's homes. Our targets were civilians."

Lewis stared out the window.

"Over the next two days it became obvious just how big the attack was going to be. Every available Superfortress was being prepped. Mechanics removed the guns and loaded additional bombs in their place. We checked and double-checked every switch, every gauge, every valve and button. Then I went back to my bunk and tried not to think about where those bombs were going to fall. Bolt was lying on his bed. He was turned away from me, muttering to himself. At first I assumed he was cursing whoever was responsible for the decision to disarm the planes, but then I realized that he was praying.

"American air squadrons stationed on Guam and Tinian were also joining the raid. There were more than three hundred aircraft in total, each one of them loaded with bombs. It took more than two hours just to get them all off the ground. Our plane was one of the last to leave the base. We took off just before seven o'clock in the evening on March 9. The plan was to fly through the night and arrive in Tokyo early the next day. Usually we flew in tight formation, but that took time and fuel. Instead every bomber navigated its own way to the target. Usually the crew talked and joked to make the journey pass quicker, but this time we hardly spoke.

"We were still pretty far from Tokyo when the attacks began.

Enemy fighter planes buzzed around us like wasps at a picnic, but of course our gun turrets were unmanned, so we couldn't defend ourselves. But there was a reason they called those planes Superfortresses. Unless they got lucky, Jap bullets couldn't down such a large aircraft. I watched the flash of gunfire from a Mitsubishi Raiden as it peppered the B-29 immediately in front of us. Sure enough, the bomber kept right on going. When the Raiden's cannons stopped blazing, its ammunition spent, I expected it to head back to base. But the pilot had other orders. He rammed his plane straight into the body of the B-29. It exploded in a massive fireball. Not even a Superfortress could survive a suicide attack like that. There wasn't enough time for the crew to bail out before the plane crashed into the water."

"What was going through your head?" I asked.

"I didn't have time to think. We were approaching the target. I could already see an orange glow on the horizon. I remember thinking that it was too early for sunrise. I was right. It wasn't the sun. It was Tokyo, burning so hard that it lit up the sky.

"Our mission was to incinerate the city, but by the time we arrived, it looked like the job was already done. The place looked like hell on earth. There were pillars of flame leaping hundreds of feet into the air. The fires started by the napalm had spread across the city, and the bombs that followed destroyed everything. There was a ribbon of darkness that ran through the city from north to south— the Sumida River. Everywhere east of its banks was a carpet of fire."

Nathan was still keeping his eyes fixed on the floor. He had begun to gnaw on his thumbnail.

"We were flying at low altitude, so the airplane was unpressurized. That meant we weren't wearing oxygen masks. We'd been able to smell the smoke for a while, but as we neared the drop zone, there was a different stench in the cabin. It was terrible. Within seconds

I'd puked up my guts. I had to grab my oxygen mask and clamp it over my mouth." Lewis's eyes were empty. "It was the smell of burning human flesh."

A strange sound emerged from the back of Nathan's throat.

"I didn't think there could be anything left to destroy, but we had our orders." Lewis paused. "Just then I saw that one of the needles on my bombsight was stuck. I tapped the dial, but it didn't move. I took the knife off my combat belt and tried to pry the glass off the dial. We were just moments away from the target. The heat from the fires beneath us was terrible, and I was sweating like a pig in my flak suit. I pulled off my gloves and began to work the blade of my knife behind the bombsight's dial. I could hear the navigator counting down the distance to the target in my headset. I was starting to panic.

"Then there was a terrible lurch, and suddenly the floor of the aircraft was rushing up toward me. My knife slipped, and the blade sliced clean through my thumb."

I closed my eyes.

"The plane was shuddering like crazy. We had been hit. I could hear the rest of the crew yelling. Then I realized that we were going *up*."

"Up?" said Nathan.

"It didn't make any sense," said Lewis. "Damaged aircraft crash to the ground, they don't go higher. Just then the shaking stopped, and I heard the pilot's shout. No damage! he yelled. No hit!"

"What had happened?" I asked.

"Aerodynamics. The heat from the fires had nowhere to go except for straight up," explained Lewis. "We'd been caught by a giant thermal gust coming from the ruins beneath us. Our bomber was tossed around like a kite in a tornado. By the time we had leveled out, we were thirteen thousand feet above the fly zone and out of position. We circled back around until we were over the target again.

The dial on the bombsight still wasn't working, but I didn't care anymore. I stared out over the flames, crazy with pain. My thumb was lying on the floor between my boots. With my good hand, I released the bombs. As soon as the doors of the bomb bays had closed again, the plane banked to the right. I didn't open my eyes for a long time.

"The flight back to Saipan was a blur. The crew's engineer stitched the skin on my hand back together, making a stump where my thumb had been. Then he wrapped my hand as tightly as he could in a bandage. It was good enough for the journey back. I didn't lose too much blood, but by God it hurt. Back at base the medics cleaned the wound and stitched it up properly. When I returned to the barracks, the bed next to mine was empty." Lewis looked sadly at us. "Bolt hadn't made it back. His prayers weren't enough to save him, in the end." He sighed. "But they didn't save the ones who got back alive, either. None of us escaped."

THIRTY-TWO

We sat for a long time without saying a word. Lewis closed his eyes. The effort of telling his story had exhausted him.

"So that's how you lost your thumb," I said.

Lewis grimaced. "That's how. But you know what? Every time I look at my hand, I think about Bolt, and all the Japanese men and women and children who died that night." He paused. "That's a pretty good way of making sure I don't feel too sorry for myself."

"Did you fly more missions after the raid on Tokyo?" I asked.

"Oh yeah. They fixed my thumb and sent me back to work. Tokyo was just the start. After that we attacked Osaka, then Kobe. On and on it went. And after we'd hit every city, we started on smaller towns. There were no strategic targets anymore, no military bases or factories. Our job was simple. We were to keep killing civilians until the government surrendered. But what the American high command never understood was that surrender is dishonorable to the Japanese. They refused to concede defeat, and so on we went, bombing them all to hell." Lewis paused. "It was an unfair fight. They had no way to defend themselves. Talk about dishonor. It was only when President Truman dropped the atom bombs that they finally gave in, and we got sent home."

"What happened then?" I asked.

Lewis looked down at his hands. "It turned out that I didn't want a hero's homecoming, after all. I needed a fresh start somewhere new. So I came to Haverford. Met your grandfather, bless his soul. He gave me a job, and I began again, as best I could."

I glanced at Nathan. He was sitting upright in his chair. I couldn't remember the last time he had spoken.

"Nathan?" I said. "Are you all right?"

"What is it like," asked Nathan, "to fly?"

Lewis looked at him. "Did you hear a word of the story I just told you?"

"Yes, but—"

"That's all the answer you need, then."

"But what happened wasn't your fault!" cried Nathan.

"I was the one who pulled the lever, Nathan. Nobody else."

"You were only following orders!"

"That argument didn't work for the Nazis, so why should it work for me?"

"You did your duty," insisted Nathan.

"You don't know what you're talking about," said Lewis, not unkindly.

"But what about when you took off on those training exercises in the desert?" said Nathan. "Don't you ever think about that?"

Lewis sighed. "Nathan—"

"*That's* what flying should be about! Escape and freedom!"

"Listen, Nathan," said Lewis, "if you want to think flying is all about swooping through the sky without a care in the world, you go right ahead."

Just then the door opened and a nurse appeared. "Visiting hours are over, boys," she told us. "Mr. Jenks needs his rest."

When Lewis did not protest, I knew it was time to go.

I stood up. "We'll come back," I promised him.

"You do that," he said softly.

I wanted to hug Lewis then but didn't know how. It was too com-plicated a transaction, on every level. I did not know which was the greater obstacle, the tubes that snaked in and out of his wrists or my own awkwardness. In the end I patted the bottom corner of his bed and slipped out of the room.

"Do you think all that stuff he told us was true?" said Nathan as we walked down the hospital corridor.

I stared at him. "Are you serious?"

"Well, all that bombing. All those deaths."

"It was a *war*, Nathan," I said.

"So how come I've never heard about it?" he said. "I mean, we all know about the atom bombs, but nobody has ever mentioned *this*."

I understood why Nathan was reluctant to believe Lewis's story. He didn't want his own romantic ideas about flight sullied by what had happened over Japan more than thirty years ago.

We unlocked our bikes and cycled to the park in silence.

The parking lot was already filling up when we arrived. Long lines had begun to form at the ticket booths. It was going to be a busy day. "Poor Dizzy," I said as we dismounted. "He's going to have to wait until tonight for another walk."

"My shift ends early today," said Nathan. "I can do it, if you like."

"That would be great." I handed him Lewis's house key. "Dog food is in the basement."

"I remember," said Nathan.

It was only as we set off in different directions that I realized we hadn't talked any more about what had happened with Faye.

It was a beautiful summer's day. The warm sun made me sleepy and I struggled to stay awake as I shuttled back and forth between the Ferris wheel and the control booth. My monk's tunic felt heavier than ever. I thought about Lewis, lying in that too-small hospital bed. I wondered what it must have been like to carry those memories around for so many years, never telling a soul, terrorized by memories that would not fade.

WHEN I GOT HOME that evening, my mother was in the kitchen, unpacking groceries. There had hardly been any food in the house for weeks. Now the fruit bowl was filled with apples. I picked one up and bit into it. It was delicious.

"How's Lewis?" she asked.

"Better, I think," I said. "But he has a lot on his mind."

"I imagine a heart attack will give you a few things to think about."

"He told Nathan and me a story this morning," I began.

"Oh, that reminds me. Nathan called. He said to meet him at the mill at seven o'clock tonight."

"Tonight?" I groaned. "Did he say why?"

"He wanted to give you Lewis's key back." My mother crossed her arms and looked at me. "Why the mill?" she asked. "That place is still locked up, isn't it?"

I hedged. "As far as I know."

"Only so much mischief the two of you can get up to, then."

I said nothing and took another bite of my apple. I looked up at the kitchen clock. It was already half past six. I had never felt so tired in my life. The last thing I wanted to do was to climb back onto my bicycle, but I realized I didn't have much choice. I needed Lewis's key back. At least Nathan hadn't asked to meet at the beach, I told myself. Maybe he'd finally accepted that he didn't stand a chance with Faye, and he wanted to start hanging out at the mill again, just the two of us.

I got back on my bike, daring to hope.

It was just after seven o'clock when I turned off Bridge Lane and into the mill's parking lot. As I dismounted I heard Nathan call my name. I looked around, not seeing him.

"Robert! Up here!"

I looked up. Nathan was standing on the top of the mill's chimney.

He waved at me and then pointed at the iron rungs that had been hammered into the chimney's brickwork. It was part of the same ladder that he used to climb in and out of the mill's broken window. "Look! It goes all the way up!"

"Nathan, what are you doing?" I shouted. "Come down!"

He looked impossibly tiny, perched on top of that tower of dark red brick. He must have been balancing on the chimney's rim. "Dad always said the world looked more beautiful from a distance," shouted Nathan. "That's why he spent so much time on the roof."

"You have to come down!" I yelled.

"Don't worry," he called. "I'm coming down. Just taking in the view first. You can see the ocean from up here." He turned to the east and my world slowed to a petrified crawl.

Lewis's parachute was strapped to Nathan's back.

"Nathan!" I shouted. "Whatever you're thinking—"

"Relax, Robert." Nathan pointed to the pack between his shoulders. "I borrowed this when I went to feed Dizzy this afternoon."

"You're not going to *jump*!"

"Of course I am!" cried Nathan cheerfully. His silhouette was almost black against the early-evening sky behind him.

"But how do you even know that thing still works? It's been sitting in Lewis's basement for thirty years! It could be rotted away!"

"It's US military issue!" said Nathan. "Best in the world!"

"It's too dangerous!"

Nathan laughed. "You think anyone would remember Philippe Petit if his stunt had been *safe?*"

I was frantic by then, desperately trying to think of anything that would make him climb back down the ladder to safety. "What about Faye?" I shouted.

He looked down at me. "What about her?"

"If it wasn't you in the dragon suit, you need to tell her that!"

He peered down at me. "You still don't believe me, do you?" he shouted.

"I can't talk to you like this," I yelled. "Come back down and let's talk about it."

Nathan looked around him for a moment. "It was easier for Dad up on the roof, you know. Sometimes he liked to keep the world at a distance."

"Please come down!" My voice was becoming hoarse with shouting.

"I used to feel that way, too, but not anymore. Now I always want to come back down to earth, Robert." He looked at me. "You remember what Betsy Cribbins said, don't you? *There's just so much to live for.*"

And with that Nathan Tilly flung himself into the clear, pale sky.

THIRTY-THREE

W hat happened next has been splashing on an endless loop inside my head for the past forty years. Nathan leaping joyfully into the sky. His single tug on the parachute. The useless cord, limp between his fingers. His limbs flailing. The soundless fall to earth, so quick, so quick. The crumple of his body against the concrete.

WORDS FOLLOWED.

Words followed, and once they began, they wouldn't stop. There were sentences, then paragraphs, then whole pages. A forest of paper sprung up around Nathan's fall, trying to make sense of what happened. There were sworn statements and police reports. There were hospital records, a coroner's verdict. There were newspaper reports, editorial pieces, and letters to the editor. Words tumbled out, thickening the air until there was no room left to breathe. There were dry recitations of terrible facts, impenetrable thickets of medical jargon, hectoring diatribes about the fecklessness of youth. There were hand-wringing regrets at the terrible waste of it all. There were lazy assumptions and ignorant accusations. There were flat-out lies.

These words rose up like a black swarm of insects, dizzyingly violent, obscuring the view. None of them made any sense. And none of them would ever bring Nathan back.

CERTAIN FACTS BECAME CLEAR. The release mechanism on the parachute had rusted shut after all those years in Lewis's damp basement. But even if the parachute had been working perfectly, Nathan would not have survived. The chimney was not tall enough. There would not have been enough time for the chute to open and slow his fall. And he would never have been able to jump far enough away from the chimney. The fabric of the parachute would have caught on the bricks, and Nathan would have slammed into the side of the building.

None of this helped.

The Haverford police carefully reconstructed a timeline of the day's events. I sat with my parents in an interview room and told two detectives everything I knew about Nathan. The detectives seemed very interested in the fact that Mr. Tilly had also fallen to his death. When I told them about Nathan's infatuation with Faye, I saw them exchange a meaningful look. I realized then that they assumed that he had committed suicide; they were just trying to find out why.

That was when I really began to talk.

Nathan did not want to kill himself, I told them. He wanted to fly, not fall. I told them about how we had set free Mr. Tilly's kites, how Nathan had watched happily as they were swept into the sky by the ocean winds. I told them how he had climbed up the roller coaster and sat alone at its highest point. I told them how he had spent an evening leaping out of my bedroom window into the snow. I told them about the nights he had spent on the Ferris wheel. Nathan Tilly was always climbing, I told them. He wanted to escape gravity, not give in to it. All Nathan wanted to do was to fly. He thought the parachute was going to work. Again and again, I repeated the last words he had shouted to me. There's just so much to live for.

I talked and I talked until the detectives had no choice but to listen. They went away, they came back. They asked more questions. In the end, they believed me. This was an accident, not a suicide. *Death by misadventure*, pronounced the final police report.

None of this helped.

THIRTY-FOUR

An eruption of green fur spilled out toward me when I opened the door of Nathan's locker. I hauled the dragon suit onto the floor and looked at it for a long time. The costume was in three parts—legs and tail, torso and wings, and head—all connected with heavy Velcro straps. The dragon's cartoon eyes gazed sightlessly up at me.

I stepped into the legs and then wriggled into the top half of the outfit. When I put on the fiberglass head I was assailed by the pungent tang of dried sweat and the burn of stale tobacco. It was as if Nathan were standing in there with me. There was a surprising amount of room inside the head. I could peer down the dragon's snout and see what was going on. I turned toward the full-length mirror at the end of the locker room. The dragon looked back at me with its usual goofy grin. I stared at myself for some time, not moving. Finally I raised my right arm. The dragon shyly waved a wing.

By then I had started to cry, but the dragon continued to smile, as cheerful as ever. I shook my ass and watched the lumpy tail sway behind me. Tears were running down my cheeks. I turned and walked unsteadily toward the door.

Nathan had been dead for three days.

THE PARK WAS HEAVING with visitors. The sun was shining, and within minutes my skin was prickling with sweat. I wandered along the paths, peering down the dragon snout as I went, keeping an eye out for small children. I was surprised how heavy the suit was. My neck began to ache from the weight of the dragon's head.

I trudged ahead, wondering how Nathan had climbed back into this suit day after day. Suddenly I was swamped by a fresh wave of loss. Inside the dragon's skin Nathan had danced for the children, and he had danced for Faye. He brought the dragon to life, and along with it, huge barrelfuls of hope.

Just then I heard an excited squeal and felt something wrap itself around my right leg. I stopped moving and looked down. There was a small girl gazing up at me with unabashed adoration.

"Dragon!" she shouted. I put out a hand and cautiously patted the top of her head.

"Lindsay, honey, come away," came a voice from out of my line of vision. The girl made a squawk of protest and squeezed my leg more tightly than ever. I carefully pivoted until Lindsay's mother came into view down the snout. She beamed at me. "I'm sorry, Mr. Dragon," she said in a chirpy, singsong voice. "Miss Lindsay here has been *so* looking forward to seeing you!"

Lindsay confirmed this by kicking my shin and shouting, "I love you, dragon!" I stifled a yelp and gave the woman a hearty thumbs-up.

"Any chance we can get a photograph?" asked Lindsay's mother. Two seconds later she was standing next to me, gripping my shoulder tightly in case I might try to escape. No chance of that: Lindsay was still fiercely clinging on to my leg. "Chet," the woman barked at her husband, who was holding a camera in front of him as if it were a hand grenade. "Hurry up!"

As the man took our photograph, something peculiar happened. Flanked on either side by Lindsay and her mother, I smiled.

This was no small grin, either. This was a full-wattage, Hollywood-style display of teeth. I was on the red carpet, facing the massed ranks of paparazzi behind the velvet rope. Only once the family had bustled off did I realize that when the family's vacation pictures came back, all Lindsay would see was the same snaggletoothed dragon grin that had stared back at me in the locker room mirror. My own smile was invisible.

But I didn't care. After that children began to swarm all over me, tugging, stealing hugs, demanding attention. They yelled in delight as I goofed around and made them laugh. I even danced a little. And every time a parent produced a camera, I stood up a little taller and grinned like a lunatic.

Now I understood exactly how Nathan had pulled on the dragon suit every day.

AFTER AN HOUR OR SO, I made my way back to the locker room. I was exhausted and hot, but I was also happy. There was such joy in giving delight to all those children. They had flocked to me with complete trust, and in the maelstrom of all that unguarded affection a little bit of my sorrow had been rubbed away.

I lifted off the dragon's head and then extracted my arms from the wings. My T-shirt was soaked through with sweat. I put each piece of the suit back into Nathan's locker. When I picked up the bottom half, I heard something roll across the inside of one of the dragon's outsize feet. I peered down into the leg. There was a faint glimmer of reflected light. I hadn't noticed anything while I'd been walking through the park. Whatever it was must have been caught in the dragon's toes until I'd dislodged it. I felt a rush of excitement.

Perhaps Nathan had left something behind, some kind of clue that would help me make sense of what had happened, or at least something to remember him by. I reached down into the leg.

I pulled out an empty miniature bottle of bourbon.

I looked at it for a long time. Then I unscrewed the lid and took a sniff.

The smell was instantly familiar, the memory of a thousand evenings of my childhood: my father, pouring himself a finger or two of whiskey when he got home from a long day at the park.

Nathan had been telling the truth.

I CLIMBED ONTO my bicycle and headed home, pursued by my shame.

Nathan hadn't lunged at Faye that night. It wasn't him I'd watched crumple to the ground in the dragon suit.

It was my father.

This was knowledge I would never outrun. The perimeters of my existence were already shifting, reluctantly expanding to make room for this new information. My father, the drunk. My father, chaser of young girls. My father, desperate and hopeless and on his knees.

WHEN I ARRIVED HOME my mother was waiting for me.

"How was it?" she asked.

"I put on the dragon suit," I told her. "I went out into the park. I waved at everyone and I danced with little kids. I got my picture taken. I did all the things Nathan used to do." I paused. "The kids just see the dragon, Mom. Nobody cares who's inside."

"It could have been Nathan," she said.

"That's what it looked like."

"So you were bringing him back to life."

"Maybe just a little."

We were silent for a moment.

"Judith Tilly called me this morning about the funeral," said my mother. "She's going to bury Nathan in the plot next to her husband."

"She can't do that," I said at once. There was nothing Nathan would have hated more than being buried, even if it was next to his father.

Just like that, I saw how I could make amends for my failure to believe him about Faye: I would convince Mrs. Tilly that Nathan's body should be cremated and his ashes scattered to the winds.

"I have to go and see her," I said.

"Maybe you should leave her be," said my mother gently.

I shook my head. "Do you remember how angry Nathan was at his father's funeral? That's because Mrs. Tilly *buried* him."

My mother looked at me for a moment, and then she nodded. "Let me drive you," she said.

As we drove out to Sebbanquik Point, I tried not to think about my father, but I couldn't push away the memory of the dragon lunging at Faye while the fireworks exploded overhead.

We parked in front of the Tillys' house. The only other car in the driveway was the blue Impala. No friends or relatives had come to console Nathan's mother.

"Oh, the poor woman," said my mother. She peered toward the house and drummed her fingers against the steering wheel. There were unshed tears at corners of her eyes, and I knew she was losing Liam all over again. I wondered which was worse, an agonized, long good-bye, or the sharp brutality of unexpected loss. Perhaps there was no way to calibrate certain kinds of heartbreak.

"I won't be long," I said.

When Mrs. Tilly opened the door, she looked at me, then at my mother waiting in the car. Her face was pale and drawn. Grief had washed her out.

"Robert," she said. "I suppose you'd better come in."

I followed her into the hallway. There were cardboard boxes everywhere. In one corner a large rug had been rolled up and was standing on its end. Several paintings were propped up against the wall, next to a small forest of unplugged lamps.

"Mrs. Tilly?" I said. "What's going on?"

"I'm packing."

"Packing?"

"That's right." She turned toward me. "I'm leaving."

"So soon?" I blurted.

"I've lost my husband here, and now my son. Are you surprised I can't wait to leave this awful place?"

I remembered our conversation over Christmas lunch. The Tillys had stayed in Maine because of me. My throat closed up. If it hadn't been for me, Nathan would have returned to Texas months ago, far away from the paper mill and Lewis's parachute.

Mrs. Tilly pulled out a pack of cigarettes from her cardigan pocket and lit one. "Why did you come, Robert?"

"Mom says you've bought the plot next to your husband's grave for Nathan."

"That's right."

"Nathan would hate to be buried, Mrs. Tilly," I said.

She took a long drag on her cigarette. "Do you think it's a coincidence, the way Nathan and his father both died?" she asked. "Because it's not. My husband might as well have pushed Nathan off that chimney himself." Her eyes darted restlessly about as she spoke, never meeting my gaze. "Leonard was a kind man, but he filled Nathan's head with stupid ideas and impossible dreams, and Nathan believed every word." She sighed. "My husband lived for pleasure, Robert. There was nothing he liked more than spending all day in his workshop, building those wretched kites, and then flying them from the roof of the house." She paused. "And yes, I *wanted* him buried in the ground. I hated the thought of his ashes being scattered, never coming to rest. I didn't want him disappearing into the sky. It would have only kept all those stupid myths alive in Nathan's head."

"He was so mad about it," I said.

"It was for his own good. All I wanted—all I *ever* wanted—was to stop him from making the same mistakes his father made, and look what happened." She took a long pull on her cigarette. "A roof, a chimney. The details don't matter much in the end."

We were silent for a moment.

"Please don't bury Nathan, Mrs. Tilly," I said. "Please don't put him in the ground."

"You need to leave now, Robert. You need to let me grieve for my son."

I stood there, robbed of all words. Nathan's mother opened the front door. I stepped outside. A few paces away was the spot where Mr. Tilly had landed from his fall. A hot bolt of anger shot through me. Mrs. Tilly was determined to blame her husband for everything that had happened, but that wasn't right.

"Do you know why your husband was on the roof on the day he died?" I asked.

"He was flying a kite," said Mrs. Tilly.

"No he wasn't," I said. "The kite was just an excuse."

"An excuse for what?"

"Before he died he told us the real reason he was up there." I swallowed. "He was watching you."

Nathan's mother had gone very still.

"He said he loved to watch you while you walked along the beach.

That's what he was really doing up there." I paused. "So don't blame him or the kite for his death, Mrs. Tilly. He was up there on that roof because of *you*."

I turned and walked back to the car. Nathan's mother rested one arm up against the frame of the front door, watching me go. Her cigarette still smoldered between her fingers, forgotten.

THIRTY-FIVE

Nathan's funeral took place the following afternoon, at the same church where we had gathered for his father's service nearly two years earlier. My parents and I arrived early. Mrs. Tilly was waiting for us in the parking lot.

"Robert," she said. "There's something I want you to see." She led me to her car and opened the trunk. Inside there was a gray, unmarked tin.

"What's that?" I asked.

"It's Nathan's ashes."

"Oh!" I said.

"He was cremated this morning."

"You changed your mind," I said. I peered into the trunk again, surprised by how big the tin was.

"Come for a ride with me after the service," said Mrs. Tilly.

IN CONTRAST to his father's funeral, the church was full for Nathan. My parents and I sat next to Mrs. Tilly in the front pew. I watched as the seats behind us filled. Most of our classmates came, together with a handful of teachers. The two detectives who had conducted the investigation into the accident showed up. There were strangers, too, lots of them. I guessed they had read about Nathan's death in the paper and were either curious or sorry, or both. Faye was there, looking very pretty in a black dress with her hair drawn back in a sober ponytail. She knelt and prayed and even wiped a tear or two away from those beautiful eyes. (Nathan would have been ecstatic.) Even Hollis appeared, tugging at his shirt collar as he sat stiffly in his pew.

I remember one thing from the service. During the minister's eulogy, my mother turned toward my father and rested her head against his shoulder. A moment later, he put his arm around her.

I kept staring straight ahead.

Hope is a curious thing. It emerges in the most unexpected places.

AFTER THE SERVICE WAS OVER, my parents stood on either side of Mrs. Tilly, soberly shaking hands with the mourners as they filed out of the church. I hovered by the door, anxious to go.

"How are you, Robert?"

Liam's old nurse, Moira, was standing in front of me.

"Not great," I confessed.

"No, I would think not." She spoke very softly. "Liam used to talk about Nathan a lot. I feel like I knew him. He was your best friend, wasn't he?"

I nodded, not trusting myself to speak.

"It's a fine thing, to have a best friend, you know," said Moira. "But goodness, what a hard year it's been for you. First your brother, now Nathan." She looked at me, her eyes full of sympathy. "My mother had a saying she was very fond of at times like this. It's an old

Irish rhyme. *Death leaves a heartache no one can heal; love leaves a memory no one can steal.*"

"I like that," I said.

Moira took my hand in hers. "You might not think so right now, Robert, but you're a lucky boy. People go their whole lives without knowing what real friendship looks like, how it feels. But you do. And even though Nathan's gone, he'll always be with you, if you let him."

"*Love leaves a memory no one can steal,*" I said.

"That's right." She smiled at me. "Don't forget him, Robert. Nathan's friendship was a gift. Just because he's gone doesn't mean you have to throw it away. It's yours to keep for as long as you choose."

"I won't forget him," I promised her.

She let go of my hand then, and walked out of the church.

A few minutes later I stepped into the afternoon sunshine. I paced up and down the sidewalk, thinking about Moira's little rhyme. It was all very well having a memory no one can steal, but there was also the heartache part to deal with. People were still coming out of the church. When Faye appeared at the door, I gave her a small wave. She walked toward me.

"Hey, Robert," she said. "Can I ask you a question?"

"Sure," I said.

"I heard you were at the mill when Nathan jumped."

I nodded. "Yeah."

Faye looked troubled. "Did he say anything about me?"

"About you? Why do you ask?"

"Something strange happened the night before Nathan died," she said. "It didn't make any sense then, and now I don't know what to think." She paused. "Do you remember we talked about him that night?"

"Of course. You were going to speak to him."

"Right, and he was waiting for me when my shift was over. Still in his dragon suit. So, just like we discussed, I told him right away that I wasn't interested. I told him he was sweet and everything, but that he was just too young." She frowned. "First of all, he wouldn't say anything. Not a word. Instead he began acting strange. He was dancing and jumping around, but really close to me, you know? I didn't like it. I told him he was scaring me. But he still wouldn't speak. All I could hear was this awful, heavy breathing coming from inside the dragon suit."

My drunk father, crazy with grief for his dead son and who knew what else.

"When I realized that he wasn't going to stop, I started to walk away. But he followed me." Faye paused. "It was creepy. He wouldn't leave me alone. He followed me almost into the woods. In the end I had to push him away." She had begun to cry. "So now I'm wondering if that had anything to do with what happened at the mill."

"Nathan didn't commit suicide," I said.

"He jumped off the chimney, didn't he?"

"Yes, but he was wearing a parachute. He thought he was going to live."

She looked at me closely. "Did he tell you what happened that night? During the fireworks?"

Faye was a kind person. None of this was her fault. "It wasn't Nathan in the dragon suit, Faye," I said.

"What do you mean?"

"Someone took the suit out of his locker that night. Nathan told me about it the next day. Besides, when I saw him at the mill, he was acting like he always did. He was still crazy about you, Faye. He wasn't a guy who had just been told no."

She frowned. "So if it wasn't Nathan in the dragon suit, then who was it?"

I paused. Faye deserved to know the truth, but perhaps not the whole truth. Then I remembered Nathan's own theory about what had happened that night.

Hollis Calhoun could take one for the team.

"Well, now," I told Faye. "Here's the thing."

A LITTLE WHILE LATER, Nathan's mother stepped out of the church, followed by my parents. All the other guests had left. Mrs. Tilly took my arm. "Come on, Robert," she said. "You and I have a job to do."

We drove in silence out to Sebbanquik Point. I heard the urn rolling around in the trunk as Mrs. Tilly took some of the sharper corners. When we pulled up outside the house, she wound down her window and stared up at the sky for several minutes. I sat there, thinking about my father's arm around my mother's shoulder. Finally Mrs. Tilly turned to me. "Why don't you take your jacket off?" she said.

I climbed out of the car and did as I was told. The ocean breeze felt good. I loosened my tie and undid the top button of my shirt.

Mrs. Tilly opened the trunk. "Get that for me, would you?" she said. I picked up the urn and followed her down the wooden staircase that led to the beach. I stumbled slightly as small pebbles gave way under my shoes. The ocean lapped peacefully across a dark ribbon of sand.

"I always liked it down here," said Mrs. Tilly. "It was peaceful. Just me and the ocean."

I looked up and down the shoreline. The columns of stones had disappeared. There was no more ghostly army scanning the horizon to the east. Now there were just small, uneven hillocks of tide-tossed rocks.

"Where are the statues?" I asked.

Nathan's mother looked out across the dark water. "Each day I came down here and built a new column," she said. "I liked walking along the beach, looking for stones. The shape and size of each one had to be just right. It was my own little ritual, a way of marking time. I built one for each day here."

"Did you knock them all down?"

She nodded. "They'd served their purpose."

We were quiet for a moment.

"Why did you change your mind, Mrs. Tilly?" I said. "Why did you have Nathan cremated after all?"

She turned toward me. "I've been angry for a long time, Robert," she said. "I couldn't forgive my husband for the stupid way he died. Falling off the roof of your own house! It was ridiculous and selfish. That was what I thought, anyway, until you told me what he was doing up there. I realized then things are always more complicated than they seem. Nobody's entirely innocent. We're all responsible, one way or another. We're all to blame." She paused. "I was angry with Nathan, too, but I realized that whatever happened, it would have been wrong to punish him for it by burying him in the ground."

I offered her the tin. She shook her head.

"You do it," she said. "He would like that."

Nathan and I used to run along the water's edge as we tried to coax his father's kites into the air before setting them free. We would splash through the waves, holding the line above our heads, waiting for an upward gust. I took off my shoes and socks. I unscrewed the lid of the urn and walked down to the ocean. Then I raised my arm above my head and started to run. Every few steps I gave the tin an ecstatic shake. Each time, a cloud of gray ash flew into the air and was taken up by the wind.

When the urn was empty, I came to a halt, my chest heaving. Nathan was gone, swept into the sky at last—just as he had always wanted.

I looked back down the beach. My footsteps had been washed away by the ocean.

2016

EPILOGUE

I drive away from the mill, the crash of the wrecking ball still ringing in my ears. I head out of town toward Sebbanquik Point. The road north was widened twenty years ago. The hedgerow on the east side of the lane was pulled up to make the extra room. It gives a better view of the ocean now.

When I reach the Tillys' old house, I pull over and lower the window. Crisp morning air fills the car. The place looks much the same as on that first afternoon I walked there with Nathan, although now there is a child's swing set in the yard, and a yellow plastic tricycle is tipped over on its side in the grass. The shed where Mr. Tilly built his kites still nestles in the shadows behind the house. I wonder what happens in there now, what adorns those whitewashed walls.

After ten minutes I put up the window and switch on the ignition. Then I put the car in drive and head back through forty years.

THE DAY AFTER Nathan's funeral, my father left the couch in his office and came home.

His station wagon pulled into the driveway just after my mother and I had finished supper, and he appeared at the kitchen doorway carrying two bags, one full of clothes, the other full of V. V. St. Cloud novels. My mother looked up at him and smiled. She had known he was coming.

I ran over to him and hugged him as hard as I could. After a moment, he put down his bags and wrapped his arms around me.

I've never asked my father why he chose to return then. I like to think that Nathan's death reminded him that life is precious and we shouldn't waste a single day of it. The alternative explanation—that it was the cocktail of humiliation and remorse after his night in the dragon suit that sent him running for the comforts of home—is less palatable.

One thing I knew as I clung to my father: now that he was back, I would do anything to keep him there. I understood instinctively that the empty bottle of bourbon I had found in the dragon suit could destroy us in any number of ways. Neither my mother nor my father could ever know that I had found it.

I never told anyone.

My silence has not been such a burden, if I'm being honest. I wanted to forget what had happened that night as much as my father did. My joy at his return had to be filtered through the prism of what I now knew. It was sobering to discover that my father wasn't the man I'd believed him to be. Our worlds are always at risk of these unexpected fracturings that require small—and sometimes not-so-small—readjustments of hope and expectation.

THERE WERE STILL several weeks of summer to get through.

The day after Nathan's funeral I reluctantly put on my monk's costume and returned to work. I watched the crowds as they waited in line, happily unaware of everything that had happened. All I could think of was how much Nathan had loved his nights alone on the Ferris wheel, how he had kept his nocturnal vigil from its summit, watching over Faye's fire crackling on the beach far below.

To my relief my father retired the dragon suit for the rest of the summer, although it wasn't clear if this was done as a mark of respect or for more practical considerations. Nathan's performances had pushed the costume to its breaking point. The wings were tattered and limp. The tail was close to falling off completely. My father boxed the thing up and sent it away to be cleaned and repaired—a process that would also conveniently eradicate all evidence of his own recent occupation of it.

I'd hoped that once the season was over and I wasn't spending every day at the park I might miss Nathan a little less, but things were no better when the new school year began. I'd sat next to him in every class, eaten lunch with him every day. If anything, I missed him more than ever. Each night I went home and cried myself to sleep.

My parents did their best to buck me up. They took me out of school for a week in October and we drove down to Orlando to visit Disney World. The trip was a disaster. My father spent every minute being lacerated by professional jealousy so acute that sometimes he actually lost the ability to speak. There was not so much as a kernel of spilled popcorn anywhere in the place. The rides were thrilling and smooth, without even a nick of paint that needed retouching. Every employee was cheerful and polite and professional. My father prowled through the Magic Kingdom like a maiden aunt at a family wedding, hunting for something to complain about. But there was nothing. I slouched through the attractions, listening to my father's anguished admiration and remembering all the adventures Nathan and I had had in our little park in Maine.

While I continued to drift in the flotsam of my loss, however, everybody else moved on. The town soon turned its attention elsewhere. Sometime during the following winter the iron rungs that had been hammered into the mill's brickwork were removed. If you knew where to look, you could still see a series of holes where the ladder had once been. That was all there was to remember Nathan Tilly by—a ghostly absence of something that was once there, long ago. Now, thanks to the wrecking ball, that has gone, too.

ON WEEKENDS I helped my father with the annual maintenance at the park. I found solace in that sea of greasy axles and high-gloss paint. I felt a small but significant shift within me that winter. I suppose, in retrospect, you might call it peace. It came, at least in part, from the understanding that, almost without realizing it, I had chosen to make the park my life. Looking back, I'm sure my decision was a subconscious attempt to ensure my father would not leave again. With every hour that we spent together in the park, I was trying to lash him closer to me, making it harder for him to slip free. After all, Liam was still dead, and whatever demons had driven him away once might yet return.

I committed myself to mastering every aspect of the park's operations. My father patiently answered all my questions and did a poor job of concealing his delight. I pretended not to notice when he turned away to hide his smiles, but I registered every one. During the rest of high school I spent most of my evenings and weekends working with him. I was acutely aware of the fragile impermanence of everything I loved, and I was happy to spend all my free time at the park, if that was what it took to keep what was left of my world in one piece.

The aftershocks of Liam's death abated over the years. My parents and I slowly found our way back to one another. It was a cautious process of forgiveness and forgetting, of recalibration and reimagination. It wasn't always easy. I tried not to think too much about my father's doomed pursuit of Faye in the dragon suit. That was when I would silently, determinedly incant my favorite line from *The Great Gatsby*: Reserving judgments is a matter of infinite hope.

Gatsby left another legacy, too. After that bewitching summer of F. Scott Fitzgerald and V. V. St. Cloud, I began to work my way through the rest of my mother's library. I read hungrily and without discrimination, which was just as well, because her literary tastes were decidedly lowbrow, although I didn't know it at the time. There were no slim volumes of gorgeous prose for her, no plotless peregrinations about the bleakness of the human condition. Blockbuster thrillers and romances were her thing. The bookshelves groaned beneath the collected works of Sidney Sheldon, Rosemary Rogers, and Jackie Collins. I gobbled them all up. There was nothing I loved more than falling under the spell of a good story. Those fat, brick-size novels were counterfeit passports that gave me a new identity and sent me on unlikely journeys into the unknown. Whole worlds opened up to me within their pages. I soon began cycling to the Haverford library every week in search of more adventures and new authors. I haven't stopped reading since.

And so we muddled on. When I graduated high school I began working at the park full-time. We agreed (my mother somewhat reluctantly) that a university education wouldn't help me much. We squeezed a second desk into my father's office. Sometimes I would look up and catch him watching me. I imagine that in those moments he was remembering Grandpa Ronald and wondering what it would have been like to have worked with him. I'm sure he was thinking about Liam, too—his firstborn, the rightful heir to the empire. But whatever wistfulness those ghosts might have caused, my father seemed happy I was there, not least because my presence meant he could take a vacation every now and then. He purchased a secondhand Winnebago, which was so enormous he had to keep it in the far corner of the parking lot. Every spring and fall he and my mother would take off on a road trip to a different part of the country. My father drove every mile of those epic journeys across America. In the weeks leading up to each trip he pored over the road atlas, tracing his finger along the freeways. My mother sat in the passenger seat and read novels aloud to him as he drove. When they arrived at their destination, they spent one night there before climbing back into the Winnebago and heading home again. The journey was the thing—barreling along unfamiliar highways, just the two of them. They could have been going anywhere, as long as they were together.

My parents sold the Winnebago a few years ago, much to my relief. They're both in their eighties now. They still enjoy their road trips, but my father likes to drive his regular car these days, and they stay in motels along the way. The open road is all very well, my mother tells me, but when you get to be our age, you want a little less freedom, and a little more of the hot showers and all-you-can-eat breakfast buffets.

WHEN I WAS TWENTY-FIVE my parents held a Christmas party at their home. This was something they had never done before, so I knew at once that something was afoot. My suspicions were confirmed when my mother casually mentioned that the daughter of a friend of hers would be attending.

Susan was a vet and worked in a small practice in a western suburb of Boston. She and I were the youngest people at the party by a decade or two. I monopolized her all evening, pouring her fruit punch and trying to make her laugh. All I got that first night was a few polite smiles, but that was enough encouragement for me. I called her a few days later. The following Saturday I drove down to

Boston and took her out to dinner. It was a long drive back to Maine that night, but I barely noticed. The next weekend I drove down again, and the weekend after that. At some point, I stopped driving home at the end of the evening.

The following year, when the lease on her apartment came up for renewal, Susan packed her bags and moved in with me. There are sick animals everywhere, she told me, but that park of yours isn't moving. She opened her own veterinary clinic in Haverford.

Two years after that we were married, and three years later our daughter was born. Nathalie is in college now. She's also training to become a vet, but she's made it clear that she won't be joining Susan at the clinic. She wants to work on farms: no cute kittens or family dogs for her. Susan has accepted her decision with rueful pride.

I've always been proud of my wife's expertise, but it's a whole other experience to watch your child conquer vast territories of knowledge whose borders will be forever closed to you. Nathalie and her mother sometimes fall into professional discussions at the dinner table that might as well be in Swedish. On these occasions I am visited by a twinge of remorse that Nathalie was never interested in taking over Fun-A-Lot. I sometimes imagine the park continuing under her, and it's fun to think of the things she might have done with the place. But that's all right. She's pursuing her own dreams, not mine.

Nathan would have approved.

I STILL SEE Hollis Calhoun most days. In the mornings he can be found in the only coffee shop in Haverford that is open all year round, yukking it up with his cronies. He's still an imposing presence physically, although over the years all that hard muscle has morphed into something softer. Still, everything Hollis does is designed to remind you he's more of a man than you are. His handshake is firmer, his shoulders are broader, his laugh is louder.

After Hollis left school he started his own business, doing lawn care in the summer and snow removal in the winter. I would some-times see him driving around town in a pickup with a ride-on mower in the back. For all his boneheadedness, Hollis Calhoun could work harder than a dog when he put his mind to it. He built that busi-ness over the years until he'd saved enough to buy a hardware store, and then another. Now he drives a Lexus and is president of the country club.

But once a bully, always a bully. Every morning in the coffee shop Hollis mocks me for the double soy skinny macchiato I order. Is that even coffee at all? he demands, brandishing his personalized mug, which the owner reluctantly keeps behind the counter for him. What's wrong with a good old-fashioned cup of regular joe? I smile politely and turn away. One problem with a double soy skinny mac-chiato is that it takes time to make, and I have to endure his boor-ishness while I wait. I amuse myself by remembering the sight of the teenage Hollis stumbling around the sixth hole of the miniature golf course with his trousers around his ankles. He and I never spoke of the Pocahontas incident again, but I like to think that from time to time he still lies awake in bed, staring into the darkness, wondering what the hell happened.

There is one other small source of satisfaction that consoles me during those waits for my morning coffee: the lie that I told outside the church after Nathan's funeral ended Hollis's pursuit of Faye for good. The next day she accused him of trying to grope her. He pro-tested his innocence, but Faye was adamant that it had been him. Hollis was furious, but what he failed to understand was that Faye *needed* to believe that it hadn't been Nathan inside the dragon suit, that his jump from the mill chimney was nothing to do with her.

And so when I fingered Hollis for the crime, she gratefully embraced my theory. The two of them never spoke to each other again.

I DIDN'T SPEAK TO Faye again after that summer, either.

She didn't return to work at Fun-A-Lot the following season, and I was grateful for that. There were already too many memories: everywhere I turned I saw Nathan Tilly dancing in the dragon suit, basking in the applause of strangers.

I watched from a cautious distance as Faye floated through her final two years of high school. Boys and girls still flocked to her, unable to resist her. Stories were whispered up and down the hallways: she was dating the quarterback, the new science teacher, her best friend's dad. I was glad Nathan wasn't around to hear any of it.

After graduation Faye left for New York City. New York, we agreed, yes, of *course*—as if there were anywhere else that she could possibly go. She was a model, we heard. She was an actress. She had done lines of cocaine with Andy Warhol at Studio 54. All of it was true. None of it was true.

I always liked to remember Faye at the beach, strumming her guitar and filling the air with her low, warm voice, and so I chose to imagine her as a modern-day troubadour, playing quiet songs of longing and regret in the coffee shops of the West Village. I pictured her in an attic, windows open to the warm Manhattan night, writing an elegy to Nathan Tilly by the light of a single, brightly burning bulb. I knew that every time she sang that song, all those world-weary New York sophisticates would weep into their drinks.

Whatever Faye's story was, she never came back to Haverford. This has allowed my little fantasy of her to endure all these years, unmolested by inconvenient facts. Whether Faye ever wrote a tribute to Nathan that made strangers cry doesn't really matter now, but the thought of it helped me back then. I liked the idea of her memorializing him in song. I needed to believe that somebody else was missing Nathan as much as I was.

TWO WEEKS AFTER his heart attack, Lewis Jenks was released from the hospital. He was told to go home and rest for a month. The following day he appeared at the park in his overalls and boots, ready to work.

My father wouldn't stand for it. He called Lewis into his office. Doctors' orders were to be followed, he insisted. He would not contemplate allowing Lewis to return to work before it was safe. Besides, my father continued, he and I could deal with anything that cropped up until Lewis was feeling better. At this Lewis stood up, let himself out of the office, and walked across the park to his shed. There he put his feet up on the desk, switched on the radio, and waited for the walkie-talkie to crackle into life.

No matter how much my father begged Lewis to stay home, he kept showing up. Lewis didn't care what the doctors said. He was going to work. His stubbornness had nothing to do with his misgivings about our competence (although those undoubtedly existed). Lewis needed to work; it was simple as that. Thirty years before he had found grace in all those run-down machines that my grandfather asked him to fix. Each time he mended another faulty circuit board, he was able to edge fractionally out from beneath the terrible weight of his guilt. His work was a sanctuary. He wasn't about to quit it now.

I was delighted to have him back. I waited expectantly for him to drop by and say hello, but he never did. From my post at the Ferris wheel I saw him trudge from one job to the next, but not once did he look in my direction. At first I was hurt, then confused. I assumed he was angry with me, that he thought Nathan's death was my fault.

In fact the opposite was true. One night my father explained that Lewis was avoiding me because he felt responsible for everything that had happened: after all, the parachute had belonged to him. The following morning I went to Lewis's hut. I barged into the room, switched off the radio, and made him promise to listen to everything that I had to say. He sat back in his chair, put his hands between his knees, and nodded once. He kept his eyes fixed on the floor as I spoke. I told Lewis everything I had told the police. I said that this was no suicide, that Nathan was happy and full of hope when he jumped. I told him that he wasn't to blame for Nathan's death. It wasn't his fault that we'd found the parachute, after all. Lewis listened, not saying a word. When I finished speaking he sat quite still for a long moment, his eyes closed.

Little by little Lewis allowed himself to believe that he might not be to blame for Nathan's death. He began to stop at the Ferris wheel again, and one afternoon he suggested I might like to come around the following weekend. He said Dizzy was missing me.

And so we began a new routine, just the two of us. We walked the dog together, chatting about whatever took our fancy while Dizzy lumbered ahead of us. Sometimes we talked about Nathan, but not always. Our friendship grew to fill the space that he had left behind.

When we returned to the house we listened to music. On that first afternoon, Lewis sat down on the couch and gestured toward the record player.

"You first," he said.

I shook my head. "I don't want to play those records anymore, Lewis. Now they remind me of Liam *and* Nathan."

He nodded. "Too much?"

"Too much," I agreed. "Also, just between you and me, I never really liked the music as much as they did, anyway."

"Ah," said Lewis.

"I feel bad saying that out loud," I confessed.

"Don't worry, Robert," said Lewis. "I promise you, I hated it more."

So Lewis got to choose all the records. No matter how hard I listened, I still couldn't be stirred by his beloved jazz. The improvised horn lines left me as baffled as ever. Still, I was happy to be there. Lewis liked to rest his head back against the cushions of the couch as the music played, his face tilted toward the ceiling. Sometimes he would whistle along with the solos, as note-perfect as ever. The music seemed to flow directly into him like some miraculous intravenous drip.

I packed up Liam's records and took them home.

DIZZY WAS ALREADY OLD when I first met him. He died two years later. Lewis called me with the news, barely able to speak. I dug a hole in Lewis's backyard while he lay on the kitchen floor with his old friend in his arms. It was early October, a perfect fall day. We carried Dizzy to the grave together. Lewis watched as I shoveled dirt back into the hole. When I had finished we went inside and sat in silence on the couch.

When he opened the front door the following week, Lewis had a tiny black Labrador puppy in his arms and a broad smile on his face. The puppy's name was Thelonious—along with Bird and Dizzy, his dogs would have made the most killer jazz band ever—but Lewis called him Theo. Theo was a bit of a scamp and gave Lewis nothing but pure, unbridled joy. Lewis and Theo adored each other unreservedly. After our walks the two of them would flop down together onto the couch. Theo would lie with his legs in the air and fondly gnaw on Lewis's makeshift thumb while Lewis scratched the puppy's belly. It was hard to tell which of them was happier.

After his heart attack, Lewis had disregarded every single piece of medical advice he'd been given. He refused to exercise. He would not change his diet. He even took up smoking cigars as long as a baby's forearm, just to spite all the doctors who had nagged him so relentlessly over the years. He was, in short, having a wonderful time. But even this happiest of hearts had its limits. Lewis suffered a second cardiac arrest in the spring of 1991, although with none of the fireworks (literal and metaphorical) that accompanied his first. He was taking Theo on their morning walk when he collapsed, half a mile from his house. Theo pushed his wet nose up against his master's cheek as Lewis lay motionless on the sidewalk. By the time the nearest passerby had reached him, it was too late.

In his will Lewis bequeathed me both his dog and his jazz albums. I'd moved into a place of my own by then, and my mother began to come around every day, ostensibly to see that I was remembering to eat, but she really just wanted to play with Theo, whom she loved with a fierceness that surprised everyone, most of all herself.

Lewis's records are packed away in boxes now, along with my brother's rock and roll albums. I am the curator of these twin monuments to musical obsession, the reluctant recipient of gifts from the departed and deeply beloved.

I don't play any of those records anymore. It's no fun to listen alone.

TRUE TO HER WORD, Mrs. Tilly left Maine a day or two after Nathan's funeral, leaving no forwarding address. I assumed she had returned to Texas, braving all those poisonous snakes without the family's pet mongoose to protect her. I thought about her occasionally but never expected to see or hear from her again.

But I did see her one last time.

It was a regular weekday a few years ago, about a month after Labor Day. For years my mornings have begun with the *New York Times*, which I always read in the same order: front page, opinion page, sports, obits. This is how I get my information. I enjoy the steady, mindful accumulation of knowledge, the slow turn of the page. I can't stand the splenetic hysteria of cable news or the breathless anarchy of the Internet. There's something to be said for going to print only once a day.

This particular morning I was sitting at the kitchen table, the paper laid out in front of me. I've always been an early riser, and pale sunlight was just beginning to fall through the windows. Susan was still asleep upstairs. My mind wasn't wholly focused on the newspaper; I was already distracted by the day ahead. I idly flipped to the obituary page, thinking about the long list of chores that needed to get done at the park. The lead piece was about a renowned molecular scientist who had died at some fantastically old age. I had never heard of him. Then I saw the next headline:

JUDITH TILLY, NOVELIST, 78

The photograph at the top of the article was unmistakably Nathan's mother. It must have been taken ten or fifteen years after I had known her, but little about her had changed. She wore the same distracted look, staring off past the camera lens as if she were reluctant to confront it directly.

Judith Tilly, began the article, *a romance writer known for her*

SETTING FREE THE KITES

somewhat overwrought prose style and outlandish plot twists, wrote twenty-six bestselling novels in a publishing career that spanned almost five decades.

Five decades? I thought.

Her books were beloved by a legion of devoted readers. For her entire career she wrote under the pen name V. V. St. Cloud.

I sat back, dumbstruck.

Those endless hours locked away in her study. The nonstop tattoo of typewriter keys echoing through the house.

Nathan had been wrong. There had always been paper in the machine.

I CALLED MY PARENTS. I knew my father would have already been up for hours.

"Did you see the *New York Times* this morning?" I asked him when he answered the telephone. "Judith Tilly died."

"She did, huh," said my father.

"Aren't you going to ask me why her obituary was in a national newspaper?"

"I would imagine it was because she was a famous writer."

"Wait a minute," I said. "You *knew* she was V. V. St. Cloud?"

"I wasn't supposed to," said my father. "Do you remember that Christmas when she and Nathan came for lunch? While you boys were outside flying that kite, Judith was admiring Mom's bookshelves. When she saw all the V. V. St. Cloud novels, she whispered to me that she'd written them. It just kind of slipped out, I guess. She'd had a couple of glasses of sherry by then. She called me the next day and begged me not to tell another soul. I promised I wouldn't, and I never did. Not even your mother."

"So that's why you started reading those books that summer," I said.

"Right. And you know what? They were pretty good."

"Nathan thought so, too," I said. "He would have been so proud of her!"

"I wonder why she never told him," mused my father.

"It's strange the secrets we keep from each other," I said lightly. Like the discovery of empty whiskey bottles in dragon outfits, I thought.

Nobody's entirely innocent, Nathan's mother had told me on the beach before I scattered her son's ashes to the ocean winds. *We're all responsible, one way or another. We're all to blame.* She was more right than she knew. She had believed that it was her husband who put all those dangerous ideas into her son's head, but it had been her words that he had yelled as he leapt off the mill chimney.

There's just so much to live for.

We're all to blame.

I said good-bye to my father and put down the telephone. I walked out of the house. The grass in the yard was still wet with early-morning dew. I looked up into the cloudless sky and imagined a single red kite hovering silently overhead, looking down on me. Nathan was still up there somewhere, I knew that much.

Nathan Tilly, who loved a good story.

Nathan Tilly, who didn't care for rules.

Nathan Tilly, who would try anything once.

Nathan Tilly, who jumped off a fucking chimney.

Nathan Tilly, who knew no fear, only hope.

I HAVE BEEN DRIVING for a lifetime.

When I arrive home, it is early afternoon. I have no idea where

I've been. I step through the front door. The house is empty. Susan is at the clinic.

After a morning of memories, I stand in the hallway and listen to the silence. And then I decide I don't want silence anymore.

I climb the ladder to the attic. Through the hatch, I squint into the shadows and wait for my eyes to adjust. Several lifetimes are crowded beneath the eaves at the top of the house. An army of old coats, their wire hangers hooked over a rusted water pipe. A chipped mirror, leaning up against the chimney stack. A wicker basket stuffed with Nathalie's old dolls.

Liam's records are in boxes near the back wall. I flick through the sleeves, old memories beneath my fingertips. Ten minutes later, I am downstairs again with the album I was looking for.

I haven't listened to this music for nearly four decades now. As I lower the needle onto the spinning vinyl, a violent blast of static chokes the speakers. I stand in the middle of the room, listening to the black hum of silence before the music begins.

First there were three of us, crammed into Liam's bedroom.

The syncopated guitar riff erupts into the room, fat with menace. I close my eyes. The music is instantly, dazzlingly familiar. By the second bar, I'm a teenager again.

Then we were two, Liam's loyal disciples. We played the music for him, and—just like he asked—we always played it LOUD.

Now comes the bass, ripping into my chest like a bullet. I rise up onto my toes. I clench my hands into fists. Richard Hell starts to sing. You know his life depends on it.

I was saying let me out of here before I was even born

And then there was just one. Just me.

The music pulls me back through the years. Here comes the chorus!

I belong to the blank generation and
I can take it or leave it each time

Look! There is Liam! There is Nathan! I can hear them singing with me as I jump up and down and wave my hands in the air.

The music carries us away.

Together we take flight.

ACKNOWLEDGMENTS

I've been incredibly lucky to have worked with two wonderful editors on this book. Amy Einhorn bought the novel before I had written a word of it, on the basis of one (admittedly quite long) breakfast somewhere in lower Manhattan. Thank you, Amy, for your faith in me. Jake Morrissey guided me through a thicket of later drafts with wit, generosity, and a slightly unnerving knack for knowing what I was trying to say even when I wasn't quite sure myself. He has helped me make this the best book it could be. Every author (and book) should be so lucky.

My thanks to everyone at G. P. Putnam's Sons and Penguin Random House, especially Kevin Murphy, Sally Kim, Ivan Held, Alexis Welby, Katie Grinch, Carrie Swetonic, and Emily Ollis. It's a pleasure and a privilege to be here. My agents, Andrew Gordon in London and Emma Sweeney in New York, steered me right and always offered first-rate counsel (and some excellent lunches). I'm grateful to them both.

My last novel, A Good American, was so warmly received and championed by booksellers across the country, and I remain grateful beyond words for that support. My thanks in particular to Vivien Jennings and Roger Doeren of Rainy Day Books, Jake Reiss of the Alabama Booksmith, and Lisa LoPorto of Barnes & Noble in Columbia, Missouri.

I first read about the devastating disease of muscular dystrophy in an essay by Penny Wolfson in the 2002 edition of The Best American Essays. Her words wormed their way inside me and steadfastly refused to budge, so I knew I had to write about it myself. The book from which the essay was extracted, *Moonrise*, is one of the most beautiful and gut-wrenching books I've ever read. Rereading it now, I realize that some of the conversations that I wrote between Sam and Mary echo the discussions between Wolfson and her husband that appear in her book. I must have internalized her words more than I knew. I also learned a lot from Christine Kehl O'Hagan's equally heartbreaking memoir, *The Book of Kehls*. The line in the novel, *The answer to most prayers is no*, comes from there.

My thanks to the many, many people who have hosted me on my trips to Maine over the years. Special thanks to Don Lindgren, Samantha Hoyt Lindgren, and Michael Magras for their insights about this state that I love so much, and for always giving me a reason to return.

Some years ago, at a fund-raiser for the Voluntary Action Center, a wonderful nonprofit organization in Columbia, people participated in an auction for the opportunity to have a character in this novel named after them. My thanks to Dr. Ron Carter for his very generous winning bid—and my apologies for killing off his namesake in such an undignified manner. My friends Shane and Mary Epping were also bidding that night. The character of Faye is named in memory of their daughter, Faye Epping.

I've thanked Louis Barfe and Richard Lewis in every novel I've ever written, and I have no intention of stopping now.

Thanks and love to my parents, Alison and Julian George, and my sisters, Amanda Passey and Bridget Shone, and their respective broods.

Every word of this novel was read and reread multiple times by Alexandra Socarides. She has offered wonderful advice, unfailing support, and endless reserves of patience. Most of all, she has given me strength when I needed it most. She is also the smartest and most generous reader a writer could wish for. I could not have written this book without her, and so I dedicate it to her.

I began writing this novel at the very bleakest time of my life. Back then, Hallam and Catherine George were the two points of hope and joy that illuminated my existence. A few years later, three more stars were added to my little firmament: Archer, Nate, and, of course, Alex. Where once there was darkness, now I am dazzled with light.